Thecla K. Alexis

ANDRÉ ALEXIS

OTHER WORLDS

André Alexis is the author of internationally acclaimed novels, story collections, and plays. His novel *Fifteen Dogs* won the Giller Prize, Canada Reads, and the Rogers Writers' Trust Fiction Prize. He is the recipient of the Windham–Campbell Prize in Fiction. His debut, *Childhood*, won the First Novel Award and the Trillium Book Award. Among his other works are *Days by Moonlight*, *The Hidden Keys*, *Pastoral*, *Asylum*, and *Despair and Other Stories of Ottawa*. Alexis lives in Toronto.

ALSO BY ANDRÉ ALEXIS

FICTION

A Quincunx

1. *Pastoral*
2. *Fifteen Dogs*
4. *The Hidden Keys*
5. *Days by Moonlight*
3. *Ring*

A

Beauty and Sadness

Asylum

Childhood

Despair and Other Stories of Ottawa

CHILDREN'S

Ingrid and the Wolf

DRAMA

Lambton Kent

OTHER WORLDS

STORIES

ANDRÉ ALEXIS

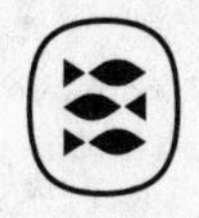

FSG ORIGINALS

FARRAR, STRAUS AND GIROUX

NEW YORK

FSG Originals
Farrar, Straus and Giroux
120 Broadway, New York 10271

Printed in the United States of America
Published simultaneously in Canada by McClelland & Stewart
and in the United States by Farrar, Straus and Giroux
First American edition, 2025

Several of these stories originally appeared in the following publications:
"Houyhnhnm" in *The New Yorker*, June 13, 2022; "A Misfortune" in
Granta 162, Winter 2023; "Consolation" in *The New Yorker*, May 12, 2024.

Grateful acknowledgment is made for permission to reprint lines from
"The Duck" by Ogden Nash. Copyright © 1936 by Ogden Nash, renewed.
Reprinted by permission of Curtis Brown, Ltd.

Library of Congress Cataloging-in-Publication Data
Names: Alexis, André, 1957– author.
Title: Other worlds : stories / André Alexis.
Description: First American edition. | New York : FSG Originals, 2025.
Identifiers: LCCN 2024056821 | ISBN 9780374611408 (paperback)
Subjects: LCGFT: Short stories.
Classification: LCC PR9199.3.A365 O84 2025 | DDC 813/.54—
dc23/eng/20241203
LC record available at https://lccn.loc.gov/2024056821

Designed by Andrew Roberts

1 3 5 7 9 10 8 6 4 2

To Elizabeth Jane Ruddell

We understand nothing about God's works if we do not take it as principle that He wished to blind some and enlighten others.

Blaise Pascal, *Pensées*

(Translated from the French by André Alexis)

CONTENTS

Contrition: An Isekai

In Memoriam Charles Officer

1. Tam Modeste

In 1857, Trinidad was green and mountainous, held in the blue palm of the ocean, the skies above it as blue as the sea, but for the clouds, those wisps of white and grey, hurried along by ocean winds.

At that time, the British were largely avoidable. One could live in the forest, say, or on the outskirts of villages, if one knew how. And this, Tamana Modeste did know. He had lived all his life on the edge of a Carib village that had no name, not far from the ocean, the wide sea expanding before him as he ventured up a mountainside, looking for the plants and minerals he needed for his trade: magic.

Tam Modeste, a Carib from generations of Carib Indians, a buyeis from generations of buyeis, was naturally wary of the British. Born in 1788, he and his family had lived through the savagery of Thomas Picton's reign, the torture and murder of anyone who so much as knew about obeah or magic. Picton had unintentionally driven the Modestes deeper inland, and this was something for which Tam was grateful, but his mistrust of the British had hardened into something like superstition.

And although he had encountered very few Britons in his life—only two, in fact—"British" was the name of a wall beyond which his curiosity did not venture.

This wall, however, was not static. It moved. It was alive, always coming his way, he felt. So, studiously avoiding places where Britons might congregate, Tam had explored—perhaps more fully than any of the Modestes before him—the interior of the land where he was born. He knew its hills, groves, grasses, rivers, minerals, and stones as well as he knew himself. He knew the cobos, mapipis, toads, howler monkeys, tatoos, iguanas, congarees, and bachac as well as he knew his own family.

If it can be said of sorcerers in general that their familiars—the animals who accompany them and help them in their tasks—are expressions of themselves, aspects of a sorcerer's being on Earth, it can be said of Tam that the entire south of Chaleibe—the Carib name for Trinidad and, thus, *his* name for it—was as alive to him and his desires as a black cat or white dog might be to a witch.

He was a man who chose solitude, one who was at home in the bush through hurricanes, blinding storms, and lightless nights. He was private and hard to find, and yet, at times, he was desperately sought by those who needed the succour that comes of obeah: curses, spells, tonics, potions, and powders. Being as great a buyeis as he was, it was inevitable that Tam should be spoken of and gossiped about, that knowledge of his whereabouts was precious, and that there was speculation about what he could actually do.

It was said of him, for instance, that he could command the winds and rains. This was an exaggeration. Tam was, rather, so sensitive to the state of the land that he could predict where and when it would rain, where and when it would not.

It was said of him that he could speak with all manner of creatures—birds in particular—so that if, say, someone had lost an important thing, however small, Tam could call on the animals to find it. This was, in essence, true. He could not so much speak to animals as he could reach the place in himself where his will and the will of the creatures around him congregated, speaking through the intercession of the land itself, communicating as beings who shared a womb might communicate. It was in this way that he tamed the various snakes that lived near his hut, including a mapipi balsain, a seven-foot-long viper who watched over his property at night and whom Tam called Koko.

It was said, finally, that although he was even-tempered, he had caused a number of deaths. The deaths had come when men, jealous of his knowledge, had tried to force him to do their bidding, with threats of violence. Most of these men were victims of snakebite, but at least two had been eaten alive by bachac. Their corpses and remains had been found far from Tam's hut, but it was known that, if you could find Tam, it was unwise to vex him.

These stories were true. Koko had bitten half a dozen men who'd approached the hut at night. Whatever their business may have been, they were bitten by the viper and five of them died. About these deaths, Tam was not unhappy. As to the bachac, those tiny tough fire ants: they had been sent by Tam as warning to a man who'd threatened him. The bachac had flooded the man's hut in such number that they were like a reddish tide, madly biting all the beings they touched. The one who'd threatened Tam survived, but his wife and child did not. And though the man never dared to approach Tam again, the death of his family was one of two profound regrets in Tam's life.

For all his wariness and willingness to punish those who threatened him, however, Tam was routinely capable of great kindness. When a woman came to him wishing to know if her husband was faithful, he would do this for a handful of chenet, if the woman was poor; for a kingfish, if she were wealthy. More: if the husband proved unfaithful, Tam would provide at no cost an undetectable herbal extraction that was guaranteed to keep the man impotent for months. If a man came asking for the means to keep his family fed, Tam would draw him a map of the vicinity, one that showed where coins, gold rings, or false teeth had been lost in the brush—or stolen for nests. If rats or manicou overran a field or grove, he would see to it that the animals left enough for the men and women who depended on the crops, entering the overrun field and drawing a wide circle around viable plants, a circle respected by rats, manicou, birds, and ants.

This last spell was done freely, when done for those in the settlement near his hut. The Caribs there were his kin if not his family. It was they who spoke his language—Garifuna—and, thus, they who lived in his world as he did in theirs. It was they who shared their milk, maize, and rice. It was they who understood his humour and his complaints. It was they who treated him best, believing that his art (not his person) was holy, visiting him only when they were in serious need—waiting patiently when he was away from his hut, as he often was, gathering the things he needed for his spells.

But those who knew Tam found it difficult to keep their admiration for him to themselves. They shared stories about the mapipi who kept watch over him, about the clouds that did his bidding, about his ability to find missing teeth, lost shillings, gold rings. And these stories spread from the south of the island to the north where, of course, they were heard by the people from elsewhere: the British.

Being civilized—that is, believing that their own superstitions were better founded than those of the natives—none of the Britons believed the stories they heard. But a shaman is a shaman and, by nature, a threat to authority. So, Captain James Edward Fernby was sent south, with two men, not to discover magic but, rather, as his commander, Major Bennet, put it: to take the temperature of the natives living there.

Captain Fernby was, even in the eyes of his own men, obnoxious. He was born to wealth and privilege and, having little talent himself, took relentless advantage of his good fortune. He was self-absorbed, wilfully ignorant, and careless of the safety of those in his charge. He was also the kind of man who found it offensive when the natives looked him in the eye.

Adding to the foulness of James Edward Fernby's naturally foul temperament was his exile. He had been sent to Trinidad, for "a time," to avoid the opprobrium that came with his responsibility in the injury of a man who, begging for shillings, was kicked by James Edward, in a fit of what his father—Sir Edward Fernby—called "misplaced consternation." The man fell to the pavement and, hitting his head on the paving stones, was injured. The man's fall had been an accident. But added to the dislike James Edward usually provoked, the incident led to his being spoken to with asperity by his peers.

Unconcerned though young Fernby was about the opinion of others, Sir Edward managed to convince him that a short stay in the colonies would allow his peers time to reconsider the unfortunate accident and would, on top of that, gain him the kind of experience that added to a man's allure, bride-wise. James was twenty-one. It was time he was married.

This last part of his father's suggestion held James's attention.

So it was that James Edward Fernby found himself lost in a country he hated, abandoned by the men he had been leading on what had been described as a routine excursion.

To be fair to the non-commissioned men who accompanied him, "abandoned" is overegging it. The captain's solitude was of his own making. He had refused to allow his men to drink the potable water they'd brought with them, until such time as he himself was thirsty. Both men being thirsty somewhere in the forest near Guayaguayare, they drank from a stream whose waters were as clear and beautiful as Venetian glass.

The following day, both were incapacitated by the stomach pains and diarrhea that were the first signs of a dysentery that might have killed them, had they not been near a settlement with a doctor who, new to the island, had read up on tropical diseases and recognized the symptoms for what they were.

Captain Fernby could have stayed with his men or, as he could do nothing to help them, he might have returned to where he was stationed, near Port of Spain. None would have blamed him for either choice. But James Edward Fernby chose to go on to the area around Basse Terre, where he was meant to communicate with the inhabitants, many of whom spoke French, a language he knew well enough.

This was an absurd decision. To begin with, the assignment had been nothing more than a way to keep a few men busy and to remove Captain Fernby from Port of Spain for a week, after which Major Bennet hoped the captain could be shipped back to England.

Even more absurd: the reason Fernby continued on to Basse Terre—the spur—was the tone of voice of one of his underlings. There was something contemptuous in the way the suffering and barely coherent man warned him not to go on his own, that it was dangerous, that he would get lost if he were not careful.

—I'm not as incompetent as you two, answered Fernby.

And he set out the following day.

And was found, two weeks later, barely alive, by Tam Modeste.

It was more of a stumbling-upon than a finding, something that happened while Tam was distracted in his search for an herb: monkey's bane (*Simia reliquit*), so-called because the smell of it was repellent to monkeys. Not that Tam ever used it to keep monkeys away. The plant was an ingredient in a powder that improved one's memory, and had he been as attentive to his surroundings as he usually was, he would have felt Fernby's presence and avoided it.

Instead, as he was walking near a storm-fed stream whose clear waters quietly rolled, he saw what he took to be a heap of clothes. He was so puzzled by the clump of muddy cloth that it took a moment for him to understand what he was looking at. Then Fernby opened an eye and spoke words that Tam could not understand. For an instant, it seemed to Tam that a mask, poised in mud, had spoken.

—Help me, said Fernby.

Although Tam did not understand his words, he knew their sense well enough, and he recognized their tone: command. He wanted nothing to do with the small living heap he'd chanced on, so he turned to go.

—Please, said Fernby. Please help me.

This new tone cut across languages and contexts. It was the sound of untarnished need and helplessness. So, despite his sense that it was best to leave things as they were, Tam pulled the body closer to the stream, the better to wash its face.

Now, there was the uncovering of something unexpectedly familiar, and not pleasing. The boy was British. His hair—dark blond—stuck like paste to a high forehead. There was a moustache, a slight beard, lips thin and blueish. Below that: a body in a mud-covered uniform that, despite its desecration, heralded an authority of which Tam was almost instinctively wary.

But Fernby must have felt Tam's wariness. So, in distress, he did the only thing his instincts suggested. He pled for a life which, to his shame and despair, he finally understood was small and extinguishable, less significant than the mud in which it was set: *something, something the need . . . the poorest thing superfluous . . . Man's life is cheap as beast's.* There it was: the voice of his education and breeding, scraps of English he hadn't even realized he'd collected. And he saw them (and himself) for what they were worth: nothing much. Why should his life be spared any more than the lives of the kiskadees he could hear calling in the distance?

Yet James Fernby wanted to live, and this longing spoke on his behalf.

After weighing his sense of foreboding against his compassion, Tam made the second decision in his life that he would deeply regret. He decided to shepherd the young man through his bout of suffering. Once he could walk on his own, Tam would lead him out of the forest and leave him where he could find his own people.

This resolution made it possible for Tam to coax, support, and drag the Englishman to a place deeper in the forest. He made sure the man was protected from the elements; fed him on mangoes, manicou, and eddoes; saw to it that he had clean water to drink; and when, after three weeks, Fernby could walk on his own, Tam accompanied him to the outskirts of Basse Terre—ten miles from where he'd found him—and sent the Englishman off in the proper direction.

These things accomplished, he put the young man out of his thoughts.

But if, for Tam, the episode was a simple matter of fear overcome by compassion, it was of much deeper significance to James Edward Fernby. His three weeks in the care of someone he'd been taught to look down on, his dependence on a native whose name he did not know, heightened the sense of his own smallness, amplifying it to such a point that James Fernby experienced, earlier than might have been expected, a revelation that comes to most at some point: that the true worth of any being is vanishingly small. He had always suspected this was true of others. It was devastating to see that it was true of himself as well.

James Edward Fernby changed his life. Returning to his peers and tasks, he was thoughtful and, source of wonder, he began to listen to others. He performed his duties without complaint or pretension, impeccably. He became a man worthy of consideration, and within weeks, the opinions of those around him changed.

Major Bennet, for instance, once anxious to send him back to England, now found reasons to delay his return home. Captain Fernby was the best one to do this, the only one to do that, the most knowledgeable about the forests, the one who knew the natives best. And this state lasted, with no word of dissent from the captain, until, a year after Fernby's "conversion" in the forest, Sir Edward requested, through channels open to a man of his standing, that his son be returned to him as expeditiously as possible.

This request was disappointing to both Captain Fernby and his commander. Major Bennet wanted the young man to stay because he had become dependable. But he had kept the captain for as long as he could. So, he put up no objection to Fernby's departure. Rather, it was Captain Fernby himself who hesitated to return to England.

—Begging your leave, said the captain. With the major's permission, I would like to remain in Trinidad for a month longer.

—A month? asked the major. Why do you need a month?

It was not that Captain Fernby did not want to return to England. He did. But he felt he had a duty to the one who'd saved his life, and this duty would not allow him to leave Trinidad without acknowledging and, to the best of his ability, rewarding the man who had helped change him for the better.

James Edward Fernby knew that the change in himself was for the better, not by the way he was treated by others—though the men around him now treated him with the deference he had previously assumed was his due—but because he had a new understanding of himself, one that was not based on social standing. Bright buttons and white shirts were not, after all, irrefutable proof of anything. Rather, he understood the words that had come back to him when he was close to death—*Man's life is cheap as beast's*—as both true and liberating. Though the writer had no doubt meant the words differently, Captain Fernby took them to mean that he was neither superior nor inferior to those with whom he shared his existence on Earth: all creatures made of carbon, water, and spirit. This exhilarating equality, which he felt most poignantly when he was called home, is what led him to look for the one who had saved his life. He did not know what he would do if he found the man, but he wanted a chance to reward him.

Although James Edward Fernby's notion of himself had changed, his idea of reward was a vestige of the privileged world from which he'd come. It was tied to the idea of renown or fame, the idea of distinction. In other words, he wanted his rescuer to be known. Moreover, he wanted him to be known in London, and he was confident that he could convince the man that a sojourn in that great city—where he would be feted and taken care of—would be a marvellous experience. So, Captain Fernby went looking for him, asking the major for two men to help him explore the area around the settlement where Tam had left him.

Leaving aside the idea of fate, for now, it should have been very difficult for Captain Fernby to find Tam at all. It had been chance that led Tam to the captain's body in the first place. Nor had Tam taken Fernby anywhere near his hut or the settlement near it. So, Fernby finding Tam should have been like lightning striking the same two people twice: unlikely. But find him he did, and easily, going as if guided to the small settlement outside Basse Terre, coming upon Tam's hut and Tam himself, as he rose in the morning to clean himself.

Tam was unpleasantly surprised by the appearance of the soldiers. It was unwanted and unexpected, but it was also, paradoxically, something he'd been awaiting. From the moment he'd washed the young soldier's face and, acting against his own instincts, helped the man survive, Tam had been expecting consequences. And here they were. He stepped from his hut and faced three British soldiers. Nor was it reassuring to see the young man's smile, to watch the man approach with his hand out. What was Tam to make of the noises he made, the dog-growling sounds of those who speak English?

What James Edward Fernby said was

—How wonderful to find you, sir!

Tam backed away from the men, looking around for something with which to defend himself. As it happened, he had left his machete, a treasure given to him by a man from Guayaguayare, planted blade-down beside the previous evening's fire. He made a move towards it.

It was not difficult to see what the old man was going for. And one of Captain Fernby's men, a young man from

Camberwell, moved quickly to subdue the seventy-year-old native. He meant to hit Tam in the shoulder, to knock him back a little, so he could not endanger the captain. But what he did was to strike Tam on the side of the head as he bent for his machete. He knocked Tam unconscious.

All of this, happening as quickly as it did, caused Fernby almost as much distress as it did Tam. He had come to thank (and reward) the man who had rescued his body and saved his soul. This new situation was alarming. He blamed himself for the violence done to the old man, though it had been an accident, and blamed himself for the decision to seek the native fellow out. This guilt complicated the choices before him: leave the unconscious body where it lay, wait until the old man had come back to his senses, or take his body to Basse Terre where there was almost certainly a doctor to care for any serious injury, to make sure the old man was all right.

Despite the absurdity of the situation, Fernby made the most reasonable decision that came to him. He sent one of his men to bring a cart in which the old man could be carried, if need be, and he sent the other to find an interpreter, someone to assure the man that he, Captain James Edward Fernby, meant no harm.

And so, when Tam came to, he was lying in a cart and looking up at a wide blue sky. Looking down at him with contrition—or was it embarrassment—were Captain Fernby, his men, and an interpreter.

As it happened, the interpreter spoke French and Spanish very well. The problem was with his English. When Captain Fernby asked the man to convey his contrition for what had happened, the man (whose name has been forgotten, though his Garifuna was beautiful) told Tam that the Englishman wanted an apology for what had taken place. When Captain Fernby explained that he wanted to reward Tam for his kindness, the interpreter suggested that Tam would pay for what he had done to the captain. And, finally, when Captain Fernby asked Tam to accompany him to London, England, where he could be properly honoured, the interpreter informed Tam that he would be taken to England to get what he deserved.

(Though he was, in a sense, responsible for Tam's death, the interpreter in question was a kind man, affable and confident. More: he considered affability and the projection of certainty to be aspects of translation itself. And although he was not as concerned with accuracy as he might have been, he was ahead of his time in believing that messages were a matter of feeling more than they were of words. Here, for instance, he had sussed out the hint of wilfulness in Fernby's desire to reward Tam, and in conveying this wilfulness, he was not fabricating unreasonably. In any case, as with any translation, chance trumps fidelity.)

At the thought of being taken from the land to which he belonged, Tam despaired. He looked up at the sky, as if it were a thing that could be stolen. And what could other skies possibly mean to him? He was seventy years old, and he had discovered as much about the world around him as any buyeis had before him. He could, if he'd wanted, fight against the Englishmen. He could call on the earth to attack them. But in that moment, as Tam looked up at his expanse of blue, the pale young Englishman seemed inevitable and strangely irrelevant. He was a harbinger of death, nothing more.

Lifting himself up in the cart, Tam asked if he could return to his hut to retrieve a few things he wanted with him. The translator conveyed this message exactly, and Tam was, of course, allowed back to his hut. There, as if he were tired—or still recovering from the blow to his head—Tam sat on the ground, his back leaning against the flimsy structure.

Closing his eyes and retreating to the depths of himself, he called on the creatures near him for help. And a mapipi who happened to be cooling itself in the crux of a mango tree came to him quietly, as the English were thanking the translator for his service.

Speaking to the mapipi in their shared language, Tam asked the snake to empty its poison in his arm. And although it was surprised by the request, the snake did so, politely sinking its fangs into the arm Tam held out, as if perhaps, though it was dubious, Tam knew more about biting than it did.

And Tam died.

Or his body experienced all the pain of envenomation: hemorrhage, edema, thrombosis, renal failure. And having suffered through the worst of all this, Tam finally lost consciousness.

Or he experienced a break in consciousness very like those moments when one is trying to stay awake, when one is resisting a sleep whose rule is proved by an awakening.

And, here, the awakening was disconcerting.

It seemed to Tam as if he had been unconscious for no more than a moment, certainly not for an hour, even less for a day. But when he opened his eyes, he found himself cradled in the arms of an extremely tall woman who, obviously distraught, was weeping over him.

In clear and measured Garifuna, Tam said

—Wuri kagi badugubei?

That is: Woman, what are you doing?

These words had an astonishing effect on the situation. The woman stopped wailing and looked down at him, still crying but now evidently confused as well. The voice—*his* voice—had startled her, though maybe not as much as it had startled Tam. It was the voice of a child.

—Kagi badugubei? he repeated.

And there it was again: the voice. It had clearly come from him, but it was so unlike his own voice that he looked up at the woman, staring at her as if asking for an explanation. She in turn stared at him, both of them as if hypnotized by each other's face.

The woman recovered first. Now crying out with irrepressible joy, exclaiming in a language he did not know, the woman took Tam's head and plunged it into her bosom.

—Paul! she said. You've come back to us!

These words were followed by the sound of heavy steps approaching, as if an invading army were rushing upstairs. Tam, whom the woman evidently mistook for some "Paul" or other, pushed her away from him as forcefully as he could—weak as he was, he barely moved her—and he cried out in Garifuna

—Kagi badugubei? Hebe, mayaronguabana!

That is: What are you doing? Stop, you'll suffocate me!

2. Beginning Again

It would be difficult to say who among those gathered in the small room in Petrolia, Ontario, was most surprised by what they witnessed.

Tam had recovered consciousness after his death, but the body his consciousness now occupied was that of a seven-year-old child, and the land in which he lay was, in its sounds, in the feel of it, perhaps even in its essence, unimaginably distant from the Trinidad in which he had, moments before, given up the ghost. In his seventy years, he had at times believed, vaguely, in some sort of afterlife. He had never believed fervently enough to actually prefigure the hereafter, but if he *had* tried, he would not have included wooden panelling, large windows, hooded lights on the ceiling, globes of light on metal poles, lampshades on which pictures of horses were painted. Everywhere he looked, everything was startling. And not in a good way, either. This afterlife reeked of settlements; the smells around him were unpleasant and unplaceable, having nothing to do with any version of Earth with which he was familiar.

That Tam was not terrified by his sudden change of circumstances had more to do with his failure to understand it than with his innate courage and grace. It felt as if he had missed an important point in a conversation that had, without his realizing, become absurd. During these first moments in Petrolia, Tam was waiting for proof that he had not lost his mind.

None came. None ever would.

Eva—the woman Tam would, after a time, reluctantly refer to as "Mom"—had, moments before Tam spoke, been weeping over the lifeless body of her only child, Paul. That her son was dead had been a certainty. Dr. Pastoureau, a reliable and compassionate man, had pronounced Paul dead, after checking for a pulse, pricking the body with a needle, and listening for a heartbeat. She had seen the sadness, sympathy, and reluctance in Pastoureau's eyes as he confirmed the death. Her husband, Roland, himself a doctor, had wept over his son's body.

In any case, she had known Paul was dead before either of them. How could she not know, she who had given birth to him? Yet, shortly after Roland and Dr. Pastoureau had left the room to give her time with her grief, Paul spoke, looking up at her with alarm, using words she did not understand. Her emotions lurched erratically up: from grief to disbelief, from disbelief to shock, from shock to hope, and from hope to elation. This trajectory was more jagged than Tam's, and it ended, after thirty seconds, with an unwordable joy, a cry that brought her husband and Dr. Pastoureau running up the stairs to see what had happened.

As her son tried to push her away, Eva clung to him.

Dr. Pastoureau was, naturally, surprised to find his former patient alive. But his surprise was mixed with curiosity, disbelief, professional dismay, and a vertiginous sense of the uncanny. In a word, he was astonished, and this, of course, cannot be compared to what was felt by Paul's mother or by Tam.

Which brings us to Roland, Paul's father, whose surprise was far more complex than Pastoureau's. He, too, felt disbelief and professional dismay. How was it possible for him, a doctor, not to know the difference between the living and the dead? Roland also felt the joy, hope, and festive love that Eva had. But his feelings were shaded differently.

Because Roland Williams was the kind of man who routinely masked his emotions, he was confused about what he ought to express. As a compulsive fornicator who regularly betrayed his wife, he was in the habit of displaying the *appropriate* emotion, the most useful one. But what attitude was one to take when a beloved child, confirmed dead, got up from the deathbed and spoke? Which was the face to show, when all faces suggested themselves at once?

If anyone had been paying attention to Roland's face in the moments after he entered his son's room, they would have seen something like a series of masks, each one briefly tried, each quickly replaced until, after a moment, there was only the face itself: disturbingly blank, unsmiling, un-anything, waiting for some hint of what it ought to show. It was a relief when, at last, his son looked up at him and, love taking over, Roland wept at the thought that his son was returned to him.

Though they were the harvest of profound emotion, Roland's tears were unnerving to Tam, feeling as he did that tears were womanish and inappropriate for a man. Also unnerving: the one weeping before him bore a resemblance to Tam's youngest brother, Tain. So much so that Tam spoke his brother's name, though he knew the man was not his brother.

When Eva and Roland had got control over their emotions—and had seemingly tired of squeezing the breath out of him—it occurred to them, at last, to speak to "Paul."

—Paul, Eva asked, how are you feeling, sweetheart?

To Tam's surprise, he understood her. But when he answered, the language that came was his own, Garifuna.

—Mama Paul niribei. Tamana niri.

He tried again and then again, but the English language—the speaking of it—was like a horizon to him, unattainable.

—Shhh, said Eva. Don't try to talk. Rest.

During his first days in Petrolia, Tam was bewildered and despairing. He had come so close to proper death: eternal darkness, the great cold, the end of becoming, the beginning of being, the *being* he knew from Trinidad, the land whose soul he shared. How unfair to be pulled back from the brink. There had to be some reason for it. Had he done something wrong? Was he being punished? Or was he meant to right someone else's wrong?

However much he meditated on his predicament, however intently he listened to the land on which he now found himself, Tam could find no trace of purpose. If he had been denied his death for a reason, the reason was beyond his understanding.

It didn't help, of course, that Eva was a constant presence in his room. It was a distraction, and an embarrassing one at that. She insisted on changing his clothes and washing his body, and in principle, he could not object. There was nothing unusual about a mother washing her seven-year-old's body. Besides, at first, Tam felt physically depleted, exhausted. He could barely stand up without feeling dizzy. But as he regained strength—warily eating the over-salted chicken, rice, and soups that were brought to him—he began to feel the humiliation of being touched everywhere by a young woman he did not, after all, know. And he, thereafter, insisted on washing himself, in private.

(The small miracle that is a bathroom—hot and cold running water, toilet, soaps, blades, brushes—was heightened for Tam by the unspoken accord that regulated the room: one was not disturbed while within, except for the occasional call to make sure one was "okay." And so, initially, Tam did much of his thinking while in the bathtub.)

As Tam recovered his strength, his English—an inheritance, it seemed, from the one whose body he now occupied—improved as well. He understood most of its words. He could not speak it fluently, but he now managed an increasing number of rudimentary sentences—"I have hunger," "I want outside"—which he delivered in an accent his parents found difficult to understand.

Given this limitation, it is understandable that Tam's first days in Petrolia were taken up with observation. When he was not sitting quietly on his bed, meditating beneath a large poster of Jackie Robinson, he spent time in the company of Eva and Roland. Rather, he spent time in their vicinity, maintaining his distance while observing them, nodding when asked if everything was okay, shaking his head when asked if he needed anything.

His parents were alarmed by the changes in their child. Paul had been bright, gregarious, and talkative, a boy with many friends, a joy to his parents. But having survived illness, their son was secretive, spoke with an accent when he spoke at all, and was more than a little sinister. They could feel themselves being observed, and this was, naturally, disconcerting. It was as if their son had escaped death only to go through an untimely puberty: glumness, purdah, and the refusal to speak.

This last idea, which Eva and Roland shared, was fanciful and not true. Tam's body was that of a seven-year-old and, at three feet and six inches tall, lower to the ground than he was used to, a reminder of how tiresome it had been to be constantly looking up. He had also forgotten how intimidating adults were, how humiliating it was to depend on their good moods. If anything, as far as Tam was concerned, puberty would have been a relief.

Not that his relationship to the young couple was always fraught. Tam quickly saw that Eva's love for him—for *Paul*—was unconditional. He would sometimes catch her gazing at him, and when she saw him looking at her, she would come to kiss his face and hold him in her arms. He was moved by her affection, by its purity. However, knowing that her affection was meant for the child whose body he occupied meant that, at times, Eva's love had to be endured. Yes, now and then, he had sensual thoughts about the woman. Given her disregard for his personal boundaries, this was inevitable. But besides Tam's natural asceticism, Eva was, at twenty-eight, too young for him.

(In fact, it was months later, when he returned to school for grade three, that Tam first felt sexual desire again. This was at the sight of Miss Heikkinen, his grade three teacher, who seemed to him an uncommonly sensual fifty-year-old, a woman who wore loose skirts and smelled faintly of starch mango.)

Another limitation: for the first while, Tam's observations were bound to what could be observed indoors. Eva and Roland were wary of anything—any activity—that might lead him to physical harm. Eva had set an invisible mark—conditions her son had to meet—before she would consider letting him outside. Even after Roland and Dr. Pastoureau had both given their approval, she defiantly insisted on her prerogative as a mother to decide what was best for her child. So, the outside world, the world Tam cherished, the elements he had spent much of his life exploring, was temporarily forbidden to him.

For Roland and Dr. Pastoureau—perhaps for most—the idea of remaining indoors was synonymous with punishment and boredom, a banishment from the variants and variations that make up Nature. For Tam, indoors was anything but boring. It was painful in its novelty.

His bedroom, for instance, with its electric lights, its large high bed, and most especially its wallpaper on which identical instances of a rat-like creature with whiskers and a tail fin balanced a large round object on its muzzle. The words "seal" and "beach ball" came to him, but they did not help him understand the image, which was bizarre, nor its proliferation, which was enigmatic.

Each of the rooms in the house held a number of small wonders.

The kitchen, for instance, was fascinating: a white-enamelled rectangle in which to keep things cool or cold (a "fridge"); an "electric range" with which to cook the meat that one kept in the fridge (Kelvinator, by name); an enamelled sink, over which a silver faucet stood watch, bird-like, as over a yellowing nest; a "dishwasher"—a perverse luxury, whose necessity was, it seemed to Tam, questionable and whose sound—rattle and groan—was terrifying.

Then, too, there was the living room with its cloth-upholstered chesterfield, its Naugahyde armchair, and its long colourful drapes. The armchair was bewildering. Tam had seen expanses of leather in his life—not often, but enough to appreciate that leather was something done to a cow or horse. This "Naugahyde," however, had nothing of the mammal to it. It was light brown, almost like the hide of a red brocket deer, but cold and glossy in a way he associated with sheets of tin. He could not stand to sit in it, but he could not stop touching it, either. And that's not even to mention the boxes of chaos: a bulky radio that stood in a corner and, in the afternoon, spoke of war, and a television, always startling, even after Tam had got used to its harsh noise and the silver-blueish images that moved on its screen.

He assumed that Roland and Eva were wealthy. They had to be, to have so many objects and a home large enough to accommodate them. But in this surmise, he was both right and wrong. They *were* wealthy, by the standards of Petrolia. But they were not "rich"—a word that had to do with profound wealth. Roland in particular seemed beguiled by the word.

—We're not rich! he'd say.

But he said this so often that being rich seemed to be a bugbear of his, or a longing.

Roland was one of three doctors in Petrolia. The men and women, farmers for the most part, who needed doctoring were, more or less, stuck with him and his prices—ever matched by the other physicians in town—unless they wanted to go to Sarnia, thirteen kilometres away, to be fleeced by some big-city doctor who would as likely charge twice as much while seeing them for half as long. The only check on Roland's earnings was the colour of his skin. He was what Tam would have called light-skinned, but as this was enough to turn off any number of Petrolians—or "hard oilers," as they called themselves—he did not thrive quite as much as he might have.

The second of the three doctors was a woman named Marilyn McBurney. As she was female, those who mistrusted women more than they did Black men went to Roland or to the third doctor, Dr. Pastoureau, whom the reader has already met and who, being French-Canadian, was shunned by those who mistrusted the French. In this way, the distribution of patients was mostly equitable, as were the doctors' earnings.

Of all the contraptions that the Williamses owned, the only one that pleased Tam outright was their automobile: a canary-yellow Chevrolet Impala, with its fins, whitewalls, and otherworldly shape. Though he was initially frightened by it, the fear turned to pleasure as soon as the thing was put in gear. So much so that, although he disliked being confined to small places, he could stand it when they drove to Sarnia, say, for Chinese food, delighted as he was by the way the world was eaten by the Impala: the farmhouses and fields blending in greys, greens, and ochres, the clouds above like white districts, the smell of the passing farms almost familiar, until the outskirts of town where the factories squatted and smoked.

During his time confined indoors, the occasional ride in the Impala was Tam's only respite from the busyness of appliances and entertainment, that and the window in his room that looked out on a wide rough field. With the window open, he could smell the field's mélange of spoor, fauna, and earth—familiar, but unfamiliar as well.

It was a relief when, some six weeks after his return to life, Eva finally allowed her son to go outside. She asked him to stay in the yard, where she could keep an eye on him, but she also encouraged him to talk to his friends—to Paul's friends—the children his age who lived on Grove Street, their names sounding exotic to Tam: Cindy, Elaine, Janet, Bob, Terry, and Phillip.

But of these two activities—going outside, talking to other children—only one was feasible. Tam did not speak English well, while all those around him did. Even if he had wanted to talk to seven-year-olds, which he did not, he could not think of a subject of interest to him that would not have terrorized them: the story of his death, the cruelty of the English, the endless suffering that human life entails, and of course, the equally inexhaustible beauty and magic of the land—his land, Trinidad, in particular.

Children were of no interest to him, and they never had been. He had, in the past, ignored them until they reached the age when they could be taught obeah. His own learning had begun when he was seven or eight, which was early, but he had been a prodigy. The children on Grove Street were thin pale primates, none mature enough to be instructed on the procedures for making love potions, curses, spells, and emetics. And, again, even if a prodigy had appeared before him, there was still the problem of language.

It was, of course, distressing to Eva and Roland that their child could not speak to them as he had, that he spoke haltingly or, at times, in a language none could identify. Eva in particular was devastated to lose this part of their intimacy. Her son had been a close ally, one she loved talking to. She was reassured, however, by Dr. Pastoureau, who insisted that it was to be expected of one who had stopped breathing for as long as Paul had, that there be some neurological damage, that Paul's case was typical. In fact, Pastoureau and Roland agreed that, all things considered, the speaking of a different language was far from the worst one could imagine, neurologically. Paul might have suffered severe brain damage. He might have lost the faculty of speech entirely. Looked at from that angle, a foreign accent was almost a boon.

Complicating the matter of language was the fact that Tam did not want to know English. The sound of it made him angry, and when he began to recognize words like "table," "chair," "lunch," and "sleep," he felt humiliated, as if the phonemes of English were a kind of vermin polluting his mind.

(Tam was reconciled to the language, gradually, through the graces of Miss Heikkinen, who was enamoured of English poetry. Of Finnish descent and with Finnish-speaking parents, Miss Heikkinen had grown to love English through the poetry of Ogden Nash, whose work she read to her seven- and eight-year-old charges. On hearing Nash's "The Duck," Tam was moved.

> Behold the duck.
> It does not cluck.
> A cluck it lacks.
> It quacks.

He was not moved by the meaning of the poem, though he loved ducks. It was the poem's incantation, its rhythm, its rhythmic resemblance to the rhythms of spells cast in his own tongue. That English could do this was already something. That it could do this while disguised as Miss Heikkinen was a revelation.)

Tam's first ventures outdoors, then, were about the land, not the children he was meant to associate with. It wasn't that the Cindys, Elaines, and Michaels didn't come to see him. It was that he ignored them or told them to go away, as he stood by the field or ventured into its grasses to see what he could find.

His anger, the anger that he had brought with him from his former life, was appeased by the land around him. His senses were more acute than they had been when he was seventy. His sense of smell, for instance, was so generous that he found it easy to isolate the odours he was seeking. He would stand still—hard to do with the hormones running through him—and concentrate, while allowing his memory of other plants to return to him.

The field beside the Williamses' house was awash with smells *close* to those of fields he had known. But whenever he approached a plant, expecting it to be one whose properties he knew, Tam inevitably found it different, as if Petrolia were a mutation of his true home. The grass, for instance, plain and faithful though it was, was not the grass he had known. The land, to which he would have gratefully surrendered himself, would not take him. The animals in the field were wary. However still he stood, the mice, moles, butterflies, snakes, and grasshoppers kept their distance.

Despite his estrangement from the earth, Tam was fortunate in the timing of his rebirth. Paul Williams died in late spring, Tam's rebirth coinciding with the months before he would be sent back to school. This allowed him some of the time he needed to familiarize himself with his body: the coursing of its blood, the growth of its skeleton, the irritations of its hormones, and the waywardness of its brain; the smell of sugar, for instance, excited him beyond reason, so that even the prospect of vanilla ice cream—a thing given to reward him for being good—was exciting. Were he actually seven, he would have been as crazed as other seven-year-olds. In fact, he was certain that the fluctuations of his body were keeping him from the prolonged stillness needed to lose oneself in the world.

But Tam, being older and a buyeis, was able to turn the hormonal chaos of his body—of Paul Williams's body—to his own uses. The chaos provided the resistance he needed to sharpen his concentration. It was the fog through which he learned to allow the world around him in. And after a while, he felt confident enough to cast simple spells: burning wild herbs in the fireless cauldron of his palms, touching plants to promote their flowering, drawing insects out of tree bark with a chant, and so on.

Prior to her son's death, Eva would have been alarmed to see him stand in a field, immobile, for longer and longer stretches of time. Prior to Paul's death, it would have been unnatural to see him like this, frightening even. He had always been a happy child and sociable, sitting still only on Saturday mornings while he watched cartoons. But although it unnerved her to see her son standing alone, some of her fears were assuaged. Though she'd given permission for him to play outside, Eva was not quite convinced that Paul's body could handle the rough and tumble of boys' play. Then, too, she was worried about his friends teasing him for his foreign accent. Believing as she did in sound minds and sound bodies, Eva was as nervous about the emotional pain he might suffer as she was about physical damage. As such, Paul's new aloneness was a relief as much as it was a cause for concern.

Eva could have had no way of knowing, of course, that the one who now occupied her son's body could not be wounded—not emotionally, anyway—by the children in the neighbourhood. Tam was often approached by other children, especially by those who'd previously played with Paul. But when they called his name, Tam looked at them with such an unsettling blankness that they were intimidated. This and the fact that their mothers had whisperingly told them that Paul was "not right" after his illness meant that, after failed efforts to recruit him for games of tag or blind man's bluff, they mostly left him alone.

(Paul's friend Phillip, a sensitive child who lived across the street, was the first who understood that *this* Paul was no longer the one he had known. Being made aware, at the age of seven, of the impermanence of what we are within changed Phillip. Twenty years later, as a result of this insight and others that flowed from it, he chose a life of celibacy and Art, becoming one of the best-known painters in Lambton County.)

The one who profited most from Paul's rebirth was his father, Roland. Besides the joy of having his son returned to him, the return was further justification for their spending time together. Roland had been, for two or three years, in the habit of taking his son with him on his dalliances with women. Claiming that he and Paul needed time together to strengthen their bond as father and son, he would, when he had arranged to meet one of his lovers, announce to Eva that "he and his son" were going out for ice cream or going out fishing or going out, period.

Roland used time with his son as a pretext for his affairs. And it was a very good pretext. The women he seduced were mollified by his affection for his child, or at least, they were reassured that here was a man who valued family, despite his attraction to women other than his wife—an infidelity that, because the attraction was to them, they forgave.

In the past, Eva could not help feeling suspicious of her husband's behaviour. She understood that Roland was using their son for some purpose, though she did not believe him capable of taking Paul to the homes of his lovers. Now, however, she approved of the closeness between father and son. She was grateful for the time on her own and grateful, too, for what Roland called a "loosening of the apron strings." What's more, now that her son was isolated from his friends, she hoped Roland could coax him from solitude and, in speaking with him, help him along with English.

This last point about language learning was one Roland himself made, on the day he and Paul visited one of Roland's patients, Annette Maillard. But he was being disingenuous. Though he did sometimes speak to his son on these erotic forays, it was only while they were in the car. And even then, Roland's biggest interest was in the flavour of ice cream Paul wanted or the type of candy or the kind of toy. These things acquired, he would leave his son with them in front of a television set, if one were available, or a colouring book, which Roland was never without.

He was ingenious in finding ways to keep his son's attention away from his lover's bedroom, the room to which he and the woman would retire "for a diagnosis"—"diagnosis" being a word his son had loved, one Paul had been encouraged to say in front of guests, to show his intelligence. But Roland was pragmatic as well. Most children having short attention spans, it sometimes took a little extra to afford him the time he and his lover needed to do their business. This extra was a teaspoon of rum mixed in with vanilla milkshake (summer) or rum and hot chocolate (winter). On those occasions when Paul was being difficult, Roland would administer the spiked drink as soon as possible.

Giving alcohol to his child was usually a measure of last resort. But on this occasion, uncertain about the new Paul and desperate for everything to go well with Annette, Roland offered him the spiked milkshake at once. Tam, who had always eschewed alcohol, spit out his first mouthful, the very taste of it an affront, and cursed Roland in Garifuna, calling him every insult he could think of in the space of a minute, from idiot to goat lover.

Roland did not understand the words the boy used, but he had been insulted often enough to understand—by the look on Paul's face, by the tone of his high-pitched voice—that he was being insulted. If he had been familiar with the word "surreal," he might have used it to describe being glared at by a seven-year-old who was almost certainly saying unpleasant things to him in a language he did not understand.

—I'm sorry, Paul, he said. You always liked milkshakes. What's wrong?

—No give alcohol, stupid, Tam answered while glaring at him.

These words were so unexpected that Roland could think of no adequate response.

—I see, he said.

And turning away from his son, he drove in the direction of Oil Springs, where Annette lived on an unprofitable farm with her husband, who was away on business in Iowa, and her children, two girls, both slightly older than Paul.

By the time they reached Oil Springs—that is, after a few minutes—Roland had more or less forgotten the contretemps with his son. Excited as he was, his thoughts had turned to speculation about what Annette would be wearing when she greeted him. Having bought his son replacements for the milkshake he'd refused—Mackintosh toffee, a G.I. Joe, a wooden spinning top—Roland left Tam in the living room with Annette's daughters, making sure to turn on a radio and informing the children that he needed private time in order to diagnose Mrs. Maillard properly.

Did they all understand this?

The girls did, but in any case they were busy with their dolls. Tam stared at Roland, still put off by the man's attempt to give him rum, but now also caught short by the man's brass. It was clear to Tam that Roland—his brother's spitting image—and Mrs. Maillard were preparing to rut. Their desire for each other was barely hidden. It was only surprising that the woman's daughters seemed oblivious to what was going on. Of course, they were children, while he was not.

Though Tam had lived much of his life as a celibate—choosing oneness with Nature over the momentary and fumbling satisfactions of coitus—he knew how strong the urge to copulate could be, how desire both distracted and focused the mind. He had experienced both the urge to mate and its satisfaction, losing his virginity to an older woman when he was seventeen. And, being the kind of man he was, Tam had sought to master the art—learning how best to please a woman—before leaving sexual intercourse behind for good, at twenty-one.

There is, of course, a dignity in fucking—a dignity consonant with life itself—and Roland shared in this dignity, as all humans do, despite the betrayal of his wife. But how Eva would have suffered, if she'd heard the muffled giggling, the muffled sighs, the muffled sound of the bedframe squeaking. All of which Tam did hear as he stood by the door, thoughtfully listening, before going out of the Maillards' home to stand at the edge of the yard behind the house, attending the wind as it soughed through the bushes that someone had planted as if to keep the woods beyond the property at bay: wilderness to keep wilderness from wilderness.

Once father and son were back in the Impala, once Roland had fastened the seatbelt for him, Tam looked at him so intently that Roland was spooked. He was already shaken up, because his habit of sleeping with his patients—with nurses, with the wives of friends, with any woman who would have him—had never brought him peace or lasting pleasure. Once he'd slept with a woman—any woman, his wife included—he felt guilt and regret until he slept with another. And so the cycle repeated. But the look his son gave him made it worse. He was convinced that, somehow, Paul knew what he'd just done and understood its implications. Roland's feelings of shame and guilt skyrocketed.

But, in fact, Tam's gaze held as much compassion as disgust. He could not help loving a man who looked so much like his younger brother. Respect, love, and longing for his own childhood rose up in him, so that he was forced to look away from Roland, turning not outward to the farm fields around Oil Springs but inward to his childhood home near Basse Terre where his brother had managed to catch an iguana on his own, the still-wriggling creature almost as tall as his brother himself: five feet from head to tail.

(How odd to long for the taste of cush-cush and 'guana while in a body that had never tasted them! And yet at the thought of cush-cush, Paul began to salivate.)

Turning back to Roland, Tam said

—Where you from?

As with much that Paul asked these days, the tone of his question was troubling.

—What do you mean? Roland asked.

—Who your family, answered Tam.

Now, this was a subject Roland liked to think about. He was proud of his heritage and was happy to delve into his own origins, as if the greatness that preceded him softened his flaws. He was born in Belmont, Trinidad. His family was, on his father's side, Creole: of mixed African and Welsh descent. He was related to Eric Williams, the second minister of the country and a brilliant man who had studied at . . .

Here, Roland rambled on about his father's people. However, none of what he recounted was of any interest to Tam who, after a while, considered asking him to stop talking. But as he was about to do so, Roland began to talk about his mother (Hilda Modeste) and her people. Roland was not proud of the Modestes. They were, to his mind, the antithesis of the brilliant and Oxford-inclined Williamses. They had been Carib, from around Basse Terre, very mysterious, the kind of people who believed in Soucouyant and La Diablesse, obeah and magic.

Tam interrupted him.

—What Hilda mother name? he asked.

Roland smiled, distracted as he was from guilt by his son's interest in their heritage.

—Your great-grandmother was Adrina Modeste, he said. And her mother was Ada Modeste. Your grandmother and great-grandmother kept the name Modeste, because they never married. That tells you what you need to know about that side of the family. You're better off concentrating on the Williamses.

In any other circumstance, this insult to his family would have angered Tam. But on hearing the name Ada, Tam was overcome by emotion. Ada had been his youngest brother's youngest child: that is, Tain's daughter. Ada, however, had looked nothing like Tain, being a replica of the young girl who was her mother. Tam had avoided holding the girl for fear he would let her fall—a fear he felt around all infants. How odd that, four generations later, Tain should be reborn in this man beside him, driving the Impala.

Tam felt, then, such a longing for home that he turned away from Roland and contemplated the sky, its bland blue expanse, in order to distract himself from longing. He felt helpless and bereft. And the full extent of his exile struck him. Why, if he had to be reborn, was he abandoned in a country so unlike the one he loved and so far away in time?

Was he meant to punish Roland or learn from him?

Was he meant to bring comfort to Eva, or was he to learn from her?

Was he meant to suffer for something he had done?

Whose agent was he? And what could he accomplish in the body of a seven-year-old?

3. Skirmishes

In relatively short time, the English language—as well as the context in which it was spoken: Petrolia, 1957—returned completely to the body Tam occupied. Two months after his rebirth, English returned so forcefully that Tam was grateful (and relieved) his own language remained.

While he had, from the first, understood English, he was now increasingly aware of its nuances—perhaps more aware than Paul had been. For instance, he could understand the messages that emanated from the television and radio, how meretricious they were. What he could not understand was why anyone would subject themself to such a flood of sound and false significance.

—Chocolate and coconut! Coconut and chocolate! Mounds by Peter Paul! Indescribably delicious!

As Tam's understanding of nuance crested, there came, as well, the ability to use the new tongue efficiently. For the first weeks, he had sometimes translated the languages within him: Garifuna to English, English to Garifuna. It had been as if he and Paul Williams had relayed meaning to each other. But now, he could feel Garifuna being pushed aside so that one day he looked up at his mother as they were eating supper and, without translating, said

—I thank you, woman, for this meal.

Eva took this well. Hiding her surprise—at the fact he'd spoken English so fluently, at the seriousness of his tone, at his proper accent, at the maturity she felt from her child—she answered

—I'm your mother, Paul. I've cooked for you every day of your life.

Thinking it over, Tam answered

—Yes, that must be true.

And a deep emotion overtook him, as he was reminded of his own mother. How different she had looked from this woman: broader-faced, bigger-bosomed, almond-eyed. And how different she had been: so modest that it had seemed, at times, as if she were not there. Or there and then somehow gone from mind, spirited away. This woman, this Eva, was more present and more attentive, no doubt because she had only one child to take care of. But looking at her, Tam was reminded of his mother, how he had watched as she made bread from cassava: cassava, salt, water, the loaves retrieved from fire, then left out to air. She had been serene, doing this thing she did so often, but seeing Tam watch her, she had smiled at him as if he were sudden sunlight. Nothing more. But his love for her flooded his soul, and in its wake, he was able to see Eva as Paul must have seen her.

—Your son loves you, he said.

It was awkward, and strangely matter-of-fact in tone, but Eva had wondered if she would ever hear words like this from her son again. And on hearing them, she was moved, getting up from the table to take her son in her arms. Which was annoying to Tam, as her embrace made it difficult for him to breathe.

The advent—or return—of English to Paul Williams's body had consequences for Tam's social life as well, such as it was. He now understood all the things spoken in his vicinity by the children who played in the field while he was there. None of what was said interested him, most of it having to do with "skipping," "Barbie," "baseball," or beings whose names were associated with images on television—Woody Woodpecker, Bugs Bunny, Sylvester, Mickey Mouse.

As it had been when Tam couldn't speak with them, the children his age left him alone. He knew now, however, that they found him scary. They were afraid, no doubt, that what had happened to him—inexplicable, unfathomable—might happen to one of them. The older children were also unnerved but, being preteens, their fears were accompanied by taunts, by the beginnings of violence, with one particularly disturbed child, John Pardew by name, slapping the back of Tam's head and calling him "retard."

It would have been ludicrous for Tam, a seventy-year-old, to take name-calling seriously. What he did take seriously was that a being twice his size—that is, Pardew—had struck him. He had felt the boy's maliciousness, and realizing that he, as a seven-year-old, would be subject to the sociopathology that was—that has always been—the rule among preteens, he decided to put a quick end to Pardew's aggression.

Though he had been cautious when it came to new-world plants and their possible effects, Tam gathered together—instinctively, relying as he did on his sense of smell and memory—weeds and wildflowers from the field near him, drying them on the windowsill in his room, grinding them together between two flat quartz stones he'd dug from the earth, each the size of his palms, both as if meant for his purpose. He could not be certain what would happen to Pardew if he inhaled the powder, because it was difficult to gauge the potency of the plants around him, difficult to guess if they would work the way plants did in Trinidad.

For all Tam knew, Pardew might die on inhaling the powder. It was a commixture he himself would have called a "useful poison." The child's death would certainly cause problems, but despite that, the next time Tam was in the field and Pardew approached with some of his friends, no sooner had Pardew called him a stupid retard and approached than Tam blew the powder in the boy's face, using a paper cone he'd made for the purpose.

The effect was gratifying. Pardew shat himself at once.

Moreover, the boy's distress was instructive both to the children who had followed Pardew and to Tam. None of the children knew for certain what had happened. But the effect of what Tam had done was unforgettable. None, not even Pardew, thought of bothering him again. And although Tam had only expected Pardew to throw up, he accepted that, under the circumstances, a ruthless laxative was at least as good as an emetic.

Petrolia being a small town, however, the matter did not end there. John Pardew's friends naturally spoke, with reverence, of what they'd seen: Paul Williams had done something—no one quite knew what—and then, right there and then, Johnny had dirtied himself. Not just a little, either. He'd soiled pants, shirt, socks, and shoes! More: John Pardew had told his father about the incident, describing what had happened, and it was in this way that the story got back to Paul's mother and father.

Roland did not believe that his seven-year-old had, somehow, administered a laxative to a child twice his size and weight. He brought the subject up while the three of them were eating supper and, barely able to contain his amusement, asked his son if he'd forced John Pardew to shit himself.

Rather than answer directly, Tam said

—What should I do if John Pardew slaps my head?

—Are you saying you gave him a laxative because he insulted you?

—Not because he insulted me, Tam said. Because he hit me.

—I don't believe you for a minute, answered Roland. You know, it's a very bad thing to lie.

—Why would I lie? Tam asked, genuinely puzzled.

Roland's attitude changed then, from amusement to annoyance. Eva tried to speak in her son's defence, but her husband cut her off without a word, bringing his palm down hard on the dining table.

—Show me how you did it, he said.

—I will not, said Tam mildly.

—You will, answered Roland, or I'll show you why boys should obey their parents.

Tam understood then, a fraction too late, that the young man before him was only marginally more mature than John Pardew. He should, he thought, have known this, given Roland's behaviour, his adultery, his willingness to intoxicate his own child. Tam had, however, taken a generous view: that Roland was suffering some crisis that clouded his judgment, that Roland was immature but capable of seeing his own flaws, that Roland, descended from the Modestes, deserved the benefit of a doubt.

How time and circumstances had belittled the Modestes!

While Pardew's immaturity was to be expected, Roland's was troubling. Tam's own father had hit him on a number of occasions, whenever he'd done anything dangerous. He had been impartial and not at all interested in subjugating his son or breaking his spirit. But Roland, it seemed, whether out of resentment or a misplaced belief that violence would serve them all, meant to tame his son. And it was unclear to Tam if Roland would unwittingly damage him. As he did not, for a number of reasons, want to be injured, he said

—Very well. If you let me, I'll get what I need from my room.

Eva again tried to intercede on her son's behalf. Roland ignored her.

—Get what you need, Roland said, and be quick about it.

Climbing down from his chair at the table, Tam did just that, returning from his room with a palmful of the powder which, approaching as if to show what he had, he blew in Roland's face, timing it so that the man breathed a lot of it in.

The effect was as immediate as it had been with Pardew. Roland soiled himself. But he had breathed in more of the dry concoction and the result was stronger, his intestinal distress more alarming. In fact, Roland and Eva were terrified by the incident. It confirmed what Roland suspected—this boy was not the son he knew. This one was mysterious and possibly dangerous.

That evening, as Tam meditated in his room, Roland—still suffering—tried to convince his wife that it would be best for all of them—their family—if they sought psychiatric help for Paul.

—He's my son as much as he is yours, said Roland. But you know he hasn't been the same, since he came back to life. It isn't only his language. It's his change of temperament.

—He's a sweet child, answered Eva. You asked him to show you what he did to that Pardew boy! Now that he showed you, you want to send him to a shrink. You're not making sense!

—*I'm* not making sense? How many seven-year-olds do you know who can make a powdered laxative? I don't know whether to punish him or send him to university!

—Well, what if Paul's a genius? Eva asked. Isn't it possible that having a near-death experience could make him smarter? He's not the same, it's true, but he's not a bad child all of a sudden.

He wasn't a bad child, and that was a problem, as far as Roland was concerned. It was one thing to send him to a psychiatrist if he were difficult, but what reason could they use, really? The present Paul was not unruly, did not make scenes, seemed mature for his age and yet showed no signs of the genius that could invent such an efficient laxative. The child was as perplexing as he was abnormal.

Though Eva had been startled by the violence of Roland's reaction to the powder, she was convinced that it proved there was something extraordinary about her child. Yes, of course he was different. As his mother, she could feel it every moment they sat together. But different was not necessarily bad. And it was no reason to send Paul to a psychiatrist in Sarnia who would be inclined to find something wrong with him anyway.

—He's not a bad child, she repeated.

—Well, I won't be taking him anywhere with me again, said Roland. And don't blame me if I stay away from home a little more, from now on.

And so, their tedious argument about power—the two-handed dispute their marriage had become—made its foul way to centre stage. Both parents cherished their son and wanted what was best for him. This was now one of the few things that kept them together. But Roland's non sequitur was just another in a long line of his threats, his excuses for staying away. In any case, Roland spent so much time away from home "working," it was difficult to imagine him spending more time away without moving out.

Eva's anger rose up in her like bile.

—How will I know you're gone more than usual? she asked.

But did not wait for an answer, going into their bedroom, closing the door behind her. Did he really believe she didn't know what he was up to? Not two days before, the husband of one of his patients had called to ask her to keep her husband away from his wife. And she had somehow found the steel, despite her shock, to say that *she* would appreciate it if his wife stayed away from her husband.

The humiliation had almost crushed her, but she had borne it on her own, silently, for Paul's sake, and because she refused to allow Roland's unspeakable behaviour to force her from her home on anyone's schedule but her own. Given all that, it was now even more clear that Paul was her only bulwark against the solitudes of her marriage. She was, after all, not one for church socials, not one for church, not one for quilting bees. Which left her the company of her husband, when he was home, the books she read, the paintings she made, and her son. Paul would have to do much worse to have her even begin to think about sending him away.

For his part, Tam was disappointed in himself. The world he had awoken to was certainly disorienting. From its tarred roadways to its endless fascination with coloured lights and loud sounds, it was still, after months of quietly acclimating, just beyond his imagining, the people in it unpredictable. Roland and Eva, though they made their way in this new world, were obviously unhappy. In his opinion, they were disastrously cut off from the land on which they lived. Still, they were half his age, and he ought to have dealt with them differently, Roland in particular.

That said, however mature he was, he was in the body of a seven-year-old, dependent on people he did not know for food, shelter, protection, and company. What had begun with the need to protect himself had descended into a small chaos. He could not help wishing for a return to Trinidad. He could feel the pull of his navel string, buried beneath a tree somewhere near Basse Terre. But how was he to return, seven years old as he was, and what guarantee that Trinidad would be as he remembered it? What hope, even?

These thoughts aside, Tam was wary of Roland. The young man was spooked, and Tam was uncertain how he would react to what had happened. There seemed no choice but to cast a further spell, one to calm Roland down. Taking a pair of Roland's socks—a pair he had stolen for the purpose—Tam pulled strands of fabric from them. Over these strands he spoke a cooling spell and placed them on a folded square of paper on which the words "otono" and "autumn" were written on one side and the word "spirit" on the other. That night, when the house was quiet and all lights were out, he opened the Kelvinator—a miraculous device, when you thought about it—and put the spell he'd made as far back in the freezer as his small arms would allow.

The next morning, Tam rose early and sat at the dining table as Eva made breakfast in the kitchen: eggs; bacon, which Tam would not eat; toast; oatmeal; and coffee, which Tam was not permitted. Roland emerged, in suit and tie, and sat at the head of the table.

—Good morning, son, he said.

If one had not known what had happened the previous evening, one would not have guessed that anything *had* happened.

—I should be mad at you, said Roland. That was a terrible thing you did. But I'm not in the mood to punish you. I'll just say: you should be careful what you blow in people's faces. I ruined a perfectly good pair of pants!

He laughed, as if the memory were a good one.

—How did you make that powder?

—I didn't mean to make it, Tam said. I put some weeds together, and this is how it turned out.

—Hmph, Roland said. Bad luck for me and young Pardew, then.

After a moment, he did as he did most mornings. He unfolded the *Sarnia Observer* and read the headlines: Khrushchev, Diefenbaker, sales at Simpsons-Sears in Northgate Mall.

The change in her husband's mood was a surprise to Eva. She had imagined having to intervene if it looked like Roland would lose his temper. But he did not. More: after eating his eggs and bacon, he complimented her cooking, something he hadn't done in years. His mildness was so unusual that it cast a light on the tension within her, the near-constant waiting for his annoyance or anger, which had become a feature of their seven years together.

Tam, who observed the two as he ate his oatmeal, was gratified by the success of his spell, unsure as he had been that it would work given the method he'd used. But Roland's presence was characteristic of someone under a spell: calm on the surface, though you could sense his feelings moving beneath. The spell was like a great sea in which Roland's will was drowning. Which meant that, as long as the packet of strands was in the Kelvinator, Roland would feel calm in his son's presence.

It also occurred to Tam, as Roland noisily shook the pages of his newspaper, that it was time to test more spells—those, for instance, that could be done without the fauna he'd seen in the field: moles, crickets, sparrows, and so on. That's not to say that he *hadn't* begun to sense the field's inner life. But it was no use asking moles and crickets for something without the ability to meet them in the place where one's will is subsumed. The mole that had approached him, for instance, and which he'd allowed onto his palm—the most beautiful creature he'd yet encountered, the soft, wriggling weight of it, its pinkish fingers splayed, its eyeless face, its palpable bewilderment as he held it.

On whom would he test his spells, though? Tam did not want to ensorcell any of the children around him. It had been a mistake, however justified, to use his gift against John Pardew. But this left only Eva and Roland, the two adults he could observe, and this naturally limited the kinds of spells he would use.

When Roland had gone for the day, after kissing the top of his son's head, Tam waited at the dining table, rather than going out to the field. When his mother had finished washing the dishes and cleaning the kitchen, she stopped to ask him if everything was all right.

—Madam, Tam answered, do you ever wish your husband loved you more than he does?

This, she thought, is the way he thinks now. She was no longer surprised by his tone, however heartbreaking it was to accept that the fever that killed him had taken something indefinable but precious with it. But "madam" was not a word she would accept from him.

—Paul, she said, I'm your mother. Please don't call me "madam." It's upsetting.

—I understand, said Tam. You're the mother of this body. But you're not the mother of this mind. May I call you Eva?

An answer she could not have imagined, let alone predicted.

—No, she said. I want you to call me Mom, like you used to.

It suddenly seemed cruel to argue with her. Eva could only see him as her son. On the other hand, the idea that she was his mother was difficult for Tam to accept. The word "mother" belonged to a woman he had loved who was long dead. Still, why shouldn't he humour one who needed the reassurance that her son was alive?

—Mother, he said, do you wish your husband loved you more than he does?

Well, "mother" was a start.

—What can a seven-year-old know about love? Eva asked.

—Isn't love the birthright of all creatures? Tam answered. Why shouldn't a seven-year-old know as much as you?

Eva laughed at this, delighted by his answer, though the conversation was already stranger than any she'd previously had with Paul. Perhaps he was a genius after all. She sat in the chair opposite him, looking into the face of her child: his thick eyebrows, large brown eyes, ears sticking out like Roland's, though the one he most looked like was her father, his grandfather—all it would take is thick glasses and a porkpie hat to make them twins! She could barely keep herself from picking him up and hugging him, though he had lately forbidden her from doing this.

—What makes you think your father doesn't love me enough? she asked.

The question took Tam by surprise. Wasn't Roland's lack of affection for his wife obvious? Of course, Tam knew that the man slept with women other than his wife—one at least. Maybe Eva did not know this, however glaring Roland's falseness seemed. Then again, in his experience, those deceived are often party to the deception: ever surprised, but ever knowing, too. Perhaps Eva chose not to see Roland for what he was.

—He's not home very often, Tam said. And he comes home at odd times. Doesn't that make you unhappy?

—Yes, she said. But I don't need him at home any more than he is.

She spoke these words resolutely, but anyone could see they were not true. They were said with too much conviction, as with someone doing their best to convince another. Tam could not help feeling sad for the woman. She was trying to convince her seven-year-old that she was happy. He decided, then, not to cast a spell for her, because he was not sure Eva would enjoy Roland being constantly home.

—I see, he answered.

—I'm curious about how you'd get your father to stay home, said Eva. But let's save that for some other time.

And, now, amused and relieved, she stood up and, before he could object, lifted him out of his chair, so she could hold him in her arms, kissing his cheek and the back of his head, enjoying the smell of her child. It was an experience that Tam found almost unbearable.

For Tam, this exchange with Eva was disappointing. He had been looking forward to observing Roland under the influence of a love spell. On the other hand, it was a signal moment in his relationship with Eva. She was obviously grateful that Tam had accepted the idea that she did not need to see more of her husband. And, in the weeks that followed, gratitude seemed to have the effect of making her more forthcoming and truthful about other matters—perhaps as a way of making up for what they both knew had been a lie.

Whatever the case, the moment Eva took him in her arms she took him into her confidence as well.

Paul Williams had died and Tam revived in May. Months passed during which a body accommodated the two souls within it, the consciousness of Tam Modeste dominant. But Tam's dominance was not as neat as that suggests. Tam was aware of Paul's emotions and, gradually, of his consciousness. The full return of the English language, for instance, was like a stage in Paul's return. Nor did Tam resent the child within him. Paul was, after all, his brother's offspring. *Au contraire*, the idea grew within Tam himself that he was shepherding Paul's body, until such time as the boy was strong enough to nudge him aside.

During these months, Tam nevertheless sought to understand the reason for his rebirth, while testing his knowledge of the new world and waiting for occasions to use obeah. He was intrigued by Petrolia and the land around it, by Lambton County as glimpsed from the windows of Roland's Impala: fields of maize, apple trees, monstrous barns, cows, horses, settlements of stone houses and streetlights. There seemed so much of it to master.

By the time Tam spoke with Eva about her husband's lack of affection, it was late August and he would, he was told, be going to school. He knew what this meant, more or less, though he had never been to school himself. But nothing could have prepared him for the *fact* of school-going, the fussiness of it.

Northgate Mall and shopping at Simpsons-Sears: these were already dismaying, the flood of things housed in tall-ceilinged places that reeked of the ungrounded. Northgate Mall was what he might have imagined—if he could have imagined it!—as the absence of all that he had known as *Fulasu*: world, land, soil. And yet, Simpsons-Sears was world, too, in a sense. The store was a mutation of the idea of abundance.

But what was of all that compared to St. Philip's Catholic School?

Despite himself, Tam felt trepidation when Eva left him in the schoolyard. The students did not intimidate him. He was being sent to grade three and most of those in the upper grades were bigger than him. But he knew them for what they were: young primates, more dangerous to themselves than to him.

What intimidated him was the school itself, the building. If Northgate Mall had seemed a perversion of the idea of Nature, St. Philip's was what Tam imagined the birth of an administration would be like. Here, this building, was the embodiment of coercion. Moreover, he could feel that many of the seven-year-olds around him—forced to line up before entering the building—felt as he did, though none seemed able to express their apprehension.

If the outside of St. Philip's made him wary, what to make of the building's interior? Tam could not be sure the tall ceilings and long corridors were unnaturally high or unusually extended. It may be that his body, compact as it was, naturally found the place outsized. But its dimensions were only part of what unnerved him. There were the gleaming doors, the smell of women and children, chalk, soap; the desks, like carvings of metal and wood, in which he was expected to insert himself; the frantic and various presences of the children around him. And it occurred to him, unnerved as he was, that it would be reasonable to leave the building and return to Paul's home—though he wasn't sure how to get back there.

It was then that he met Miss Heikkinen. Seeing him at the back of the classroom, she approached and asked him if he was feeling poorly. When he said nothing, she put an arm around his shoulder and asked his name. Without thinking, he said

—Tam.

—Oh, she said. And all this time, I thought you were Paul. I'll call you Tam if you want.

He was bewitched by her tone of voice. It was as if they were sharing a private story.

—No, he said, I'm Paul
and allowed himself to be guided to a desk at the front of the class.

Miss Heikkinen's kindness was a welcome distraction, but he was not distracted for long. The world of St. Philip's was as intimidating from the front of the classroom as it was from anywhere else. To begin with, they were made to stand and then encouraged to sing an anthem that, interpreted by seven-year-olds, sounded like a cry of surrender. After which they stood up to say their names.

—My name, said Tam, is Paul Williams
and he bowed to Miss Heikkinen. After that, there was reading and dictation, both of which, to his own surprise, Tam

found he could do, though his handwriting was shaky, there being two selves at the pencil: his consciousness mixed with Paul's learning.

It was no doubt fated that recess would be a problem. Though John Pardew did not attend St. Philip's, a number of his friends did, and they had all heard about Paul Williams. One in particular, Roger Flynn, was anxious to see what the fuss was about. So, although Tam kept to one corner of the yard, away from everyone else, Flynn and a few of the boys from grade eight approached him.

—Hey, you little twerp, said Flynn. What'd you do to my friend John?

Tam had a good idea of where this exchange was going, as you could have felt the boy's malice from miles away. Already spooked by St. Philip's and more conscious of his stewardship of Paul's body, it occurred to Tam that, though the business with Pardew had been a mistake, this was a good moment to make an example of someone.

—You are a child of chickens from a long line of chickens, he said to Flynn.

Tam then chanted a spell in Garifuna while looking in the boy's eyes, as one does when encountering a snake for the first time. The chant finished, Tam opened his arms wide, as if to set the spell free, and almost immediately, Roger Flynn crouched down, put his thumbs under his arms, and began murmuring contentedly, clucking as he waddled away from the boys around them.

The spell was effective in most of the ways Tam intended. First, it dealt with Roger Flynn. He was now more concerned with the grass in the yard than he was with Tam. Then, it frightened those who had come to see a fight. Their incomprehension was so great that it grew into the kind of terror one feels on a dark night of the soul. From that moment, none of the boys—in fact, none of the children attending St. Philip's—would ever trouble Paul Williams again.

On the other hand, the spell also overstepped its mark. He was at a Catholic school just down the road from a Catholic church of the same name, St. Philip's, and Catholicism was not like the religion in which Tam was raised. When the principal of St. Philip's, Omer St. Pierre, was told that one of the children in third grade had turned Roger Flynn into a chicken, there were really only two attitudes for him to take. The first was to assume that someone was mistaken. But the counter to this was at hand. Roger Flynn had been herded into the principal's office murmuring, clucking, and squatting with his thumbs tucked under his arms. Nor did calling his name or threatening him make the least difference.

That left the idea that this was a case of demonic possession. And if Paul Williams was actually responsible for Roger Flynn's state, the news was even worse. It would be proof that Satan was working through a seven-year-old. But although Mr. St. Pierre was fervently Catholic, and though he knew very well that it was his duty to expose evil and help expunge it, he did not trust his own faith where matters like demonic possession were at issue.

So, he did two things. He called for the parish priest, Father Fernby, to come to the school as soon as he could. And when Fernby had arrived and seen for himself the state young Flynn was in, Mr. St. Pierre asked the priest to examine Paul Williams. Though the boy was only seven, there was not, as far as Mr. St. Pierre knew, a minimum age for satanic proxies. Besides, as he understood it, Paul Williams had been on the brink of death—had died, if rumours were true—so there was, perhaps, something wrong with the boy.

—Let's hope the child is not *actually* possessed, said Father Fernby, kindly.

—I'm sure there's a better explanation, said Mr. St. Pierre. I mean, I hope there is, Father, because I don't want to tell Roger's parents that he's been cursed any more than I want to tell Dr. Williams that his son is possessed by Satan.

In the first moments after Paul entered the principal's office, it really did appear that the boy was possessed. Paul looked at Father Fernby and, as far as Mr. St. Pierre could tell, began to speak in tongues. And though what he said sounded like gibberish, the child was clearly furious. Just the reaction you'd expect from Satan when faced with God's representative.

Things, however, were even more complicated than Mr. St. Pierre imagined. Tam *was* angry, but he was not spewing nonsense. He was speaking in his own tongue and what he said was

—Mafia haruti buguya abuha ya!

That is: You white devil! So here you are!

And Father Fernby, to general astonishment, answered in Tam's language:

—Haruti nuguya pero mama nuguya mafia.

Which is to say:

—I am white, but I am not the devil here.

4. History Is Not What It Seems, It Seems

It would be difficult to precisely describe all the impressions, reactions, and surprises of those in Mr. St. Pierre's office. The general mood was bewilderment, but the tenor of the bewilderment varied with each person: from the alarmed but relieved incomprehension of the principal—relieved that Paul seemed to be speaking a known language—to the startlement of his secretary, Miss Lewis, who was at the office door, listening in, though she should have been calling Eva Williams to let her know that her son was in trouble; from the gentle confusion of Miss Heikkinen—confusion rooted in concern for the boys involved—to the thoughtful clucking of Roger Flynn who, it seemed, was searching for grain on the floor of the office.

That said, the most complex feelings were those of Tam and Father Fernby.

Father James Fernby, named in honour of James Edward Fernby, a distant relative, was almost identical in appearance to the Captain Fernby responsible for Tam's death. Moreover, he was around the same age as Captain Fernby had been—somewhat older, but still. Tam recognized his face, and in recognizing Fernby, he believed that he had finally been given the reason for his rebirth: revenge. His being in this place (Petrolia) at this time (1957) was a matter of restitution, the world's apology for what it had put him through.

But, if so, it would be a difficult revenge. He was trapped in the body of a seven-year-old. He still had all his knowledge, true, but there was only so much a child could do by way of revenge. And why was he thrown into a world of which he understood so little? The people around him had strayed so far from sense that their culture was ungraspable. If, for instance, Tam had encountered Donald Duck in the wild, he would have killed him, to protect Nature itself.

Adding to the complexity of Tam's reaction: after recognizing the man who'd brought about his death, Tam almost immediately realized that this was not quite the man, despite the resemblance. His look was similar but the spirit was different. And this one could speak Garifuna, a fact that brought Tam pleasure, despite his desire for restitution.

—Ida liya basubiduru ladimerahoun Garifuna?

—I learned it, Fernby answered. The question is how *you* know it. I have known you since your birth. You've never spoken Garifuna.

The nuances of Father Fernby's question were partially hidden by his reasonable tone. It was, for those in Principal St. Pierre's office, as if a man and boy were exchanging banalities: no raised voices, no accusations, no sudden movements. But Father Fernby, who had assumed he'd been called to the school for some small matter, was faced with something beyond his experience as a priest: demonic possession. There could be no doubt that the being before him—a child he'd baptized—was not Paul Williams. As such, there were protocols that he was meant to follow. But looking at a child he knew while knowing it was not the child he knew was unsettling.

Tam could feel Father Fernby's fright. He was, after all, the more mature of the two. And realizing that he had made an irretrievable mistake in speaking Garifuna, Tam answered Fernby calmly, in English.

—When I woke from my sickness, he said, this language was in my head. Sometimes it just comes out.

This was the right answer, and it brought relief to all of those present.

—But why, asked Father Fernby, did you speak to me in that language? How did you know I spoke it?

—I didn't mean to speak it, said Tam. I can't help it.

This was even better. All those present knew that Paul had almost died. What's more, all had assumed that there would be repercussions, that no one got close to death without suffering consequences. This made sense of—or excused—the changes in the child. Of course, there was still the question of Roger Flynn.

—Paul, asked Mr. St. Pierre, did you do something to Roger?

Up to this point, Tam had been calm. He spoke with the voice of a seven-year-old, and this lent his words a certain pathos (for Mr. St. Pierre, Miss Heikkinen) or made them troubling (for Father Fernby, Miss Lewis). It occurred to Tam, though, that he had not used the one weapon a child possessed: tears. Given the circumstances, it would be reasonable for Paul to break down, reasonable and helpful to Tam. That said, it had been sixty-something years since Tam had cried in order to gain sympathy. He no longer remembered how it was done. But when Principal St. Pierre repeated the question

—What did you do to Roger? Did you . . . fowlify him?

Tam rubbed his eyes, thought of something sad—the last time he saw his father—and made a sound that he associated with crying: something between a wail and a complaint.

Whether this forced crying would, on its own, have gained him the distraction he wanted, Tam would never know because, as he was pretending to cry, Paul Williams came upstage in their shared consciousness and began to cry in earnest, so that all the adults—Father Fernby included—felt obliged to comfort him. And after they had comforted him for a few minutes, Tam managed to say

—I didn't do anything, sir!

Which pushed the question about Roger Flynn aside, while changing the focus of attention to Paul himself. Paul Williams was the younger of the two boys and, on reflection, unlikely to have influenced the behaviour of a child almost twice his age and size.

And as often happens when authority encounters the singular, the easiest explanation for what had happened was the one that received the quickest credence. Once Paul's strange language was understood as a "neurological" phenomenon and after the Flynn child's condition was marked down as "psychological," Paul was sent back to his classroom with Miss Heikkinen, while the adults who remained tried to decide how best to deal with Roger Flynn; that is, how best to explain to the child's mother the little they understood about his behaviour—behaviour that lasted for two whole days before the boy suddenly returned to himself while roosting on his bed beneath a picture of Mickey Mantle.

But Father Fernby remained unsatisfied by the conclusion of the incident. He could not dislodge his first impression: Paul Williams was possessed. The child he'd spoken to in Mr. St. Pierre's office had none of the innocence, curiosity, and good temper of the child he'd baptized and watched grow. Moreover, it seemed unlikely that Paul would suddenly learn a language that was spoken by so few people and, having miraculously learned it, speak it to the one person—within a two- or three-thousand-mile radius—who understood it.

It all felt as if this encounter with Paul Williams was a test. But what kind of test? Was it a test of his faith or his humanity? Were these things separable? Yes, to an extent, they were.

Faith demanded, if the child was possessed, that he seek advice from those whose knowledge of spiritual matters was deeper than his. There was, in fact, a procedure. But exorcisms were elaborate and potentially dangerous. There had been cases when, though the demon was ousted, the possessed did not survive.

Humanity required that he think first of the possible consequences to the child, one whose mother, Eva, was a woman he both pitied and admired. The idea of leaving such a woman bereft of the one joyous thing in her life was unbearable.

His pity for Eva came from direct knowledge. He had heard the confessions of women who'd come seeking forgiveness for their affairs with Dr. Williams, including one—Mrs. Helen Richards of Oil City—who confessed weekly, one summer, to being unable to resist the "Black devil." And Fernby had no doubt that Eva suspected her husband's infidelity, because she had confessed to her suspicions and had sought God's forgiveness for doubting her husband. The irony of asking God to forgive a woman for suspecting the truth was, at times, difficult for Father Fernby to accept.

The important thing, he decided, was to spend time with Paul Williams, or with the being that lived in Paul's body. To do justice to both faith and humanity, he would have to look at things the right way. He would have to see clearly, which was easy to suggest, though seeing clearly was, in his experience, a difficult thing, the obstructions—internal and external—being so unpredictable.

One evening, days after the incident with Roger Flynn, Father Fernby visited the Williamses' home unannounced, his pretext being a concern for Paul's state of mind. Roland was not yet home. Paul was in his room. So, Fernby and Eva were able to speak openly about the changes in the boy. It was a relief for Eva to talk about these things dispassionately, without worrying about a negative reaction. Roland seemed to have decided that the best way to deal with the changes in his son was to ignore them. He became upset if she mentioned her fears about Paul's state, Paul's life, or Paul's future.

Seeing in Father Fernby a temperate man, and believing that he had Paul's best interests in mind, she suggested that his guidance would be helpful. For the priest, still unsure if Paul was possessed or not, this was a chance to observe the boy, discreetly.

—What are his interests? asked Father Fernby.

—I don't know anymore, Eva answered. A few months ago, he was interested in the same things his friends were. Now, it seems he's fascinated by the field beside us. I've never known a child who could stand still for as long as he does, just staring in the distance. He doesn't play with any of his friends from school or from the neighbourhood. He stands there looking at the field or walking around in it.

—Maybe we can use that, said Father Fernby. There's a greenhouse beside the rectory. Let him come over a few times a week and help me with the greenhouse and the rectory garden. I don't know if it'll bring him out of his shell, but it can't hurt. And if he doesn't like gardening, there's no reason to force him. We can try something else.

It was settled, then, subject to Roland's approval and Paul's willingness.

On hearing the proposal, Tam was noncommittal. But he decided, in the end, that afternoons with the priest would provide the occasions he needed to revenge himself on Fernby or, at least, to teach him what it meant to be stripped of dignity.

It was difficult to imagine how this would be done, but before going to the rectory for the first time, he stepped up his practice with spells and made longer forays in the fields near his house and farther away—by the golf course on Glenview, for instance—looking for plants, stones, and carcasses he might use: something to make the priest hallucinate, say, something to make the man's mind pliable, a way to make him feel what those who'd practiced obeah had experienced thanks to his people, the British—for whom Tam had a resentment that had transcended death.

Of course, Tam's resentment and anger were fiery because his betrayal by an English soldier was, for him, recent. It felt as if only moments had passed since the mapipi had freed him from capture. The Father Fernby he had encountered in Mr. St. Pierre's office was a glaring reminder of his own demise. That said, his anger and resentment were not unclouded. He was distracted from them by a thought he could not quite keep in mind, one that made it difficult for him to maintain hatred of any depth: who was this priest, exactly?

It became even more difficult after his first afternoon at the rectory.

Autumn was coming. It was already colder than Tam liked, and when his contemporaries in grade three dared to tease him at all, they would snicker at the winter coat he'd begun wearing in late September. The teasing did not rile him, but he was unhappily aware of a rift between his deepening love of Canada—the land, the sky, the sensual world—and his dislike of cold—an almost instinctive fear of it.

The autumn air itself was disorienting. It was as if the land had gradually begun to smell less like itself, growing fainter, though the cool weather made some smells sharper, too: dry leaves, dry leaves burning, the yellowing reeds and pale grasses in the fields.

Tam had expected to be greeted by Father Fernby at the door to the rectory. Instead, he was greeted by an older woman—almost as old as he was and attractive, her long white hair held behind by a clip that reminded Tam of a beetle. She looked down and smiled.

—You must be Paul, she said. I was expecting you.

She led him through a living room that was dark wood and crimson carpeting to a back door that looked out on a yard with a long garden, at the far end of which Father Fernby was working. Without looking at Tam, he smiled at his housekeeper.

—Thank you, Mrs. Barry, he said. We'll take it from here.

And when she had returned to the rectory, closing the door behind her, Father Fernby turned to Tam and spoke in Garifuna.

—Kagi Biri? he asked.

What is your name? The question was put to him so lightly that Tam was tempted to respond in kind. What stopped him was Father Fernby's accent. His Garifuna was good enough to be understood, but it was still that of a foreigner. And in the moment it took to parse the accent, Tam suppressed the part of himself that would have answered in kind.

In that moment, however, he also conveyed the thing he'd meant to keep to himself: his understanding. Tam had understood Father Fernby's words and the priest knew it. Which meant that he had to choose how he would respond. He chose to acknowledge his understanding, while answering in English.

—I understand this language, he said, but I can't really speak it.

—I'll help you with it, said the priest. It'll help me to practice with you.

From then on, Father Fernby spoke to Tam in Garifuna, though there were gaps in the priest's vocabulary and he found it difficult to say relatively simple things like "Please pass me the secateurs" or "We need to cut the lilacs back."

It was not clear to Tam that the priest had ulterior motives for his kindness. The man's chief interest seemed really to be the garden, the devotion he showed to it being more than what one gives to a pretext. In fact, in the days that followed, as they prepared the garden for winter, Tam came to trust Fernby enough to devote his attention to the plants in the garden and greenhouse. The priest described the perennials in Garifuna, while naming them in English: purple echinacea, bee balm, white feather hosta (which the priest ruthlessly cut back), bearded iris, lobelia (which they protected with mulch).

How similar some of these plants were to those Tam had known in Trinidad! But the similarities and differences—the green intensities of coriander and shadow benny, for instance—were as fleeting to him as idle thoughts, and just as hard to keep in mind.

Tam grew closer to the priest, but not by choice. He would have preferred to keep the greatest emotional distance possible between himself and Father Fernby, in anticipation of finding punishment for the man. But the incidents with John Pardew and Roger Flynn continued to influence how his contemporaries thought of him, so that even those who had known Paul most of his life were now careful around him. This isolation was painful not to Tam, but to the boy whose consciousness was now more constant. As such, isolation was a distress that Tam could, increasingly, feel. So, he was grateful for the distraction that gardening brought and for the priest's company.

In November, after the first snowfall, Tam asked if he could help Father Fernby five days a week instead of one or two. There wasn't much for Tam to do, but Father Fernby agreed, in the hope that, in time, Paul would learn to take care of the plants in the greenhouse himself, freeing part of the day for the priest's other duties.

And one day, his doubts about revenge rife, and as he was culling basil for Mrs. Barry, Tam at last spoke to the priest in Garifuna.

—Ida liya basubiduru ladimerahoun Garifuna? he asked.

It could be said that this "breakthrough" was one the priest had been waiting for. Father Fernby had been certain that the being that possessed Paul Williams was one that spoke Garifuna, and it had been the priest's intention, once the spirit spoke to him, to denounce it to the bishop. But in the months during which the priest had observed Paul and the spirit within him, Father Fernby had come to accept that Paul had been changed by his brush with death, and he no longer believed the change was malevolent.

—How did I learn the language? Father Fernby answered. I learned it when I was younger.

—You were raised by people from Trinidad?

—No, no, said Fernby. I learned it when I was in my teens. You see, I admired the man I was named after, my great-great-grandfather, James Edward Fernby. He was a very devout man who'd had a religious conversion in Trinidad. A native man saved his life, but my great-great-grandfather never had the chance to thank him. And it's part of my family's folklore that James Edward used to always say that the one regret in his life was that he hadn't learned the language to thank the man. That really impressed me, the idea of learning a language to thank someone. So I decided to learn Garifuna myself, in honour of my great-great-grandfather. Not that I've ever used it with anyone except the people around Basse Terre where I spent summers for a while. And now you, of course. I use it with you.

—This ancestor, he looked like you? asked Tam.

—I've only ever seen paintings of him, said Father Fernby. And those were paintings of an old man. So, I can't say if I look like him or not. But learning a difficult language is the kind of idea I used to get when I hit puberty.

Tam stared at the priest, struck again by his resemblance to the man in his memory. Father Fernby, on the other hand, took Tam's scrutiny for doubt.

—I know it's difficult to believe, he said, but it's true. That really is the reason I learned this language. Anyway, when you come tomorrow, I'll tell you all about my great-great-grandfather. He was an extraordinary man. I've never regretted learning a language in his honour.

The following day was a Friday, a busy day for the priest, but Father Fernby kept his word. Paul found the greenhouse locked, and when he rang at the front door, he was greeted by Mrs. Barry who shepherded him into the room with crimson carpets and dark wood: the living room, a room heated by a fireplace whose flames were so hesitant they seemed to serve the dark as well as the light.

Tam did not notice the card table that had been set up by a window that looked onto the front porch until Mrs. Barry turned on the overhead light, a small chandelier whose glass tears hid its three lightbulbs.

—I hate turning this light on, she said. It's too strong.

It was very bright, but it left no doubt as to what was on the table. Three things: a single volume of the *Encyclopedia Britannica*, 11th edition, opened to page 281, a white plate on which there were two ginger snaps, and . . .

—Would you like a glass of milk? asked Mrs. Barry.

. . . and something that caught Tam's attention and held it, so that he did not care about milk or books or anything else: a bronze death mask (full face, eyes closed) mounted on a metal pole that was embedded in a block of white marble. The mask would have been unusual in any circumstance, but it was more so, now, as the likeness was familiar to him and yet vague, like something from a dream: sharp but unplaceable.

—Would you like a glass of milk? Mrs. Barry repeated.

Tam was too puzzled to answer, but he was spared the need. Father Fernby came into the room, bringing a glass of milk for Paul, tea for himself.

—I've got the milk for him, Edna, he said. And don't worry. We'll wipe down the table when we're done. I just saw another mouse in the kitchen. Poor thing. How are you, Paul?

Tam looked at the man and, still baffled, asked

—That's your great-great-grandfather?

—No, no, not at all, answered Father Fernby. That's the man who *saved* my great-great-grandfather. He was bitten by a poisonous snake just when James Edward was trying to thank him. Bad luck, but the man died. A real tragedy. But James Edward insisted on having this death mask made, and he kept it with him for the rest of his life. So, whenever I think about my great-great-grandfather, I think about this man's face, because James Edward kept it with him, wherever he was, for fifty years. It was like a shrine for him, something sacred. It reminded him how vulnerable humans are. My father's father inherited it, then my father, then me, because I was the only one of my brothers who was interested in it, I guess. It's such a serene face. I like to think it's the face of a religious man, but nobody knows. The story is that he was some sort of shaman.

—What is a shaman? asked Tam.

—We've gotten way ahead of ourselves, answered Father Fernby. Let me tell you about James Edward, my great-great-grandfather.

Tam was distracted by the death mask, the way one is distracted by a small, persistent doubt—*did* you lock the door or *is* the stove off or was your appointment for *today*?—but he listened as intently as he could to Father Fernby's account of his ancestor's life: a pious man, apparently, and reverent.

He listened as Father Fernby read him the entry on "Fernby, James Edward" in the *Encyclopedia Britannica*, an entry which recounted the man's role as benefactor to the many Trinidadians who, in James Edward Fernby's name, were given scholarships to study in England.

> **Fernby, James Edward** *(1835–) English politician, first son of Edward, 8th Viscount Rochefort, by Margaret, daughter of John Sandhurst, of Stowe in Buckinghamshire, was born in 1835 and educated at Winchester and at New College, Oxford. After a year at Oxford, he left without taking a degree, joining the British Army in 1855 and travelling abroad to the island of Trinidad where he was posted . . .*

He listened with growing understanding as Father Fernby explained how unusual it was that the death mask before them existed at all, that the mask was almost certainly imbued with the spirits of both James Edward Fernby and the unnamed native who, by saving James Edward's life, had changed its course. The priest found it auspicious that men who had died so long before his birth had nevertheless influenced his life so vividly that he thought of them as intimates, particularly the unknown man whose face he had been meditating on, but about whom no one knew anything.

—My mother, said Father Fernby, used to swear that the people most in need of killing are almost always dead already. But I think those most deserving of thanks are usually gone, too. Would you like another ginger snap?

It was as Father Fernby proffered the white porcelain plate on which a dark orange circle lay that a realization came to Tam all at once, like a coagulate of reason and memory finally leading to understanding: the story of James Edward Fernby, the presence of the death mask; a distorted face seen in clear water (his), a face glimpsed in a smooth piece of obsidian (also his), a brief glimpse of his face in a mirror brought to the settlement by someone who'd been to Port of Spain. The death mask was of his own face, a face he had not seen more than a dozen times in his life, but which he now recognized and knew to be his own.

It was not a view of himself that he could have imagined. For one thing, he had never in his seventy years seen a death mask and could not imagine wanting to capture a face in this way. For another, the mask was like the face of one who slept, of himself sleeping.

Seeing the boy transfixed by the mask, Father Fernby said

—Are you all right, Paul? I know history can be a little overwhelming.

In this, the priest was not wrong, but it was not history that Tam found transfixing. It was the fact of his face, above all, and then a deepening wonder about the years James Edward Fernby had spent remembering it. The man had spent fifty years reminding himself of Tam's death!

What was one to make of that?

Tam turned down the ginger snap when it was offered a third time, and when the priest had exhausted his store of anecdotes about his family, he thanked Father Fernby and walked home, so thoughtful that anyone encountering him would have been surprised, it being rare to see a seven-year-old walking in the evening, as if contemplating the sense of some obscurity.

It was a bright night. The moon and stars were partially obscured by clouds, but snow had fallen, and the new whiteness—it crepitated as Tam walked—was itself a kind of illumination, comprehending as it did the light from house windows, passing headlights, and streetlamps. The dark of this winter evening could not be compared to the dark of a walk at night in Trinidad. There, the dark was so deep he'd often made his way home by habit, instinct, touch, smell, and feel.

Night in Trinidad had been warmer and more lively. There, the spirits at play had been almost palpable. Tam had seen many a Soucouyant, the ball of light above him flying away after he'd cursed it. He'd felt the evening malevolence of Dwens crying by a river. And once, on the night of a full moon, he had stared down a La Diablesse, his will much stronger than hers.

You couldn't compare such nights to nights like these, which were like the earth refusing to fall asleep. But as he walked home from the rectory, Tam did compare them, and he felt compassion for the boy whose body he inhabited.

The sight of his own face had been a shock, not least because it resonated so variously within him: the shock of recognition, a sense of indignity, sympathy for the man who had had the mask made.

History, the story as it was in the encyclopedia, was not what he had lived. The past seemed not to have noticed James Edward Fernby's cruelty, for instance. But there could be no doubt that Fernby had come to recognize his sins and repent for them. More: in keeping the death mask with him, he had forced himself to live in the presence of his misdeeds. It would have been as if Tam had kept mementoes of the woman and child whose deaths he had caused. Though he believed he was as sorry for his fault as James Edward Fernby had been, he had never thought to commemorate it.

Then again: is it weakness to live in the constant presence of the sins one has committed, or is it strength to constantly face them? Had James Edward Fernby lived in self-forgiving (the present) or self-condemnation (the past)?

Too late by a century, Tam was curious about the man.

In any case, his thoughts of retribution faded along with his anger and his sense of purpose. Was he meant to wander this new world in the body of a child until the child grew, grew old, grew decrepit, and death came for this body? Was he meant to live a better life than the one he had? Was this purgatory called Petrolia his punishment for the anger that had burned in him along with the mapipi's venom?

At the thought of the snake sinking its fangs into his arm, it occurred to Tam, as he observed Roland quietly eating across the table from him, that in all his equations and tergiversations, his bitter memories and longing for revenge, he had not once thought about the mapipi. He recalled its surprise and kindness.

Roland, feeling Tam's gaze, looked at his son and smiled.

—You poor unhappy man, Tam thought and smiled back.

5. An Inheritance

As unpredictable and quick as Tam's rebirth had been, his return to the edges of Paul Williams's consciousness was deliberate and unhurried. Paul's consciousness, which had in any case been growing stronger, grew stronger still, until the child's concerns and desires began to occupy Tam's thoughts so that, in the end, Tam was forced to pay attention to Paul as Paul had been paying attention to Tam.

The seven-year-old's experience of his body's takeover was, at first, comforting. Paul had felt himself being gently called back from the loving and peaceful darkness to which he had given himself up. But as he grew more conscious and more aware of time, he lost the feeling of great love and peace and experienced instead the sometimes peculiar—but always extraordinary—sensations of seeing, touching, hearing, and tasting at second hand; like seeing through his own eyes as if they were someone else's or tasting foods he knew he loved—his mother's omelets, for instance—as if with another person's tongue.

(For the rest of his life, he would keep this episode to himself, unable as he was to describe his experience without feeling absurd.)

No, Paul's return was not at all the end of Tam's consciousness. For years, Paul was aware of his ancestor's presence, however faint it was at times. He retained all the knowledge that had belonged to Tam. That is, the memories and experiences of Tam Modeste were now Paul Williams's as well. Tam was like an ancestor whose life and history were a boon and a burden to their inheritor.

As well, Tam had spent months gathering weeds, florals, wings, and hairs, rehearsing spells and curses, grinding salts and fingernails. Tam had rehearsed his lifetime of knowledge, in order to be sure of what he remembered. And all of this had been passed on to Paul, as if Tam had performed a long demonstration for his benefit. So, dangerous or not, Paul was familiar with the knowledge, skill, and subtlety of a seventy-year-old obeah man. He was, at seven, a buyeis of considerable skill.

If, say, Paul had wanted to have his father confess his infidelity, it would have been as simple as grinding bluebell roots, basil, lizard dung (from a five-lined skink), and calcified thistle sap with Roland's breakfast. Moreover, these ingredients and many more had been left in envelopes, shoeboxes, and glass jars—all nicely sequestered at the back of the closet in his room, all neatly labelled in Garifuna, knowledge of which he retained as well. In the end, he could have had his father fall more deeply in love with his mother. He could cast the same spell that had turned Roger Flynn into a chicken. He could have had Miss Heikkinen feel for him as he felt for her: a not-quite-innocent longing that was mixed up with the sounds he had heard from the Maillards' bedroom when his father had been with Mrs. Maillard.

But here, too, Tam's presence was influential. Whenever Paul considered using obeah, he felt the weight of Tam's experience and caution, his restraint, his awareness of the unintended consequences of magic, and the feeling of injustice that accompanies the coercion of others. In this in particular, Tam was with him, a guide, a conscience.

The things inherited from Tam—along with Tam's gradually retreating consciousness—could be put, however tentatively, on the positive side of a ledger. They were counterbalanced by a loss of innocence for which the seven-year-old was not prepared. It was humiliating to know what he now knew about his father, difficult to live with the knowledge of his mother's humiliation, and deeply confusing—intensely pleasing—to imagine himself in the arms of Miss Heikkinen, his own body a stranger to him.

If Paul was spared an alienation that would have further cut him off from the world around him, however, it was thanks to the hard fleck of optimism in his nature, an instinct like that of a plant leaning towards sunlight, whatever its circumstances. That is, Paul was gregarious, despite his secret knowledge, and he was desperate to recover his friends. In order to do this, he resolved to speak as little as possible about his experiences since his brush with darkness, his new abilities, his command of Garifuna.

As it happened, the first of Paul's friends to notice his return to normalcy—if that is the word—was David Lindsey, who lived two houses down, on Grove Street. David did not want to hear anything at all about Paul's experiences. They had known each other from the earliest age, their mothers having been pregnant at the same time, and that was enough for him.

David had naturally been troubled by the changes in his friend. The difference between Paul before sickness and the Paul who'd come afterwards had been unfathomable to the seven-year-old. It wasn't only that Paul had stopped acknowledging his friends, refusing to answer when spoken to, it was the realization that the new Paul, the Paul who'd recovered, was not Paul at all. What words were there to describe being beside a friend and knowing it was not your friend?

David's mother, Deirdre, a superstitious woman, was the only adult who took the change in Paul seriously. She had frightened her children by telling them that, as far as she was concerned, Paul Williams was possessed by Satan, and though David did not understand the significance of demonic possession, his mother's was the only explanation anyone had offered. So, he half allowed the idea that Paul was now, somehow, "unclean."

But then one afternoon in December, Paul rang at the Lindseys' front door. David's mother was not at home. She would not have let her son go anywhere with Paul. Instead, David's little sister had opened the door and let Paul in, shouting

—It's Paul! It's Paul! It's Paul!

until David, the only other one home, came to see what was the matter and saw Paul standing by the door, and knew at once that it was really Paul, recognizing a familiar presence the way any animal might: by his senses.

—What you doing, Paul? he asked.

And Paul answered

—Not much.

—You were really sick, eh? said David.

—Yeah, I guess, said Paul. Want to come over?

It was as if they had, in a heartbeat, sorted the past months out, as if there had been no break in their friendship, as if the last time they had spoken had been the day before, not seven months gone. David had to take care of his little sister (Denise) until his older sister (Darlene) or his older brother (Doug) came home, but after that the boys went to Paul's house—to Eva's pleased surprise—where they played with Paul's toy trucks—which had languished beneath his desk—and watched television until *The Woody Woodpecker Show* was over and it was time for David to go home.

The pleasure of imagining that the rug in his bedroom was a construction site was satisfying to Paul, though somewhere inside of himself he knew it was childish. It was particularly gratifying to play with someone who knew the rules, as David did. For instance: the Caterpillar hydraulic excavator and the dump trucks left their imaginary payloads somewhere beneath the bed, which everyone—that is, he and David—knew was the dumping ground.

After such camaraderie, the desire to return to his old self felt urgent. Though the journey back to friendship was more difficult with those he had not known well—his schoolmates at St. Philip's, for instance—Paul was diligent in talking to anyone who approached him and joining in the impromptu games of Red Rover or tag that broke out at recess.

(As the tide turned in Paul's favour, it was accepted by all the children at St. Philip's that Roger Flynn had been lucky. To be "chickenated" was one thing, but what if he'd been turned into a grasshopper or a hummingbird? The consensus was that these, involving flying and jumping as they did, would have been much worse.)

Once his schoolmates accepted that he was not dangerous, Paul became a kind of talisman: popular, in the way that all well-liked (and feared) children are. So that by the spring of 1958, things could be said to have returned to normal for Paul, both at school and, to an extent, at home.

Of course, this return to a kinder version of the status quo involved a heroic amount of repression. All that was Tam Modeste, all that was obeah, all that was ancestral had to be held in check. He did not use the spells he knew, did not concoct any potions, did not help others find things they had lost. He devoted himself so entirely to play that playing almost ceased to be play.

He did, however, through this challenging time, carry on helping Father Fernby with the gardening. There had been less to do in winter, just a handful of mundane tasks in the greenhouse: watering, culling herbs for Mrs. Barry, spraying some of the plants with a solution of water and Miracle-Gro. But when spring came, Paul took pleasure in preparing the outdoor garden for the annuals: spreading compost, turning the soil over, looking through the garden catalogue from Simpsons-Sears, helping choose the flowers and vegetables they would plant in the yard.

This gardening was, for a time, the most direct connection to Tam that Paul had. He could feel Tam's pleasure at fussing with the ground. But then one evening in May, when they had finished watering the plants in the greenhouse, Paul surprised himself by asking Father Fernby if he could have the death mask.

Caught off guard, the priest answered

—I don't think I *can* give it to you. It belongs to my family. But why do you want it?

—I don't know, answered Paul.

—To be honest, said Father Fernby, the first time I saw your father's face, I was surprised by his resemblance to the mask. It didn't surprise me to hear that your family's from Trinidad. You're probably related to that mask, somehow. So, how about this? If your mother's okay with it and if she doesn't mind my visiting more often, we can share it, you and me.

Paul looked to see if there was something contrary or troubling in the priest's look—an ulterior motive, a longing for his mother, for instance. No longer innocent himself, he could no longer assume the innocence of others. But there was nothing but kindness in the priest's look. Father Fernby, it seemed, was genuine.

—That would be swell, Paul said.

He felt an elation at the thought of Tam's face being in his bedroom. And on his walk home, the town of Petrolia, Ontario—*his* town, the one he loved—from Queen to Dufferin, Dufferin to Glenview, and Glenview to Grove—was alive for the twenty minutes it took him to reach his destination.

It would normally have taken less time, but along Glenview, by the park, Paul saw a pair of scarlet tanagers perched on the children's carousel like two preening flames. As one of them flew off, Paul greeted the other in Garifuna as Tam must often have done to other birds in his part of the world. The tanager turned its head so that its eye faced him. It chirruped before flying off. Then, as if it had forgotten something, it returned to its place on the carousel.

—Good evening to you, said the tanager

before flying off again in the direction of the golf course.

This encounter with the bird was a surprise, in that he had forgotten that he could do this, but it was not disturbing, as it might have been just six months before. Still, Paul felt Tam's presence within him as strong as it had ever been and, so, had an intimation of the rift in his world between past and present, surface and depth, land and home, as he walked towards the place where he did and did not belong.

Houyhnhnm

For Roo Borson

My dad, Robert auf der Horst, died seven years ago. He was a successful doctor, and for most of his life, he divided the world into two categories: what he thought useful (science) and what he thought frivolous (almost everything else). It wasn't that he disdained other things—art, for instance. It was that he couldn't see the point of pretending that knowledge, the fruit of science, was comparable to entertainment.

For the most part, we were in agreement about this. But he was disappointed when I decided to study math, at Amherst. Math was tricky ground for him: it could be useful, but was often frivolous. He saw math as the thin edge of the entertainment wedge, as if once you engaged with Fermat's Last Theorem, reality TV was not far behind.

I mention Dad's preference for evidence-based reasoning not because I have any grievances to air. I loved him, whatever our differences, and I never doubted that he loved me. It's just that I'd like it to be clear, from the outset, that my dad was a rational person.

That being said: like many serious men, my dad could at times be playful. For instance, when talking about his lifelong fascination with horses, he would point to his—and, of course, my—family name: auf der Horst, a German name, though my dad was born in the Caribbean, to Black Caribbean parents. The name isn't interesting in itself, but "auf der Horst" sounds like "auf der Horse," and this homonym allowed Dad to suggest that it was inevitable he would own horses.

And own horses he did: five in the course of his adult life.

And I assumed it had something to do with his playful side when, shortly after buying his fifth and final horse, a nameless gelding that he'd saved from slaughter, he called me into his office at home and asked me to do him a favour.

—Paul, he said, I want you to make me a catalogue of the most famous horses in literature.

—In literature? I thought you said literature's useless.

—It is, mostly, he said. But I've got my reasons. I'll pay you for the trouble.

I almost asked if he was joking, but that would have been pointless. My dad could not tell a joke to save his life. The last time I remember him telling one was sometime in the eighties: Three logicians walk into a bar. The barman asks, "Would all of you like a drink?" The first logician says, "I don't know." The second one says, "I don't know." The third one says, "Yes." I also recall my mom forbidding him to ever tell jokes again, a ban we both thought necessary.

In any event, I was happy to create a catalogue of horses for him. It was the first time he'd asked me to do research, and it pleased me to be useful. Of course, I hadn't realized how exhausting the task would be. Literature is so replete with horses, I could have written a full thesis just to give him a sense of how influential horses have been in the human imagination.

(Some fifteen years later, I don't remember much about the research I did, save the intense boredom I felt as I combed the *Poetic Edda* for mentions of a horse named Glad or perused

Celtic mythology for stories about kelpies, demons who take the form of horses. It was a relief, back then, to write about Frou-Frou and Rocinante, Black Beauty and Cigarette—literary horses I was already familiar with.)

After I'd listed, indexed, and described hundreds of horses, I was naturally curious about why he'd asked me to do this in the first place. But no reason was forthcoming. He paid me a hundred dollars—that is, not much—and then refused to say anything more about it. I had to settle for the fact that he named his gelding Xan, which I took to be an allusion to Xanthus, one of Achilles's horses.

I assume that this name was the result of my research, but the horse himself offered no clue to Dad's state of mind. Xan was average height (five feet seven from hooves to withers) and average weight (somewhere around a thousand pounds). He was a purebred Friesian, with a shiny black coat and a white spot on his forehead in the shape of a lozenge. His flanks rippled at a touch, and his mane was long and thick, because although Dad groomed him, he never dressed Xan's mane or tail.

In a word, Xan was unremarkable.

What was remarkable was the relationship between Dad and Xan. It was close and grew closer. I was not living at home—that is, in Amherst—at the time. I'd moved to New York to go to grad school at Columbia, so I took in their relationship only at Thanksgivings and Christmases. This means that Dad's closeness to Xan likely seemed more dramatic to me than it did to, say, my mom. She would call me every so often to make sure I had everything I needed, and in the course of our conversations, she would mention, for instance, that Dad had had a large heated brick-and-mortar barn built for Xan, or that he'd had a pond dug in the field behind our house and had filled it with goldfish, because Xan loved fish, apparently, or that he'd walk beside Xan for hours, going around our two square acres even in the rain, or that she'd both seen and heard Dad reading books to the horse.

—What kind of books? I asked her.

—Oh, I don't know, sweetie, she answered. Isaac Asimov, mostly.

On hearing my mom's accounts of Dad's behaviour, I admit I grew anxious. The man she described resembled my father less and less. Then not at all. Yet whenever I returned home, I could see for myself that Dad spent hours with Xan, talking to the horse, walking him around the man-made pond, and reading to him—or was he reading to himself?—from Asimov's non-fiction.

Further complicating matters was the fact that Dad would not discuss Xan. If he said anything at all, it was that the time he spent with his horse was private. We were free to admire and pet Xan whenever we liked, Mom and I, but he made it clear that their solitude—his and Xan's—was beneficial to and craved by both of them.

I thought he was losing his mind, and I began to mourn him from the moment I first saw them—Xan and Dad—walking in their fenced-in emerald world, Dad laughing at God knows what, as if deep in conversation with the horse.

This state of affairs—I thought of it as a decline—went on for eight years. And despite the pain I feel at having lost my dad, I'm now grateful for that time. For one thing, after a while my mom's stories stopped alarming me. It was almost amusing to learn that Dad had ordered an oversized mattress for the horse, that he'd had taps installed in the barn from which Xan could drink fresh water whenever he wanted, that he'd had a library built there, that he'd hooked up a contraption that allowed Xan to listen to music whenever he had trouble sleeping, et cetera.

Those years were good for my mom, too, I believe. Her husband was not an invalid. He earned a great living as a doctor—a respected and popular MD—until he retired. And though she liked having him around, she learned to treasure the time she had for herself—that is, the mornings and evenings when Dad was communing with his horse.

Up until my dad's death, my parents' lives were what you could call eccentric but normal. Moreover, this new normal was very like the old one, save that Dad treated his horse with the kind of deference usually reserved for presidents (when they are worthy) or potentates.

The first of the deaths I'll speak of here was sudden and devastating. It descended on my dad like an Olympian decree—swift and merciless. On a Sunday, he began to feel unwell and went to the hospital in Northampton. We spoke the next day, Monday, in the morning, just before he went in for surgery to drain the uric acid that had backed up and was poisoning him. He died on the operating table around noon. I think he knew his time had come. His last words to me, that morning, had been

—If I die, Paul, please take care of Xan. You'll have to keep him company. He's very sensitive.

—It's like Xan's your son, I said.

—No, not my son, exactly, Dad answered.

Though I promised to look after the horse and swore I'd do it well, it was at least a week after Dad's death before I was really conscious of anything I did. I was derailed not just by grief but by the sheer depths of my emotions. I mechanically shovelled feed into Xan's copper trough, leaving mounds of alfalfa and clover in his vicinity. Even following the letter, rather than the spirit, of my promise was difficult, because Xan's barn reminded me so much of my dad: the chairs in which he'd sat while talking to Xan, the books on Xan's bookshelves, and Xan himself, whom Dad had clearly loved.

It isn't accurate to say that dealing with Xan diverted me from grief. Nothing could have done that. But as I became more conscious of what I was doing—feeding, cleaning, and even (occasionally) talking to Xan—I found the discipline, the responsibility, and the schedule comforting. I'd been teaching at UMass Amherst for years by the time Dad died. And I was living just off South Pleasant, less than two miles away from my parents' home, off Mill Valley.

Every day of the week, I would get up at five in the morning and spend two hours with Xan. On weekday evenings around six—earlier on weekends—I'd go back to feed Xan supper, to keep him company awhile, and to spend time with my mom, watching the Nollywood films she consumes.

I liked knowing where I would, or should, be at these times, and I began to feel at ease in Xan's company. I had never shared my dad's fascination with horses. In fact, I'd disliked them ever since I was thrown by one of his mares when I was eleven or twelve. The difference now was that I came to know Xan's personality. He was, in the days after Dad's death, even-tempered, gentle, and as quiet as if he had no vocal cords. The other word I would use to describe him—though I'd never have used it before we grew close—is "searching." Even in those early days, I felt in Xan what I've often felt in my brighter students: an inquisitive nature.

Of course, Xan was also physically intimidating, as most horses are. If you have never been around horses, I'm not sure I can convey their heft. It's a density that's as psychological as it is physical, so that one approaches a horse with the idea of its stature as one of its dimensions. I don't know if this is the right way to say it, but one brings a sense of horseness to one's encounters with horses.

It's possible that this thought was inspired by my research, and I now suspect that, by having me create a catalogue of literary horses, Dad was trying to prepare me for life with Xan. But none of my thoughts, feelings, or ideas could really have prepared me for the moment when Xan spoke. I'm still surprised at how calm I was when, after we had spent months in each other's company, Xan said

—I don't suppose Robert is coming back.

I thought, when I heard those words, that I was talking to myself, that I'd finally reached the limits of grief.

—No, I said. Dad isn't coming back.

—I don't mean to criticize, said Xan, but you could have told me earlier.

I nodded, I think, or made some sign that I understood. But I went on brushing his flanks, and when that was done, I left him. I went home, and cried again for the loss of my dad.

Over the next few days, Xan was his serene and wordless self, and I felt closer to him, amused that my grief had manifested in such an unexpected way—in my imagining that a horse could articulate my sense of loss.

The second time Xan spoke, I was frightened—not by Xan but by the thought that, grieving or not, I was losing my mind.

It was a morning in mid-March. Xan and I were walking in the field, where clumps of granular snow clung to the ground in unpredictable places. The field was muddy, but it was solid enough if we kept away from the outer edges where we often walked. I was thinking about grass seed, wondering how many bags of Scotts Turf Builder I'd need, when Xan said

—I'd like it if you'd read to me, Paul.

His head was near mine but above it. I hadn't seen his mouth and tongue move. So, with what seems, in retrospect, like incredible sang-froid, I asked Xan to repeat what he'd said. And this he did, his lips moving discreetly, his tongue barely shifting, his breath escaping in a small cloud. Watching him speak was like watching an elephant gracefully pick up a pea.

I suppose my sense of wonder overcame my fear. Thinking about the anatomy of a horse, its mouth in particular, I felt it should not have been possible for Xan to produce the sounds he did, as elegantly as he did. The "l"s in "like" and "Paul" and the "d"s in "I'd," "you'd," and "read"—which were distinct from the "t" in "it"—were skilfully done. Only the "e"s in "me" and "read" were unusual, as if half whistled. To be fair, this was likely because of his buckteeth.

—It should be impossible for you to speak, I said.

—It's taken a lot of work, he answered. There are words I still can't say properly.

—That explains your accent, I said.

—I don't have an accent, said Xan.

This was the first of many instances in which I found it impossible to judge his attitude. Had I offended him when I mentioned his accent, or was he teasing me when he denied having one? His face was placid and unchanging. One of his eyes was looking at me, until he raised his head and his mane veiled it.

We walked on in silence then, until I remembered his request.

—What would you like me to read? I asked.

One of the most valuable aspects of my time with Xan was that, in speaking with him, I understood—truly understood—that words can only hint at what a psyche wants or needs. Although Xan and I spoke often after this moment, I was never certain—despite his use of words—if he possessed great depth, or, in fact, any depth at all. This was no doubt because his speaking was without affect, clear without being expressive.

—Poetry, he answered. I'd like poetry. Or Gertrude Stein.

—Did Dad read you poetry? I asked.

—Yes, Xan said, but he preferred science.

When I inspected the books in Xan's library, I saw that there were, indeed, several volumes of poetry. This was unsettling, because it was not easy to imagine my dad buying poetry for himself. In fact, it was like discovering a secret side to him, although, of course, technically speaking, this side of my dad belonged to Xan.

—What do you like about poetry? I asked.

—I don't have to think about what it means, he answered. Your father told me it doesn't mean anything.

Just the answer Dad would have given, though, for Dad, this would not have been any kind of recommendation. I was left wondering whether Xan actually liked poetry, whether he thought of it as a kind of intriguing chatter—like birdsong—or whether he listened to it in defiance of Dad.

It did not occur to me to seek professional help. I took solace in my situation, despite knowing how unreal it was. Moreover, I didn't want my time with Xan to end, because it was, in a way, time with my dad. I mean, Xan was a being Dad had loved. When I was with him, I felt my dad's personality and, to some extent, his presence, even. But time with Xan was time with Dad in another way, too.

By his own admission, Xan knew very little about the world. He had been, he said, an outsider all his life. His experience had been of stalls, fields, and tracks. His exposure to other horses had been incidental and not intimate. Dad had often asked him what it was like to be a horse. But if it was true that, for Dad, Xan represented a means to understanding another species, it was also true that, for Xan, my dad was a road to the human. And Xan, a being at least as observant as my dad, had made an intense study of Robert auf der Horst: his personality, his habits, his sense of humour.

Dad's sense of humour, in particular, seemed to fascinate Xan. I imagine that, after Mom and I discouraged him from telling jokes, Dad needed an outlet. And so Xan became his audience—captive, quiet, and, no doubt, perplexed.

Here, I'd like to point out that my dad's jokes, when told by Xan, were still pointless. They were, however, funnier and more striking. In fact, it is difficult to convey the range of emotion I felt whenever Xan told me one of Dad's jokes. For instance, one day Xan asked

—What do you call a reindeer with one eye?

—What? I answered.

—No idea, Xan said.

I had, of course, heard it before. It had only ever been slightly funny to me, and that was only because Dad thought it was funny. But looking up at Xan as he told it, watching his lips and tongue move together as if dancing, hearing it in his slightly wobbly voice, I felt a confusion that must have shown on my face.

—I didn't get it, either, said Xan.

I explained to him then the play on words that gave the joke its purpose: the play of "eye" and "I," the complicated pun on "no-eye deer" and "no idea."

—I understand, Xan said, but did Robert really find this funny?

This was one of the most unexpectedly tricky questions I've ever been asked. I assured Xan that some humans do find puns droll. Beyond that, though, was the question: Why did Robert auf der Horst find this joke funny? I couldn't think of a clear answer. Dad's love of puns was part of what had made him who he was, but the reason for his love was, for me at least, undiscoverable, *terra incognita*. And at that moment, standing beside Xan, I was struck by the strangeness of my dad's having remembered this joke in particular, and the even stranger fact of his having related it to a horse.

—Did *you* like his jokes? I asked.

—I found them hilarious, said Xan, even the ones I didn't get. That is why I remember them.

I saw then that in asking me if Dad found this joke funny, Xan had been testing me. He'd been trying to discover my sense of humour, not Dad's. In fact, in the first year that I knew Xan, I often felt as if I were being tested or observed.

Though Xan admitted to liking my dad's sense of humour, I never heard him laugh at any of Dad's jokes. He did laugh, though, on occasion. And although I know that what we call laughter encompasses a range of sounds, I expected Xan's to be something like an unhinged whinny or a prolonged neigh, but it was nothing like either of those. It was, in fact, exactly like my dad's laugh, a faithful imitation. The first time I heard it was as I read to him from Kant's *Critique of Pure Reason*. I was reading this at his request. It was, apparently, a text that he and my dad often read together, one that both found hilarious.

I didn't know where the humour lay, but when I read the sentence "The more true deductions we have from a given conception, the more criteria of its objective reality," Xan laughed and had to drink water before I could go on reading.

Sad though it is to admit, our time together, mine and Xan's, was mostly unremarkable. I mean, I'm aware how unusual it is to spend so many hours talking with a horse. But when, for instance, my mom asked what Xan and I talked about—or, rather, what it was that I was saying to the "poor horse"—I could think of very little to tell her. Not because I was ashamed to talk about my relationship with Xan but because, as in most relationships, what was actually said was evanescent. The important thing was that we spoke, not what we spoke about as we tried, mutually, I think, to understand each other. Here, let me say that I find it funny to think that humans struggle to imagine what aliens might be like when, for all intents and purposes, aliens already share the planet with us. As I came to a better understanding of Xan, some of the questions I had about what "alien perception" might be were answered. For instance, Xan found sunsets unappealing and assumed that they had some physiological effect on humans, because they were so often mentioned in books or poems. He was surprised to learn that we find sunsets aesthetically pleasing, and nothing more. For further instance, Xan found ants terrifying, unsure as he was of just how many of them there were beneath the surface of the Earth. It alarmed him to think that both he and the planet could, at any time, be overrun. As a means of explaining to Xan what a devil might be, my dad had asked him to think of Satan as the essence of ants. And it was in this way that Xan had come to an appreciation of human religion.

Our five years together, mine and Xan's, though mostly unperturbed by catastrophe, were among the most memorable I've spent on Earth. They leave a residue in my mind that grows in significance as time passes. I do wish I could remember more, though—more of the particulars. Talking to Xan became part of my daily routine. And after a while, I stopped being aware that I was talking to a horse.

(It has always seemed to me that intimacy is oddly timeless. When intimacy exists, it feels as if it had always existed, so that I'm surprised when I think that, for instance, there was a time when I did not know Xan, a time when I did not know the taste of cherries, or the sounds of New York, or the feel of snow on my eyelashes, and so on through all the small things that seem timeless before coming to an end.)

The main problem with my lack of awareness is that now, when I try to remember who Xan was, I find it difficult to describe his personality. He was gentle, but that's a feeling, not a fact. He was witty: another subjective perception. Was Xan really witty, or was he witty for a horse? He was kind. Yes, he was. He would ask what was on my mind and pay attention to my concerns. There was nothing I couldn't tell him, and, rarer in my experience, he was not critical. He did not laugh easily, but he wasn't overly serious, either. I felt with him not as I felt with my mom or with friends. I felt when I was in Xan's company as if I were privileged to be with someone so noble. Of course, nobility is as difficult to define as any other quality. But it is the word I feel compelled to use when I think of him.

I remember the smell of Xan's breath: like sour grass.

I remember the smell of Xan's sweat: like rancid meat mixed with hay. I remember the movement of his teeth and tongue as he spoke.

I remember the swishing of his tail: deliberate at times, at times random. I remember the frissons that traversed his flanks.

I remember his eyes, great and glaucous, on either side of his head. There are incidents that I remember, too, of course.

I remember the moment I realized that my mom had, in fact, heard Xan speak, had likely heard his voice often. It was one morning as we were eating breakfast together. Apropos of nothing at all, Mom said

—I see you have the same talent as your dad.

—What talent is that? I asked.

—Ventriloquism, she answered.

I didn't know what to say.

—But it's interesting, she said. Your horse voice is the same as your dad's. Did he teach you?

—Mom, I'm not a ventriloquist.

—Oh, I see. You're not going to admit it. Well, like father, like son. But Rob was better at it than you, you know. I can see your lips move when you do the horse. I never could with Rob.

I remember when one of the neighbours confronted me about "my behaviour."

—Now, look, he said. Your dad was a good guy. But he was a little funny, the way he was with that horse. If I didn't know Doc better, I'd say he and that horse were bunking together. You know what I'm saying? I'm not saying your dad was a liberal, but who buys a house for a horse? And now it's looking a little like you're going that way, too. And I would feel better . . . we would all feel better if we knew there wasn't anything funny with you and that horse.

I'm not an angry man, not given to violence, but if the neighbour in question hadn't been in his eighties, I'd have hit him—for me, for Dad, and for Xan.

I remember the first time we walked into town. We took back fields before coming out on South Pleasant, then walked to Amherst Coffee and turned back. I recall this walk not because it was so different from others we would take but because, somewhere past the golf course, Xan stopped for a long while, looked over at the green valley in the distance, and asked if I knew the number of ants there were likely to be on Earth.

The moment before he spoke, I'd have sworn he was admiring the landscape.

Despite this handful of vivid impressions and memorable moments, Xan's gradual decline is what has left the deepest mark on me. It is the thing I can't help remembering.

I suspect it began before I noticed it. The moment of noticing transfigures the moments that preceded it. So that, thinking back, the line is slightly blurred. But I began to notice his decline in part because Xan, who could do a fair imitation of Dad, failed while telling one of Dad's worst jokes.

—Why is it bad to trust atoms?

—Because they make up everything, I answered.

—Oh, said Xan. That's right.

Not two minutes later, he asked again.

—Why is it bad to trust atoms?

Thinking he had some reason for wanting to say the punchline, I said

—Why?

But he didn't answer.

A minute later, the third time he told the joke, Xan said

—Why is it bad to trust fish?

He laughed, then said

—Because they make everything up.

I let this go, thinking it was some kind of meta-humour, Xan's attempt at absurdism, say. And he changed the subject. He began talking about sun flares. I remember this specifically, because I wondered if he was making a connection between atoms and flares of the sun. But he wasn't.

A few days later, when Xan told me Dad's joke about tuna, I began to trace his confusion.

—What kind of fish is made of two sodium atoms? Xan asked.

—Two Na, I answered.

—No, he said. Tuna make everything up.

He had confused one joke with another. But the sad thing was not the misplaced punchline. It was Xan's momentary distress. He was the same Xan. His expression was as unreadable as always. But the feel of him, the energy, was something like embarrassment.

One of my mom's favourite sayings came from a philosopher named Epictetus: "No great thing comes into being all at once." Dad hated this, of course. He'd bring up the big bang and say that the greatest thing of all (the universe) had come into being all at once, before time, even! On balance, big bang excluded, I agree with Epictetus: most great things take time to happen. And so do catastrophes.

That was the idea that pursued me, as Xan grew less and less like himself.

The weeks following his punchline mix-up were, more or less, normal: I walked with him in the morning, spent time with him when I could. We spoke, as usual, of the things that interested us—my dad, the strangeness of Earth, the pleasures of a good lawn, the way life felt from Xan's perspective, the meaning of God, the meaning of evil, and so on.

Jokes, however, were now a source of pain. Xan simply could not tell them properly. He mixed them up or forgot their punchlines or, eventually, lost the sense and rhythm of them. They became a kind of gibberish to him, and he had to ask me, repeatedly, more and more bewildered, why it is funny when, say, a horse walks into a bar or a dog sits on sandpaper. In fact, I think the only reason he kept telling jokes—until he stopped speaking entirely—was his slowly fading memory of their meaningfulness.

I found this loss particularly difficult. For one thing, Xan's jokes reminded me of Dad, and for another, it was like watching

Xan gradually lose his humanity—if that's the right word for it. (It is funny, in a way, that for months I longed for him to succeed at telling jokes that I would have discouraged anyone else from repeating.)

But how do you chart the loss of normal? The constant acceptance of declining normals, each lesser than the one before? Though Xan was forgetting jokes or mixing them up, we could still talk about math, for instance. And then one day, we simply couldn't, because numeration left him. All of a sudden, quadratic equations meant nothing to him. After that, we could still talk about the sun, until sunlight, heat, the growth of the soil . . . until none of that meant anything to Xan. These things had been interesting to him, and then they weren't. And his lack of interest was signalled only by his prolonged silence.

The subject that held his interest the longest was my dad. But then, somewhere near the end, just before Xan lost language—human language, anyway—he asked me

—Who is Robert?

—My dad, I answered. The one who looked after you, before me.

—Oh, yes, he said.

But I could tell he didn't remember, and after that we did not speak about Dad.

As strange as it was to discover that Xan could speak, it was stranger still when he stopped. I went out to him one morning, as usual. It was early June. And I greeted him as always.

—Good morning, Xan, I said. Did you sleep well?

His usual answer was "Thank you. Yes."

Though sometimes he could be more critical. "I slept poorly," he'd say. "The mattress is lumpy. I would prefer straw."

But on this morning, Xan neighed and shook his head. Then he snorted, anxious to go out, it seemed. More than that: he had shit all over the living room and had strewn books about, having bitten them and eaten some of their pages.

—Is everything all right? I asked.

But again he neighed, making a sound I associated with his unguarded moments, not with our conversations. And it's putting it mildly to say that I found his behaviour disturbing. It was as if I had entered someone's home and been confronted by a farm animal, though Xan had never been that.

When I spoke, earlier, of declining normalcy, I was referring to my sense of Xan's decreasing mental faculties. There had been a physical decline as well, but it wasn't until he stopped speaking that it finally registered with me. I mean, it wasn't until he stopped speaking that I understood that his increasing sleekness, as I described it to my mom, was not a sign of good health. In fact, thinking about it now, I'm ashamed that I could have attributed the gradual protrusion of Xan's rib cage to anything other than decline.

By the time I called Dr. Antony, a local vet, Xan had become whatever it is you call a dying creature who was once noble. He was still a horse, I guess, but that designation had never suited him, and although his decline had made him more horselike, "horse" still didn't suit him. At least not to my mind, because I could not forget his manner of speaking, his way of being, all the things that had distinguished him from the simply equine.

I called the vet because, several weeks before he died, Xan tried to bite me.

He'd grown listless. He walked around the field slowly, as if he resented the effort it took. And he stopped for long stretches of time, lost in thought or maybe just bewildered. On one of those occasions, when he'd been immobile for twenty minutes or so, I tried to coax him into moving. I spoke to him and stroked his neck. I meant the touch as an act of affection, but Xan turned to me and tried to bite my hand, distractedly snapping in my direction, his teeth clacking.

The vet was more worried about me than about Xan. Had he actually managed to bite me, it could have been serious. As far as Dr. Antony was concerned, Xan was old and there was nothing to be done about that. He advised me to have "the animal" put down. His intention was to save Xan from suffering, and he offered to do it for me and arrange to have the carcass taken away.

There was no question of allowing Xan to suffer, but neither would I allow him to be carted away and rendered. I struggled, trying to decide what to do and how to do it. I also struggled with the question of whether I was more upset by Xan's decline or by the fact that he had turned into a mere horse.

What settled the matter was Xan himself. On a morning three weeks after Dr. Antony's visit, Xan allowed himself to be led from his now more barnlike house. The place smelled of manure, urine, and uneaten feed. Xan followed me to the field and then, when we'd reached its centre, refused to move. He lay down in the grass, his mane unkempt, snorting and kicking out whenever I tried to coax him up. His eye on me then was glacial. And I was certain that he was asking for help to put an end to his confusion.

I did this the only way I knew how.

I shot him and had his body buried in the field where he'd fallen.

So another grief—lesser, but still intense—followed the death of my dad. In fact, I think of it as an echo of the grief I felt at Dad's passing, a grief that I had, ironically, begun to overcome right around the time that Xan began his final decline.

My mom, of course, felt differently about all of this. She had suffered at the death of her husband, and because my own grief was all-encompassing, she had largely suffered alone, dependent on a handful of friends for comfort. I see now that she must have resented Xan's hold on my attention. As Xan's body was put into the pit I'd had dug in the yard, she said

—Well, that's that, at least.

—What do you mean? I asked.

—Honestly! You and your dad were obsessed with that horse. I'm glad it's over. I was worried about Rob for years. And now it's been years with you. I forbid you to get another horse while I'm still alive.

Her attitude took me by surprise. Not just what she said but how she said it—with such bitterness. To me, it was as if a close friend had died and I was watching someone spit on his grave.

It was only then that I began to wonder about the exact nature of Mom's relationship with Xan, that I began to consider the intrusions of Xan into her life, that I had my first inkling of how selfish my grief had made me. And in the days that followed, I found it difficult to speak to her.

But then: after Xan's death, I was able to gauge the extent of my isolation and loneliness. I was aware of how much I had given up to walk with him every morning and evening. It was like those times when you're too busy to be sick. Your work is too demanding, your nerves too frayed. But as soon as the work lessens and the nerves subside, your body surrenders to illness. And so it was that when Xan died, I understood at last how alone I had been, and I longed for company.

But then, too, you'll recall that, at the start of this account, I stressed that my dad had prized science and reason above all. He could be a little eccentric in his preference, but it was one of the characteristics that defined him. My mom—who had never easily tolerated his worship of (in her words) "reason, the bringer of nightmares"—had, through her reaction to Xan's death, drawn a line between herself and Xan, Dad, and me. Or, rather, Mom's response had thickened the line that already existed.

It is a line that I've resolved to eradicate. I love my mom as much as I loved my father and Xan. But Mom's indifference to Xan's death had, in its way, comforted me, suggesting as it did that, in this matter at least, Dad and I had been close. We had shared the knowledge that Xan was extraordinary.

Winter, or A Town Near Palgrave

After Tommaso Landolfi

One of the most amusing things about being a writer is how often others share what they think will inspire you. For instance, a man from Perth once tried to introduce me to his mother, who knitted socks that, from a certain angle, resembled the Virgin Mary. A woman from Preston Lake thought I should write about her cat, Mittens, a legendary mouser in a town where there are more mice than people.

The suggestions people offer reveal their interests, their assumptions about writing, their thoughts about my work. The suggestion that I write a biography of Mittens, for instance, likely springs from the fact that I've written about dogs. Then, too, I've always been obsessed with the idea of God, so socks that resemble the Virgin Mary are within my purview—just.

That said, I rarely use anyone else's suggestions for stories. The ideas that come to me need to have germinated in my imagination. They need to be mine—or have influenced mine—so I can explore them without getting lost.

But some time ago, a fellow writer—Michael Redhill, as it happens—suggested that I visit the town of L—, somewhere near Palgrave, north of Toronto. He was vague about L— because he hadn't been there himself. But he'd heard rumours about it and thought it might be "my kind of place," the kind of place I'd find inspiring. I took this to mean that Michael thought the place was eccentric—a word he often used to describe my work.

To be polite, I told him that I'd keep L— in mind.

It isn't so easy to keep a small town in mind, though. Time passes. One falls in or out of love. One deals with regrets and recriminations. Life goes on. It wasn't until years later that I heard the name L— again. This time under very different circumstances: a report in the *Toronto Star* about skeletons found in Palgrave, the skeletons of a dozen cows. There was no suggestion that anyone from L— had taken them, but a local farmer swore that, in his opinion, L— was just the kind of place where you'd expect people to abuse cows.

The farmer's words reminded me of what Michael had told me about L—, that it might be of interest to me. Having grown up in a small town, I am fascinated by odd behaviour in isolated places. So, that July, on an excursion north of Toronto with my brother-in-law Ray, I asked if he'd mind stopping in L— for lunch.

My first impression of the town was one of normalcy. The buildings along its main street, the houses on the streets that branched out from it were unremarkable. So much so that you'd have thought yourself in a southern Ontario of southern Ontarios, an Ontario of the mind, like a small town outside Plato's cave.

My second impression, after half an hour of walking around, was that the place was odd. It was a district of absences:

no restaurants, no gas station, no bars, no taverns—no place where you might stop for a rest or for lunch.

There were people around. It was not a ghost town. But my third impression of L— was that its strangeness resided in its people. Those we encountered that day were white, but not in the sense of Caucasian; there were people of various racial origins. Like the town itself, L—'s residents were somewhat erased. I could not, for instance, have told you the age of anyone we passed in the street. Certainly, some were younger than others, but L— was like a town of people who were "young for their age," even the infants, two of whom I saw in the arms of their ageless mothers.

If I was not at all put off by any of this, it may be because the feel of it—what the town evoked in me—was the specific emotional state I had felt when I was four years old coming to Canada for the first time from Trinidad: terror and wonder and an excitement like playing in a vast abandoned house. Ray, on the other hand, was weirded out. He'd wanted to leave from the moment we arrived. He'd humoured me for half an hour as we walked about. Now, he began to insist we leave, assuring me that he'd take the car and go, with me or without.

—He's a bit of an ass, your friend, isn't he?

The woman speaking to us was short, thin, and of Asian descent. She did not look like the others we'd seen in L—. She looked every minute of her—as it turned out—seventy-something years. And as neither Ray nor I had seen her approach, we jumped when she spoke. I laughed, once I got over my startlement. Ray did not.

—No, no, I said. It's my fault. I told him we'd grab lunch here. But we haven't found a place to eat, and we've been wandering around for a while.

—If you wanted to eat, she said, you should have eaten in Palgrave. Not that there's much there. But there's nothing here, even in summer. Your friend's definitely an ass. Next time you're here, you'll come see me first.

—There won't be a next time, said Ray.

—Not for you, she answered.

The woman, whose name was Furaha Yao, did not live in L— full-time. She lived there in mid-autumn and winter. Her home was Kingston. In fact, she wasn't usually in L— in July, but something had called her. Neither of us believed it was chance that she'd been in L— on the same day as me. I don't believe in chance. But Furaha gave greater weight to our encounter than I did. She spoke of our fate: not of mine and hers, but of a fate we shared.

Before I'd made plans to return to L—, before I'd thought about returning, even, she found me via the simplest means: by phone. Warning me that she would not be in Toronto long, she insisted we speak before she went back to Kingston.

—Do you have any idea how to massage leather? she asked.

A question connected, it seemed, to L—, nor could I help remembering the news about cows, their carcasses.

—What makes you think I'm going back to L—? I asked.

—Oh, said Furaha, because you remind me of me. And I know myself pretty well!

She was convinced that I'd return to L—, that I needed her advice. And in spite of myself, I was influenced by her conviction. For those who have a strong will and refuse to be put off their chosen roads, my decision to listen to Furaha might be difficult to understand. But part of my disbelief in chance is tied to my sense that my fate is, in some way, guided. As a result,

I am, at times, susceptible to those who seem to know—or, even, pretend to know—things about me that I don't. This has led to some complications in my personal life.

It is, for instance, what led me to the Tim's at King and Bathurst where I agreed to have coffee with Furaha.

(An aside: I often wonder how important I am in my own life. Like David Copperfield, I'm not convinced I am the hero of my story. My parents, my sisters, my loves, my friends: all of them seem more prominent than me. I felt that way about Furaha, too. Though I've met the woman only three times, and I assume I will never meet her again, it sometimes feels as if I were her shadow.)

—You don't have to look at me like that, Furaha said as she drank her coffee. There's nothing mysterious going on here. I'm a seventy-eight-year-old second-generation Chinese woman from Actinolite. I've been making quilts for forty years. My quilts are all over the world, and my work and my children are the most important thing to me. I passed through L— one summer day ten years ago, and I've been spending winters there for the last ten years. You're the first interesting outsider I've met in L— in all this time, so it's natural that I see you as . . . significant. The way I see it, you must have some connection to the place, and I can help you deepen your ties to it. Whatever else you can say about L—, it's a good place to find the depths. And that's what this is all about. I don't need anything from you, you know.

She spoke in the most reasonable tone imaginable, daintily sipping on her double-double and hiding her mouth each time she bit her old-fashioned plain. I remember there was a moment when I was struck by the thought that she was making sense. But, of course, the situation was absurd. The assumption that because she had seen me in L—, I needed to deepen my acquaintance with the place? That made no sense at all, though I was intrigued by the idea of depths, that a place could help you find them.

Through Furaha, it felt as if L— itself were addressing me. Not politely, but without aggression.

—How are you going to deepen my connection to L—? I asked.

—I'll take you there for the winter, she answered. Bring your work with you. You'll stay at the house on Riverdale. It's a good place for the soul.

Driving into L— at the end of November, with Furaha, I had the same thought as when I'd driven in with Ray: the place was too general to describe. The feel of it was sharper this time, though. L— had the feel of a great city—Rome, say—a place that is lordly in its indifference, because it knows it doesn't need you. L—, though it has not a speck of Rome's grandeur, seemed almost palpably unconcerned with Furaha and me.

On my first visit, I had seen no restaurants, gas stations, or general stores. I was wrong to think there were none, though. The general store and the gas station were on Riverdale, at the house Furaha lived in, the house I would be staying in for a while, to write. That said, the store and station were not usual. The station's tank was filled once a year, on October 11th, but, according to Furaha, it was little used and never sank beneath the halfway mark. The general store was, in reality, Furaha's kitchen and consisted of two bookshelves and a small fridge. The fridge was filled with boxes of Allen's apple juice. One of the bookshelves held tins of vegetables, beef consommé, and cream of mushroom soup, while the other was stacked with metal containers of Vermont's Original Bag Balm.

There were so many of the bright green tins of Bag Balm that you'd have sworn Furaha was a promoter of the stuff; either that or that L— was afflicted by dry skin and cracked udders, the chief use of Bag Balm being the soothing of these things. And just to be clear: there was not a single living cow within kilometres of L—, the nearest farms being closer to Palgrave, Caledon Village, or Mono Mills.

The kitchen/general store appeared to be a late addition to the house, or perhaps a gazebo that had been converted, insulated, and wired for the fridge and stove. It was the only unusual part of the house. The rest of it—single storey, yellowing plaster walls, brick fireplace—held two large bedrooms, a living room, a modest bathroom, and a number of closets. Furaha had converted one of the bedrooms into a workspace. It was crowded with boxes of colourful fabrics. And there were quilts—the ugliest quilts I have ever seen—draped here and there, so that the room looked as if it were padded in spots.

The ugliness of the quilts was a surprise, because I had looked at Furaha Yao's work online and had been impressed by its colour, precision, and play. These quilts looked like the outcome of a nasty argument among modernists.

Furaha held up her hands, trying to obstruct my view of the quilts.

—Don't look at these, she said. I don't know why I made them! I'll clear them out. You should set up your work in here. There's a desk under all this. You'll see.

And then, shooing me out of the room and changing the subject, she said

—Tomorrow, I'll introduce you to someone you have to meet. But don't take his brusqueness to heart. Everyone around here is . . . difficult. It's why outsiders don't come back once they've been here.

—Except for you, I said.

I'd meant the words lightly, but Furaha thought about it before saying

—Yes, and now you, too.

The following day was Furaha's last in L— and my first.

I woke in the morning, after a deep and dreamless sleep, to discover that Furaha had taken her things—boxes of fabric, ugly quilts—out of the second bedroom. Now the room was clean and tidy. A writing desk stood before a picture window that looked out onto a backyard that seemed endless and endlessly autumnal; the grasses dun, though, here and there, greenish at the roots; the maple trees near the house barren, their dead leaves brown with spots of red, yellow, and black.

The house smelled of oatmeal and peanut butter which, as it happens, was breakfast. And when we had finished eating, Furaha showed me around town, a tour that took a leisurely hour, during which she tried to prepare me for my meeting with Mayor Roberts, the highest authority in L—, if L— can be said to have any kind of echelon.

(I would like the reader to keep in mind, here, before they meet Mayor Roberts, that all those who live in L— are unpleasant. But their unpleasantness is rooted in their situation. So, in the three years I've wintered there, I have come to . . . not accept it, exactly, but to appreciate it, to take the unpleasantness lightly, because I understand it.)

Mayor Roberts was tall, gruff, and fat, his hands and fingers as if swollen, his cheeks flush and saggy, his neck like a monstrous sausage supporting his head. Cradled in his left arm, there was a blue metal box that had once held—or perhaps still held—Danish sand cookies.

—This is A—, said Furaha. He'll be staying on Riverdale for a while. He's a writer.

To Furaha, Mayor Roberts said

—He'll be minding the store? Is this the best you can do?

And then, to me:

—You look incompetent.

—Mr. Mayor, said Furaha, you didn't like me, either, you know.

—*Didn't* like you? said Mayor Roberts. I still don't like you. How many of us have suffered while you were sewing your rags? We should have eaten you before winter and gotten someone else to look out for us.

—But you didn't, said Furaha, and here we are. And now you have your someone else.

—Hmmph, said Mayor Roberts.

He watch me cut-eye, as Trinidadians say, before opening the cookie tin and taking out three hundred-dollar bills, which he held up as if offering sardines to a cat.

—This is what you want, isn't it? he asked.

But aside from the fact that it would have felt demeaning to take the bills from him, there was also the fact that the bills were greasy and in no way attractive. Plus, I had no idea what the man was talking about or what he expected me to do for the money he was offering.

—What do you want me to do with that? I asked. Mayor Roberts—surprised, it seemed—turned to Furaha.

—Is he stupid? he asked.

—No, said Furaha, he just doesn't know how to deal with your rudeness.

—So, he's . . . sensitive?

And then, to me, with almost blistering sarcasm

—Listen, my good sir, I expect of you the most ardent commission of your duties. This stipend I offer is meant to assure that any prickish tendencies you possess will be forthwith suppressed. It is an incitement for you to diligently and correctly perform your duties to me and my family. Do you see?

I didn't see. I was even more baffled after the explanation than I had been before it. But Furaha took the three bills and thanked him, after which Mayor Roberts shut the door in our faces, without another word.

Two things struck me as we walked away. Firstly, I had not yet agreed to stay in L—, not for a day, not for a month, not for any length of time. As such, it felt as if Furaha and Mayor Roberts were colluding against me. Or was it, and this resonates with me still, that in coming to L— with my writing and my suitcase of clothes, I had tacitly agreed to stay? Secondly, Mayor Roberts's fatness—his corporality—seemed out of place. On first visiting L— in July, I thought all the citizens of the town, save Furaha, looked young for their ages. They had all been svelte, athletic-looking. In Mayor Roberts I had found one who was ungraceful, adipose, old for his age. Was Mayor Roberts an exception? No. As it turned out, all those I'd meet or see in the coming weeks would be grossly overweight; not hairy, but ursine.

In November, everyone in L— looked old for their age.

The moment I should have reconsidered staying in L— came as I spoke to Furaha for the last time, that evening.

All day, she had been kind, but mysteriously circumspect as well. She had shown me how to run the store. She had given me keys to the truck I could use, if ever I wanted to go to Palgrave, say, or Caledon East.

—You never know, she said. You might want some relief from the solitude.

But then, as if she wanted to get everything out with a final push, she handed me a page on which she had printed a set of rules.

—I didn't mention any of this before, she said, because I didn't want to put you off. But there are a few things—not that difficult!—you're expected to do over the winter. I've printed them out for you. You'll see, there's nothing too difficult.

1. Do not go into anyone's house until December 15th, at the earliest. They will not welcome you.
2. After December 15th, visit every house in town once a month, more often if you've been paid for it by a homeowner.
3. There will be a number of large lumpy sacks (of various sizes) hanging from the rafters of the houses. On each visit, rub the bottoms and sides of these sacks with Bag Balm. In December, do this carefully. Stop immediately if you hear groaning. After December, you can rub as vigorously as you like.
4. In the event you enter a home and smell something rotten, find the bag that stinks, cut it down, take it to the field behind the house on Riverdale, and burn it. If the bag moves while it is in transit, take it back to the house where you found it and try to burn it later, if the stink persists or worsens. Use your judgment. (There is a wagon in the garage for this purpose. It's best not to carry or drag the sacks yourself.)
5. Leave L— before March 15th. You may take the truck as far as Palgrave, but leave it at 57 Fenton Road. Take the bus from Palgrave to wherever you are going.

—What does all this mean? I asked.

—Well, said Furaha, L— is a town that hibernates. I mean, I believe that's what they call it. It's a tradition. You won't see anyone between mid-December and mid-March. I don't really know what goes on, and I've never wanted to know. It's not my business. I come here to do my work. If I have to humour a few people along the way, well, what about it? No one gets hurt. I don't know if it's essential that you do these things, but if you want to come back, you should. I've been coming for ten years, myself. Ten winters. I think it's enough.

Even as she confessed these things, I felt she was being evasive.

She gave me the keys to the house and patted my hand. And looking down at her thin and hunched-over body aswim in its overcoat, her white hair combed back, the traces of the comb like furrows in silk, her kind smile . . . I was reminded of my mother and felt a surprising wave of emotion.

—I'll do my best, I said.

—Good, good, answered Furaha. But . . . just one more little thing. I have to be truthful, you know, but I've never done good work while I've been here. I don't know why, but everything I make here is just terrible. But I always come away feeling renewed, and that's when I do my best work: when I leave. So, don't get discouraged if your writing doesn't go well. The inspiration will come when you least expect it.

—I'll give it a month, I said. If things don't feel right, I'll go.

These words clearly troubled her. She frowned.

—I'm certain, she said, that you'll stay till March. I feel it. I have faith in you. I'm certain you'll be fine.

She didn't look all that certain, and I had the unexpected sense that my leaving would be a serious problem—I wasn't sure for whom. I trusted her faith in me, however, and I told her so.

—Good, good, she said, smiling at me as she drove off in her Hyundai.

Despite the instructions she'd given me, I took the word "hibernate" to be metaphorical. I took it as Furaha's fanciful way of suggesting that the town of L— is preternaturally quiet in winter. I thought it was a figure of speech right up until December 11th.

Up until mid-December, the town was quiet and my days were relatively peaceful. Although my kitchen was the so-called general store, there was little traffic: one or two people a day, corpulent and sullen, interested in nothing but Bag Balm. Even at that, I sold no more than a dozen tins of Vermont's Original. Most of those who came in seemed more interested in sizing me up. They stared at me, as if I'd done something to provoke them. A few did only that: they stared, then left without a word.

On the day in question, no one had come to the general store/my kitchen. I had the impression that anyone in town who'd wanted to see me had done so. More than that: on my daily walks around L—, I saw no one on the street and little traffic to speak of.

All those who wished to be in L— were, it seemed, present, and those who wished to leave had, apparently, gone. The winter had effectively begun, but I wasn't quite prepared for it. My routine was not set. I had not yet portioned out my day. As a result, I missed the presence of others and I walked about—here and there, once or twice—just to see if there was anyone around.

That evening, however, I was driven by more than just the desire to see a fellow human. I'd begun to fear that Furaha was right. Despite my quiet surroundings and the creative excitement I felt, I was troubled that nothing I'd written since my arrival was any good. During my first weeks in L—, I was prey to wild ideas. For instance, I'd spent three whole days translating the first pages of my novel *Seventeen Dogs* into Middle English: *Oon effning wher tres ayenstonden in water is, ye Godes Hermes ond Apollo* . . . and so on. Three days wasted.

So, I went out for a walk to clear my mind of its idle enthusiasms. I went just after sunset, walking by early moonlight in the field behind my residence. The world smelled of late-autumn rot and stagnant water. It was not cold, but the air was bracing, and I strolled along the edge of the field, which a number of houses abutted.

I suppose I must have noticed the backs of the houses, windows yellowed by the lights inside, when I went out. But it wasn't until I was coming back that I paid attention to them. Most of the windows were shuttered or curtained, but one was not. And through it I saw a man and a woman, naked in the middle of what looked to be a living room.

The sight was not appealing, and I would have turned away, but I was struck by what they were doing. The man, corpulent and awkward, looking like a monstrously oversized baby, was climbing a ladder, a bale of thick rope around his forearm. Unfurling the rope, he threw the bulk of it over a beam and, coming down, gave his wife the other end, before climbing up again with another bale of rope.

How quickly one falls into other lives!

Seeing ropes being thrown over thick beams, I assumed I was watching the initial stages of a double suicide, and I felt it was my duty to save the two, though I did not relish the idea of rushing in on a naked couple who were about to hang themselves from the rafters of their living room. So, as I watched the ritual unfold, I tried to calculate, despite my distress, the best moment for me to intervene: now, while they were still preparing, or later, when the nooses were tied.

I opted to wait for the nooses, which was just as well because, as time went on, what I had taken to be a preparation for death evolved into something else. With a precision and cooperation that could only have come from long experience, the two began to prepare harnesses: ropes attached to the four corners of what looked like deep leather hammocks. Feeling, then, that I had intruded on sexual ritual, I was horrified and left the scene at once.

I have mentioned that this incident happened on December 11th. I've insisted on the date because it coincides with the onset of my feeling that the town had been abandoned. It had not been abandoned. At night, one or two of the lights were on in all the houses, but it felt, as the saying goes, as if no one was home.

There was no one on the streets, no one walking about by day, no smoke rising from chimneys, no smell of cooking, no children's voices, no errant curses, no laughter, no cars passing through. It was as if I were nowhere. So by the 15th, when I was meant to make my rounds, I wondered if there was any point.

I went, however, because I'd given my word and, after writing all morning on the 15th, I needed a break. It was a bright day, the dead leaves reminding me of basement windows and late-season gardens. L— was, of course, quiet. And maybe because I'd been more intimidated by Mayor Roberts than I realized, I went to his home first.

—

The front door was unlocked, and there was a light on in the foyer. The place smelled of mildew, but there was a hint of air freshener, along with a hint of fresh air. The first thing I saw as I entered was a table on which there were tins of Bag Balm. Before the tins was a note addressed to me: "We are in the living room." And I went to the unlit living room, expecting to find Mayor Roberts and his family sitting around, waiting.

What I found instead were four misshapen whitish globes suspended by ropes from beams along the ceiling. They were like hammocks, in that they hung down from the rafters. But they were not elongated, as hammocks are, like canvas smiles. Rather, they were in the shape of teardrops or giant Baci chocolates. Each globe was some distance from the others, and each swayed slightly. The material out of which the hammocks were made was leather and something porous, an off-white brushed cotton, maybe. And, of course, in each one there was a human body.

I say "of course" because, in Mayor Roberts's home, I finally accepted that L— was a town where hibernation was not a metaphor. I could not see into the hammocks. So, I had no idea who was where. Nor could I distinguish on the basis of size. Everyone, it seemed, was large, and each hammock swayed, now and then, as one of the bodies inside moved or sighed.

The reader may be wondering, as I have sometimes wondered, why I was so calm, given the circumstances. It is not often that one enters the darkened living room of people who have suspended themselves in leather-and-fabric cocoons. But I was not entirely unprepared for something like this. Though I had not quite believed her, Furaha had told me about winter. And then, too, I found the situation pleasing. Maybe even a little exhilarating, suggestive of some potentially useful metaphor or another.

In other words, I couldn't help thinking this was good for my work.

The situation was also unexpectedly intimate. I was careful, as I rubbed Bag Balm on the outside of each of the hammocks. I was gentle, understanding that the objective was to keep the leather supple without disturbing any of those within. This concern connected me to each person in his or her cocoon. And, naturally, I couldn't help trying to guess whose hammock I was anointing: a man, a woman, someone young, someone old? And what exactly was I touching: a head, buttocks, a belly?

I felt maternal or, at least, what I imagine maternal to be, the feeling coming with a memory of my mother's hands smelling of liniment. Only once, during that first ministration, did anyone within make a sound: a groan or, perhaps, a muffled fart. Hard to say which. The rest of that day, while it was still light out, I tended to other houses in L—, all of them set up much as the Robertses' had been: darkened living rooms, bodies suspended from rafters, Bag Balm waiting.

Though I was, from the first, at ease with my task and my surroundings, I only ever visited people's houses in daylight. I could not have imagined walking through the town by moonlight by myself. So, it took me a week to look after all the inhabitants of L—.

Much of my time in L—, that winter, was spent in contemplation. I was, after all, alone with my thoughts. Or accompanied by the muted presences of others.

But contemplation was not the result of my circumstances and my nature alone. It was also the product of my ritualized relationship to L— and its inhabitants. I mean, as Christmas approached, I began to long for my time in the houses of others, rubbing balm on suspended bodies in darkened rooms: the approach, the unique density that is human presence, even when it's stifled, the silence that ushered me into a house. In effect, I grew somewhat dependent on the sensual details that came with my task.

No, "dependent" is not the word. Nor is "longing." Those things come from within, whereas what I felt started with the inhabitants of L—. Their vulnerability was an active part of the emotion I felt. I don't believe that a word's origins are necessarily in play when one uses a word. (I was not, for instance, thinking of the origin of the word "prick"—from the Old English *prica*, a sharp point, puncture, minute mark made by sticking or piercing—the last time I referred to my father as one.) But, here, the origin of the word "care" comes to mind: from the Old English word *carian*, which means to be anxious or solicitous; to grieve; to feel concern. Yes, I was anxious for them, grieving, though grief was not really called for, as they were all, I believe, still alive, however little they moved about in their winter confines.

I felt this sense of care most poignantly one day in January. The world was covered in snow after a storm. None of the walkways had been cleared, so it was difficult to move from house to house. The sky was blue as only a Canadian sky can be: slightly muted, apologetically blue, but still infinite, while the clouds were solitary and white.

In the distance, along one of the side streets, I saw a hulking figure—pale and white—walking. It was an unsettling moment. I had not seen anyone walking about in weeks, and I felt my own vulnerability as I watched the figure struggle through the snow. What did the person want? What was the protocol with strangers? How far was I expected to go, in defence of my charges? How much of myself was I meant to surrender?

But all these questions were the effluvia of a heartbeat. After a few seconds, I realized that the person before me was naked, someone who had, no doubt, awakened before she was meant to. Moreover, this particular sleepwalker was particularly fortunate. I'd discovered her not twenty yards from her house, the door to which was still open. I could imagine what might have happened had I not arrived when I did: her death on a cold road or in a snowy field.

Recognizing the situation did not make things easier for me. Disoriented people are sometimes dangerous, and as the person in question was unclothed and walking about in January snow, I assumed she was, at the very least, disoriented. So, I was wary and my concerns were entirely practical: how should I lead this woman—her breasts blue-veined and snow-flecked—back to her home, back to her hammock?

(It was then that I realized how conventional my feelings were. My reservations and pudeur were a menace to the person stumbling before me.)

When I caught up to the woman, she was mumbling to herself, mumbling so softly that I was beside her before I realized she was repeating the words

—Their horses are swifter than leopards . . .

over and over as she forded the snow. She was, in other words, praying as she went or, simply, clinging to a passage from the Bible. And recognizing the prayer, I took her hand and led her home, leaving her to return to the cocoon by herself.

It has occurred to me since that I should have waited for her to get back to the hammock. But that seemed an intimacy too far, going past a border I didn't want to cross. As a result, I still have no idea how the people of L— insinuate themselves into their suspended cocoons. The next time I went to her home, the following day, all was as it should be, and you could not have told that any had left their winter places.

After that, I was more aware of the dangers and vulnerabilities faced by those who wintered in L—. I now understood that the Bag Balm was a pretext. The leather-and-cotton cocoons did not need monthly anointing. What was needed was attention, vigilance, care. The money that each of the households had given me—three or four thousand dollars in all—had been given to assure themselves of the quality of my attentiveness. But as there was no way to guarantee my attention, their contributions were an attempt to reassure themselves, as if my desire for money were a warrant of fidelity.

And, of course, the more I understood the extent of their vulnerability, the more the resentment and scorn the inhabitants of L— had shown me revealed itself for what it was: a mask for their fears. It was not just that any one of them might wake early and wander to their death. It was not just that any might die while cocooned. It was that, had I chosen it, there was nothing any could do to prevent me from murdering them as they hibernated or from abandoning them to the depredations of strangers.

They had taken a chance on me, on Furaha, on all those who had come before us. Aware of this, I was also aware of the endless darkness that would have come for L— had they been wrong about any of us. For that reason, and because what I wrote in L— was unusable, I did less and less writing during the two months that remained of winter. Instead, I performed my tasks more often.

Nor was I bothered by this fall in word production. It seemed to me that the experience of caring was immense for my psyche. As it must have been for Furaha. As it must have been for the ones before her, not all of whom would have been able to say—as I was when March came—that that year, none had died in their hammocks, and none had wandered to their death. None that I know of, anyway.

I was tempted to stay beyond the 15th, to be in L— when the town emerged from winter. But two distinct ideas—or feelings, if you like—stopped me.

First, I felt as if my presence would have been an intrusion. No one is at their best when waking or, for that matter, when being born. And there was, as spring came and the snow grew granular before melting, a sense of renewal, of rebirth. Maybe if I'd been invited, I might have stayed on to greet those who awakened. But I had not been invited. I had been warned to leave.

Second, as I was looking out my window, one morning around the 1st of March, I saw a deer with her fawns nonchalantly crossing the field behind my house. As far as the deer knew, she and her children were alone and safe. The sight of them called to mind the idea of maternity. And it was suddenly mysterious to me, this "maternity," a thing that stretched from the deer before me, as she stopped and listened, to the crab spider, one that gives up her body as food for the spiders to whom she gives birth. And it seemed to me, in that moment, that at the heart of maternity—at the heart of care—there is discretion and sacrifice.

I did not think that the inhabitants of L— would eat me when they awakened—not necessarily. But it felt as if my desire to stay, to feel L—'s gratitude, was selfish and small. Besides, I did not know how they would react or what frenzy rebirth might bring. So I felt intimidated whenever I thought about staying.

In the three years since that first winter, the thing that still amazes me is the path I took to L—: a word spoken by an acquaintance, a story in a newspaper, and the encouragement of a quilt-maker from Kingston. How uncertain it all was, considering how important L— has become to me, how predestined our relationship feels. I have come to accept that my soul and the soul of a place can share a trajectory without either of us knowing it.

(Or is it that places know these things, while humans belatedly learn them?)

In any case, the wondering about L— is its legacy, the source of its appeal. It is, for instance, the reason I have written this memoir, "Winter." The questions L— provokes have occupied me since I left the place that first year, on the 11th of March, driving Furaha's truck—as I still think of it—to Palgrave, though, of course, L— is not near Palgrave and is no place you are likely to have been.

A Certain Likeness

There can be no world of the Buddha
without the world of the devil.
Yasunari Kawabata

Kisasi O'Hara, an archivist at the Art Gallery of Ontario, took the train from Montreal to Toronto often: five hours, the land going by in familiar waves—the sprawl of Montreal, relieved by views of the St. Lawrence River, then farmlands and farm fields, rocks and trees, small towns, then Kingston, the shores of Lake Ontario seen, hidden, seen again, before the return of concrete sprawl, and finally Toronto, home.

She had made the trip countless times in her life, because Montreal had always been a haven to her, a relief from the banality of Toronto or the tarnish of Bewdley, the small town where her mother was born and where she died. Younger, Kisasi had visited friends in Montreal. Now, in her forties, she spent most weekends there with her partner, Alain, returning to the city of her birth on Mondays or Tuesdays.

It hardly mattered when she travelled. The journey was inevitably dull or comforting in almost equal measure, variation provided by the time of year. In winter, for instance, whiteness predominated, bearding the land and greying the lake. In spring, the freshly shaven face of Earth, its brown fields and soft-leafed trees, made the lake seem innocent. While in summer, all was colour and breeze in the countryside, cement in the cities, various indigos on the lake.

On this particular trip, it was autumn, and although she was by a window, Kisasi was not interested in the landscape. She was in business class—for the first time in her life, on a whim—and she was sitting beside Misha van Zandt, a well-known artist, who had permitted her to sit beside him in a bay of four seats, all of which he'd bought for himself.

On the pretext that she was feeling motion-sick, she had approached the man and demurely asked if it would inconvenience him to have her sit in one of the forward-facing seats. He had looked up at her face, as if searching for something.

—I prefer the aisle, he said. And I like facing forward myself. I also *prefer* . . . being left alone. But if you don't mind sitting beside me, you can sit by the window until you feel better.

—It's very kind of you, she said. Thank you.

He had stood up, then, to let her pass and Kisasi could feel his presence, smell his cologne, appreciate the fact that although the man was in his sixties—hair mostly grey, impeccably dressed, but wearing running shoes as if in defiance of his demeanour—he was attractive. Women found him attractive.

She found him attractive, though the feeling disturbed her.

Whatever else she had in mind, Kisasi was determined not to overstay her welcome. It was enough, for the moment, to have met him. So, just before Kingston, she told him that she felt much better, and thanking him again, she stood up to return to her seat.

Though he had not spoken to her nor seemed aware of her presence, he said

—You've been good company. You can stay here, if you want. You never know. You might start to feel motion sick again. Then what would you do?

His tone of voice was just this side of sarcasm, but Kisasi wondered what he meant by "good company." She nodded and sat back down, careful to suppress her emotion, but smiling in a distant way, as if she were remembering some past goodness.

Van Zandt turned towards her.

—What's your name? he asked.

—Kisasi, she answered. Kisasi O'Hara.

—Kisasi. Is that African?

—No, she lied. It's Japanese.

—You remind me of someone, Kisasi. Have we met before?

She met his look and tilted her head slightly, as if seriously considering his question.

—No, she said. We've never met.

—You've got a fascinating face, he said. Gorgeous cheekbones, lovely eyebrows.

She took no pleasure from his words, but she smiled as if she did. He had assessed her not to compliment, exactly, but not to belittle, either. Then, as if he'd said all that needed saying, Misha van Zandt turned back to the magazine he was reading, on the cover of which a man was talking to a deer—or was it an elk?—that had massive antlers: *Artforum*.

Kisasi was grateful to have been dismissed in this way. For one thing, she did not have to show gratitude for this assessment of her "gorgeous cheekbones and lovely eyebrows"—both features she shared with her mother. And then: she knew he was the kind of man who liked the sound of his own voice and (in her mother's words) liked to hear its echo. She was happy to accommodate him in this.

Looking out the window, she at last took in the autumn gallery: fiery red, orange, and yellow, mixed with fading greens, a raw blue sky traversed by thin grey clouds, the dandelion clocks by the side of the tracks shivering as the train passed.

Her mother came back to her, then.

An impression rather than a memory: Kika's hair clinging to one side of her face like wet dark threads. The impression was fleeting but vivid, no doubt tied to some deeper moment between them. But the envelope that held the impression—the place and the time—would not be coaxed back. Not that this caused Kisasi the least anxiety or sadness. The love she felt for her mother was independent of place or moment—more so, now that Kika was dead.

Kisasi's childhood had been an interesting one. Her mother, Kika, a single parent, had made certain that Kisasi wanted for nothing. Within her limited capacities, Kika had pampered her daughter, while instilling a reverence for certain virtues: truth, justice, courage, devotion. She had instilled these things without homilies or injunctions, sharing with her daughter her love for music and nature, so that virtue—or the idea of virtue—had come, for Kisasi, along with attention to the beautiful things in the world. By the time she was eleven, Kisasi could name most of the trees, plants, and flowers in or around Toronto.

She would not have changed a thing about the first years of her life, but that's not to say that Kisasi's childhood was without pain, fear, or sadness. Despite her mother's bouts of joy, there were also times—intense and scalding—when Kika seemed beyond her reach. Nor could Kisasi predict when these moments might come. Once when they'd been sitting together, side by side at their small dining room table, her mother disappeared:

not materially, of course. Kika was there beside her, but a subdued presence had supplanted her mother's, so that it was, suddenly, like sitting beside a block of wood. She had been eight at the time, and the experience had terrified her.

In the years that followed, these withdrawals gained two names that stuck. The comforting name, which Kisasi learned at eight, was "bipolar." Her mother was bipolar. She was a depressive, subject to bouts of depression and elation. Due to her condition, Kika could not help behaving as she did. In other words, the withdrawals had nothing to do with her daughter. It was not, as Kisasi had feared, her fault. It was, perhaps, no one's fault. And that being the case, Kisasi willingly became her mother's caretaker: cleaning the house and cooking whenever Kika's depression took hold. She fell into the habit of suppressing her own emotions whenever Kika was at her worst, but Kisasi never resented the housework. It was an occupation for which she was grateful, allowing her as it did her own version of not-being-there.

(Naturally, Kika's condition had other, deeper influences on Kisasi's life. It was, for instance, at the root of Kisasi's mistrust of emotional entanglements, her coldness at the idea of family. In fact, it seemed a small miracle that she had met Alain Tournier, a man as sybaritic as she was, and just as allergic to the gooey emotions he called "fleurs bleues.")

The second name for her mother's depression was more mysterious: Misha van Zandt.

Kisasi could not have said when, exactly, Misha's name first came into her life, nor the first time she recognized it. It was certainly after Kika's first disappearance, the moment when mother and daughter were sitting beside each other at their table. But the significance of the name came later still. "Misha van Zandt" was, to begin, just the name of someone whose memory was upsetting to her mother. Then it was a name that seemed to precede her mother's bouts of depression; not immediately, but close enough to seem a harbinger of pain. And then when Kisasi was eleven, her mother at last confided in her.

—Mom, Kisasi asked, what does my name mean, really?

It was a question she'd asked before. But previous to this, her mother had answered evasively.

—It means I love you, she'd say. Why else would I give you such a beautiful name.

Or

—Never mind that, now. Come and help me with . . .

And there seemed always to be something more important to do or talk about. So, Kisasi had looked "Kisasi" up online and discovered that it was the Swahili word for revenge. A coincidence, she assumed, because she could not imagine Kika choosing such a name for her.

But that day, Kika answered plainly.

—Kisasi is Swahili for revenge, she said.

—Why did you call me that? Kisasi asked.

—Because the first time I saw you, I could tell how good you were, and it felt like you were my answer to all the terrible things in the world, like sunlight is God's revenge on darkness.

Then why had she hidden this from her in the first place?

—I didn't hide it, said Kika. I waited till you could understand.

This was credible, not only because it was typical of her mother's thoughtfulness, but also because the Kika who loved the world and nature *would* think of sunlight as a revenge on darkness. On top of which, the eleven-year-old Kisasi was thrilled that she had finally reached the age of understanding.

But the unaccommodating mother, the one who could not be reconciled to the world, let it slip that, on second thought, the revenge she wanted had something to do with men in general, and with Misha van Zandt in particular. That is, she hoped her beautiful daughter would ruin as many men's lives as she was able. And if it were possible, if circumstances ever arose, Kisasi should particularly ruin Misha van Zandt.

The story of Kika's relationship to van Zandt was complicated and it varied at each telling, depending on her mother's emotions at the time. But, in brief: Kika met Misha van Zandt in 1975, when she was seventeen, not long after she'd left her parents' home in Bewdley. She had found work in Toronto, modelling for visual artists. It was work she loved, allowing her as it did the kind of contemplation that helped her stay grounded while also being, at times, physically challenging. Van Zandt was, for a time, just one of a number of painters for whom she modelled. But then he had asked if she minded working for him alone, and though he could not afford much more than she usually made, he did offer more.

The sessions with him were wonderful. Though she did not always feel comfortable posing for one artist alone, she was at ease in Misha's company from the start. The warmth of his attention was constant but unobtrusive, like a light left on in another room, so that, after a while, the fact of his looking at her was somehow unimportant. Misha was attentive in so many ways: making sure she was comfortable, taking breaks for food he made himself, entertaining her with gossip both ancient and modern—from Montaigne's love for his friend La Boétie to Eartha Kitt's threesome with James Dean and Paul Newman, from the significance of Socrates's acceptance of political lies to recipes that Misha had memorized from the medieval cookbooks that fascinated him.

In a word, he was beguiling, someone she would have been happy to listen to whenever he chose to speak. It was the first time she'd met anyone who moved her in this way. But beyond that, he embodied the reason she'd left Bewdley, a town so hateful to her that she never returned to it. Why would she return when there were people like Misha—smart, funny, urbane—elsewhere?

She had been naive, of course; naive in a number of ways.

While it was true that Misha was unlike anyone she'd known, he was not representative of Toronto. He was more talented, more easily confident, more broadly learnèd than most of those she met in the city. Then, too, he did not think about his art as she did. Painting was not noble to him, not something that separated him from the day-to-day. And finally: although he was genuinely interested in her body as an aesthetic proposition, he was not uninterested in her erotic self. All things considered, he was as interested in fucking her as any number of boys in Bewdley had been.

But why should Misha's desire offend her? Kika was not interested in virginity. Her love of nature included a love for her body and its pleasures—which love she passed on to her daughter. But she had, perhaps unconsciously, drawn a line between those with whom she slept and those whose interest in her body was professional. This distinction was part of what allowed her to model without anxiety. It had been important to her to distinguish between men-as-such and people-who-painted. So, sleeping with Misha had been more of an event than it should have been. Not much more, but enough so that it was painful when Misha was done with her, when he had finished three portraits of Kika Hedden and dismissed her—"ghosted her" is what her daughter would have called it.

What disappointed, what rankled, was that their final parting had been much like those that preceded it. They had held each other and kissed. But he had added, as she left his studio, that he would be away for a while—away in Europe where, he said, he was to have a vernissage in Paris before visiting friends in Berlin.

—I'll see you when I get back, he'd said.

But Kika never saw him again, nor even heard from him.

She blamed Misha van Zandt for the suffering that the waiting and uncertainty brought her. A clean break was, she felt, the least he'd owed her, and this resentment was at the heart of her dislike for Misha; it was the grounds of her hatred.

But other things rankled as well, things that were not Misha's fault but for which she blamed him nevertheless. For instance, her decision to sleep with Francis O'Hara, another painter, as a way to punish Misha, though, in the end, it was self-punishment, really. And this "lying, lousy, good-for-nothing prick" was, as it happened, Kisasi's father. Were it not for Kisasi, Kika would have blotted him from memory. As it was, the only things she remembered about Francis O'Hara were his "stupid-looking beard" and that, despite his Irish name, he was Black.

(These scant details were all that Kisasi knew about her father—he was a prick and he had a beard. There were any number of "Francis O'Hara"s online, but none of those she looked up corresponded to the one her mother described. Nor were there any whom she resembled, none whose image Kika would acknowledge as "the sperm donor." Perhaps he'd ceased to be an artist or had left Canada or had died. Whatever the case, this Francis O'Hara was one of the thorns in Kisasi's relationship with her mother.

—If you hated him so much, Kisasi asked, why do I have his last name?

—I don't know, Kika answered. I guess, at the time, I hated the name Hedden more than O'Hara. I still do!

That Francis O'Hara was her daughter's father and that this was significant to Kisasi did not seem to influence Kika at all. She chose not to talk about him.)

The most malignant spur to Kika's hatred for van Zandt had almost nothing to do with the man himself. The three portraits that he had painted of Kika before leaving for Europe became iconic, representative of Misha van Zandt's "early genius"—as a critic in *Art in America* had put it. Two of the three were sold to an American billionaire who, shortly before his death, bequeathed them to the Art Gallery of Ontario. This was tremendously prestigious, both for the artist and the country that had produced him, such that, whenever there was an article about van Zandt, one or another of the so-called "portraits of KH" that had sold were used as illustration.

At times, Kika found this union of herself and Misha van Zandt bemusing, at times fateful. It ate at her, though, and she began to see something sinister in it, something unnameable, until it occurred to her that Misha had knowingly used her to advance his own career. He had known, as she had, that the paintings captured her depths: her sensuality, love, and vulnerability. He had put her essence on display, in order to advance himself. Seeing it in this way, it became clear to Kika that he'd abandoned her for the basest of reasons: he had not wanted to share an iota of credit for the creation of his masterpieces.

After a while, this idea, credible or not, became a keystone of her grievances, a justification not only for her hatred of van Zandt, which was poisonous, but for her turning away from the world. And it seemed to Kisasi, in the months before her mother's first attempted suicide, to be the only subject Kika would entertain. Nothing else mattered.

—

As the train approached Toronto, Kisasi began to consider what she should do about van Zandt. It was something of a miracle that she'd met him, but was there a point to the encounter, a deeper meaning? Or was it only a brief and fleeting coincidence?

Interrupting her thoughts, Misha van Zandt said

—I'm an artist, a painter. If you're up for it, I'd like to paint you. Here's my business card.

—I'm flattered, said Kisasi.

—Don't be, he answered. I'm not interested in anything but painting you. If you like the idea, call my secretary. We may be able to arrange dates and times. I'll need about forty-eight hours altogether. We can stretch it over two or three months. If you're not interested or you don't have the time, it was nice sitting with you. It's not very often that I meet young people who know how to keep still.

—Will I have to pose naked? she asked ironically.

He frowned and shook his head.

—I'm not interested in nudes, he said. I'd like to do a portrait of you with your clothes on. Besides, men representing women's bodies isn't a thing anymore, and hasn't been since I was young.

That Kisasi was not convinced by these words had, in part, to do with her mistrust of his denials. Why *shouldn't* she be flattered by his desire to capture her? It was also due to her surprise at van Zandt's earnest answer to a teasingly asked question. It was arresting that he'd been so quick to reassure her. But beyond all that, there was the bland truth that she was no longer young, no longer impressed by others—unless she chose to be.

She found the man interesting, but the man who interested her was not, strictly speaking, the one she'd met. "Misha van Zandt" was an amalgam of a living being and a man who'd been so often described to her by Kika that she could not untangle the one in her imagination and the one beside her.

There was, besides all that, a feeling that she owed her mother's ghost something. Kika would have been unhappy to learn that her daughter had met van Zandt and done nothing to avenge her. That said, didn't Kisasi owe it to herself—to the sense of justice Kika had instilled in her—to see what kind of man van Zandt actually was? She could not imagine taking revenge without knowing what he deserved. She was not so naive as to think that her mother had been objective about him.

In the weeks that followed their meeting, Kisasi gradually convinced herself that there could be no harm in posing for Misha van Zandt. So, a month after their meeting, she called the man's secretary and set aside a block of time to pose for him.

A number of things occurred to Kisasi, as she was shepherded to van Zandt's studio in Leslieville. Foremost among them were the words a fellow archivist at the AGO had spoken when she learned Kisasi was going to model for van Zandt.

—Why would you do that? she'd asked. He's a dirty old man!

As the woman was in charge of van Zandt's correspondence in the gallery's archive, Kisasi did not dismiss her opinion. Rather, she asked if anything had happened recently. In the seventies, when van Zandt came to prominence, painters used to talk about "painting with their cocks," as if mind and desire were irreconcilable. Kika herself had told her this, and though Kisasi did not accept it as reason or excuse for chauvinism, she had felt her mother's sympathy for the idea and could not condemn Misha for an attitude that, according to Kika, had been universal among male artists at the time.

—No, the archivist answered. I haven't heard about anything recent. From what I hear, he keeps his secretary in the studio while he's painting, so he's got a witness. There's no chance he'll be accused of anything obvious. But, you know, Kisasi, I've read a lot of his correspondence, and knowing what an entitled bastard he is, I can't stand to be in the same room with his paintings. He thinks he's regal, just because he's talented.

The archivist made a face, as if a sewer main had just then broken nearby.

But van Zandt's studio, filled with his work, had nothing regal about it. There were a number of canvases, in various stages of completion, against the walls: from an almost-blank and gessoed canvas at the centre of which were two meticulously painted eyes to an oversized portrait of a well-known Toronto couple—she sitting, he standing with his hand on her shoulder. Kisasi did not feel the least revulsion in the presence of van Zandt's work. If anything, the serenity they exuded was a reminder that an artist and his work are, effectively, an estranged couple, that it is possible to choose one over the other.

The other thing Kisasi noted was that the two of them were in the studio by themselves. His secretary—a young man whose hair was wisp-thin, so that, in places, his scalp showed through—had left them to themselves, very soon after he asked if she needed anything. When she said she did not, he pointed to a refrigerator at the far end of the studio, beside which was a red trolley bearing an electric kettle, a jar of instant coffee, a white porcelain teapot, and a package of Moroccan mint tea.

Just before leaving, and in a kind voice, the secretary said

—My office is in the next room, if you need anything at all.

Misha, who had been intently looking at her from the moment she entered the studio, finally spoke.

—I think you'll feel more comfortable sitting. Or do you want to stand? For most people, it's harder to stand for long periods. So, it takes longer.

He was all kindness, now, his tone of voice avuncular. But then this, she thought, was his domain. He had done hundreds of portraits; very few still lives, and no landscapes she knew of. So, his expertise would naturally include putting his subjects at ease. Knowing this made her more, not less, uncomfortable.

—Don't worry, he said. It's not painful. It's mostly getting used to someone staring at you. You know, I wanted to feel what it was like, so I sat for Gord Rayner, who was my mentor. One of the least boring men I've ever known, but the only way I could get through it was I started looking at Gord as if *I* was the one doing the painting. I don't know if that would help you. Depends on your orientation, if you're visual or not. What kind of person are you, Kisasi?

This question, an invitation to think about what she wanted, was helpful. She relaxed, then answered

—I'm more of a word person

and chose to sit in an armchair.

—Are you going to keep your coat on? Misha asked. You'll end up wearing it for hours and hours, if you do.

Kisasi hadn't realized that she'd kept her coat on. She was tempted to leave it on, too, as if the coat—dark blue, full length—would keep him at a manageable distance. But on second thought she took it off, choosing instead to have her jeans and t-shirt commemorated.

After the first three or four sessions, she saw that most of his energy had been devoted to her eyes and forehead.

—I start with the face, said van Zandt. It's an anchor.

He worked slowly, deliberately and talked most often about Renaissance poetry, once he learned that her partner was a writer. In fact, Alain was a journalist, and he was amused when he heard that he was the cause of van Zandt's going on about obscure Italian poets. But, to be fair, Misha was interesting on the subject, and he often branched out into related matter—spending one session comparing the meaning of bears in Renaissance bestiaries to more modern representations of them; in Werner Herzog's *Grizzly Man*, for instance.

What Kika had said about van Zandt was still true: he was a charming raconteur.

Whatever Kisasi imagined she was doing when she sat beside Misha van Zandt on the train, there evolved between artist and model an ease tinged, on her part, with fascination. This was a surprise to Kisasi. She could not have imagined feeling anything of the sort for a man whose mentor was Gord Rayner and whose major influences were Lucian Freud and Max Beckmann: manly men who manfully painted in manful ways.

But there you are: in Misha, at least, she thought she could see past the bravado to the insufficiency that propped it up. He was a sensitive soul, hiding behind a pantomime version of masculinity. And this, of course, made her all the more curious about what, exactly, had happened between Misha and her mother. Had Kika fallen for the show of masculinity or for the sensitivity behind it? Or was it, rather, both? How convenient to find one whose physical longing was front and forward, while their sensitivity was deep enough to keep your interest when you were sated. Given the circumstances, it was inevitable, wasn't it, that she imagined herself in Kika's place? What surprised her was how appealing she found the situation.

By mid-winter, when bright colours had ceded the world to faded blues, greys, and whites, Kisasi felt sufficiently at ease to ask Misha more personal questions:

Where was he born? Glencoe, Ontario.
Who were his parents? His father had been a shoemaker, his mother a part-time maid, who worked when the family needed money, which they often did, because his father, an alcoholic, drank his earnings.
Why had he chosen to become a painter? Because, in the end, he had admired how his father had worked with his hands. In fact, Misha believed that hands were the most significant human appendage, and he swore he could tell more from a person's fingers than he could from their thinking or the symmetry of their face or the timbre of their voice. And it had given him the greatest pleasure to learn that he shared this belief with Pierre-Auguste Renoir, a painter he now respected more than admired, though he had (when he was nineteen) spent two months in Paris, living in Montmartre, at 14 rue Houdon, not far from where Renoir himself had lived and painted, downhill from Sacré-Coeur.

Misha's questions became more personal as well. But perhaps because he valued his own privacy—at times answering her with an asperity bordering on complaint—his questions allowed her room to hide things from him. And she took advantage of this. She did not, for instance, mention Kika, reasoning that she would tell him all about her childhood and her mother when the time was right; that is, when she had heard for herself his thoughts about Kika.

It was Alain who first noticed the change in her attitude to van Zandt. He teased her about it, one evening as they lay in bed watching the snow drift across their bedroom window.

—You two are getting very close, he said. I approve. Get him to give you a canvas. We could use a new stove!

—What are you talking about? she said. He's painting me and that's all there is to it, for now. I don't think you can help feeling closer to someone you spend so much time with, can you?

Alain's was a fair question, but it confirmed that her acquaintance with Misha had become more complicated. Alain, who was not the least jealous or concerned, repeated his suggestion, adding that there might be enough profit from the sale of a van Zandt to pay for renovations to both their condominiums—in Montreal and Toronto.

They laughed at the idea of Misha helping them to renovate. But later, as she drifted to sleep, Kisasi wondered: what did she actually think about Misha? Up to this point, all had been unconscious (on her part), instinctive, even. She had pursued a connection to Kika that had presented itself on the train home. From there, she'd formed a growing bond with a man whose chief worth was in his knowledge of her mother—a young girl at the time, much younger than Kisasi was now. And she enjoyed the time they spent together.

What could be more natural? There was nothing deep to think about. In fact, she resented Alain for bringing the matter up in the way he had, though he had been kidding and she knew it.

No, there was nothing deep to think about, and yet there were decisions to make, like how to prolong their friendship now that the painting was approaching its end, her image in bloom on the canvas, with only the background left to do. Did he really need her at all? There were more pressing matters as well, like whether to accompany him to a vernissage to which he'd been invited by one of his younger contemporaries.

This was the first time he had invited her to accompany him anywhere, and it surprised her, his studio having been a safe haven that held whatever intimacies they chose to reveal. She had told him about Alain. This was an aspect of her life that she was comfortable exposing. Foremost, because she was happy with Alain and had been for fifteen years. They had had their problems, of course; the distance between Montreal and Toronto being as much an irritant as it was a boon. She had small doubts about how he conducted himself when she was away from him. He was an exciting and entertaining partner. She had reason to be jealous, but she was not jealous. She could not take what he did while away from her too deeply to heart, refusing to give their time apart the same weight as the hours they spent together.

She reminded Misha of Alain's importance to her when he asked her to the vernissage.

—It's on a Thursday, she said. I usually talk to Alain on Thursday nights. I'll ask if he minds giving up some of his time.

—Do you think he will? Misha asked.

—I don't think so, she answered. He's very generous.

Not that she bothered to call Alain or otherwise ask if he minded her going to an art opening with Misha. He would not have minded, and in any case, Thursdays were in no way significant to either of them. The point had been to stress the importance of her relationship, because she could sense, behind Misha's invite, the assumption that she would be thrilled.

Kisasi had been to any number of opening nights: for books, exhibitions, film premieres. She found them not exciting, exactly, but not unexciting, either. There was pleasure in being in a room filled with people who wished an artist well, who were curious about a work, who had a sense of occasion. She enjoyed the emotions—from boredom (the onlookers) to terror (the artists)—and the hiding of emotions that made these occasions a feast of feelings.

She herself had felt a range of things on these occasions. For instance, when Alain launched a collection of essays called *Montréal et autres cimes*, she had shared his nervousness, his relief at the sight of friends, his frantic gaiety. She supposed that if she ever published her monograph on the Art Gallery of Ontario's archives, as Alain often encouraged her to do, she would understand the distress creators feel from a different angle, but that vantage did not seem mysterious or unattainable.

What she had not experienced, and what she could not have imagined, was an evening with Misha in public. Having agreed to go with him, she was surprised when, as they entered the gallery on Queen Street where the event was held, the painter she knew became Misha van Zandt, Artist. He was recognized by many in the gallery, and the regard for him was expressed in lingering glances, respectful greetings, a raising of the social temperature, though very few actually approached him. It was strange, and strangely interesting, to vicariously experience celebrity. Misha smiled. He stood up straight. He was polite and friendly while, at the same time, being neither of those things, since you could feel the way the room reinterpreted his qualities, which (to Kisasi) was like watching a man being fitted for quotation marks.

This odd sensation did not last long. After a short while, it seemed to be accepted that Misha van Zandt was in attendance, and so the attention faded, without quite disappearing. What was left, Kisasi supposed, was what could be called his aura. That and a curiosity that seemed to take her in, lightly, as if she were interesting for having entered a room with him.

—And who's the lovely young woman with you? asked the artist whose vernissage it was.

—Kisasi O'Hara, said Misha. A young friend of mine.

—It's nice to meet you, said the artist.

But with that, his interest in her went out like a blown bulb. Turning to Misha, he said

—I can't thank you enough for coming. I haven't seen you in so long, I wondered if you'd left the country again.

It would have been enough, as far as Kisasi was concerned, if her evening had included no further novelty. She would have enjoyed the vernissage, meeting the artist, and observing how Misha was treated. But Misha's attitude to her was an added pleasure. Without at all fussing over her, he made it known that she was his companion for the evening, introducing her to his acquaintances. At the same time, he shared with her his thoughts about them. For instance, the artist whose work they'd come to see was, he said, "on the spectrum." Whether this was true or not, Misha disapproved of the way he had abruptly turned away from Kisasi after greeting her and mocked the man for his gaucheness. On the other hand, those who expressed interest in Kisasi—a handful of the thirty or forty people in the gallery—he treated kindly, turning his attention to them when they spoke to her.

It was pleasing, the fact that he took her feelings into consideration, and it was impressive to have him do it without drawing attention to himself, without making it seem that he was protecting her—as if he were some art-world chevalier. His consideration was not something she would have said she needed or wanted, but it put her at ease in the way she usually felt when out with Alain.

Both men were charming; one was older and had slept with her mother.

This fact had not impinged so starkly on her thoughts as it did at the vernissage. In part because, at first, it was slightly embarrassing, an idea for which she could find no cool place in her mind. Not thinking about it was easiest. Seeing Misha for the first time on the train, she had been led by curiosity, by fascination, by the memory of her mother. Now, however, the thought of Misha and Kika making love was more interesting than embarrassing. For one thing, she could see what her mother had seen in him. He was in his sixties and was well-built, tall, a little intimidating, dressed (now that he was out of his studio) in an elegant dark-blue suit with a light-yellow shirt, unbuttoned to the first sprig of grey hair on his chest.

He had been, in his younger years, *un homme à femmes*, a man who preferred the company of women and slept with many. Seeing him out and about, feeling his aggression and finesse, you'd have had to be in denial to doubt it—the number of women, that is. And it was not unpleasant to wonder what he was like in bed. Or whether he would have been different with Kika than he might be with her.

But that, as it happened, was a thought too far. She blushed, and though she smiled politely when Misha looked at her, she was certain that he both noticed her embarrassment and understood its cause.

—

As she and Misha lay in bed together a few weeks later, Kisasi wondered if she had been seduced. Or if she had been the seducer. Not that the answer was important. Both of them being willing and enthusiastic, could it really matter who had initiated what had turned out to be—for her, in any case—such an absorbingly erotic turn of events?

In fact, their sessions together, hers and Misha's, making love in his studio, had been such that some part of Kisasi was now jealous of her mother, almost resentful that Kika had been with Misha before her, or even at all. And what a feeling that was! One of a number of emotions that made her feel that what she did with Misha was somehow wrong and, of course, more arousing than it might otherwise have been. Though there was little chance they would be interrupted—Misha had seen to it—it felt as if they might be discovered at any moment, that his secretary would walk in on them, which made everything seem urgent, exceptional, a shared transgression.

All of which is to say that, although she had, on first seeing Misha, vague ideas about getting to know her mother through him, she was now in a different state of mind and would not have brought Kika up herself. But when he had finished her portrait in February, he suggested she spend the night with him at his house in Moore Park.

(It was interesting to have been painted by Misha. She imagined that she could trace the growth of his longing for her. He'd begun with her eyes, of course, and they were precisely done, but the portrait gained emotion as he painted the rest of her and the surroundings. It was, in her opinion, a very good painting of a subject whom she did not know—unknown, because she had never seen herself from Misha's perspective, given Misha's flaws, limitations, gifts, habits, age, knowledge, and artistic goals. She did not feel that he had captured her, and that was, at least at first, a disappointment, though she accepted that she might grow into his portrait or that the portrait might grow into her.)

A night with him in Moore Park? It was a surprisingly complicated request to grant. Though she was fascinated by Misha, or at least entranced by the physical pleasure of their relationship, she was not prepared to leave Alain, and she had told Misha this. Staying overnight at his home was more than she wanted to do, wary as she was of a relationship that would bring flowers, chocolates, and long silences. That she agreed to spend the night with him was less a matter of wanting than it was an unwillingness to hurt his feelings, a not-quite-readiness to end what she had hoped, when she first slept with him, would be a physically exciting interlude—which it had been.

The house, of course, was not the problem. It was in a part of town filled with gorgeous houses and properties. Misha's home was close to a park which, in its late-February guise, looked sterile, its hard-looking ground haunted by streetlight and traces of snow. Inside, it seemed less a home than a gallery for Misha's work. His paintings hid many of the walls, taking pride of place over furniture or furnishings.

—I have a house a few streets away, he said, where I entertain. But this is where I live.

He said this matter-of-factly or wryly; she couldn't tell which, in part because she couldn't imagine what it would be like to live with so many fragments of your soul. She felt uneasy even before they went up to his bedroom where, on the wall above his bed, there was a painting of Kika that she had never seen. It was some six feet by five feet, overwhelming even if it weren't a painting of one's mother.

Nor was the fact of the painting the most interesting thing about it. The painting itself was like a collaboration between

Misha and Holbein the Younger, so smooth was its surface, so precise the details (Kika's skin, lips, eyes, body, as well as the objects on shelves behind her: a glass apple, an hourglass, a wasp poised on a piece of bread), so classical the composition, so bright its palette and vibrant its colours. And then there was Kika herself: her large breasts subtended by her folded arms, her hair bobbed like Louise Brooks's, her expression as enigmatic as La Gioconda's but more severe, as if she were waiting for the answer to a question.

It was the Kika of the more famous paintings, but here she was painted as a sphinx.

Sensing Kisasi's confusion but taking it for admiration, Misha allowed her time to take the painting in, before he said

—It's the only painting I've ever done like this. This style was a dead end. But it's a precious dead end. I've turned down a lot of offers for it. It's a good life lesson, that there are some failures more precious than all your successes. Not many! But still, this is one of mine.

—Isn't this a model you used a few times? said Kisasi.

—Yes, Misha said, but nothing good ever comes from talking about the past. Sleeping dogs and all that.

He began to undress as he said this, but the last thing Kisasi wanted, under the circumstances, was to touch or be touched. She agreed with his sentiment about the past. Nor did she want to talk about the woman staring down at her from above the bed. But given the choice between making love and talking about her mother, she (to her own surprise) chose the latter. She encouraged Misha to tell her about the woman.

—What was her name?

—*Was*? he answered. For all I know Kika's still alive. She was younger than me. You look like her. Are you sure you're not related?

He smiled as he said this, and Kisasi answered while staring at the painting.

—I've never seen this person in my life.

—There isn't much to say about her, Misha said. We knew each other when we were very young. She was a troubled person, what we used to call manic-depressive. Fun to be with when she was manic and difficult when she was depressed.

—And that's why you stopped seeing her?

Misha laughed.

—It must be hard for you to imagine this, he said, but she left me! I shouldn't laugh. It was pretty stressful at the time. She was pregnant, and I wanted her to keep the child. It would have been my first, my *only*, but she went into one of her dark phases and got it into her head that I was a terrible person. So, she had an abortion. I don't know what happened to her after that. The thing about this painting is that it's one of the few I ever painted from memory. It's the first. Maybe that's why it's no good *and* why I like it so much.

Puzzled, because Kika had never told her of any abortion, Kisasi asked

—Are you sure she had an abortion, though?

It was a question Misha answered with a sigh.

—If she didn't, he said, I suppose I have a child out there somewhere. It would be just like Kika to change her mind, too. Maybe someday, someone will come and call me Daddy. Listen, let's stop talking about this. I need a drink.

For a moment, while looking up at a version of her mother's face, Kisasi wrestled with the idea that she had been making love to her biological father. The timing was believable. Kika had had her not long after her break-up with Misha. And if she were actually Misha's child, it might explain why her mother had told her so little about Francis O'Hara, her supposed father.

—I'd like a drink, too, she said. I saw some wine downstairs. I'll have some with you.

Before he could say anything, she walked out of the room, went down the stairs, and, collecting her coat, left Misha's house, there being nothing she could imagine saying at that moment, nor anything she wanted to hear.

Kisasi was not the type to live in her head or give too much weight to her thoughts. It was not until she told Alain all that had happened that her vagrant thoughts came home. It wasn't the confessing that stirred her. She hadn't done anything for which she felt guilty. It was, rather, Alain's reaction. While he was sorry for her unsettled state, he could not help finding the whole episode absurd and, for that reason, darkly droll.

Having listened to what had happened, he said

—This is exactly why you shouldn't sleep with older men! It's Oedipus, but gender-reversed!

He laughed, which is when Kisasi began to wonder about it all.

—Is there any chance he's your father? Alain asked.

Without hesitation, she said

—There's no chance. If I'd been his daughter, Kika would have told me. All those years of running him down and I'm his daughter? No chance. She'd have wanted me to get whatever I could out of him. Anyway, Misha van Zandt wasn't any kind of father to me. I slept with an interesting man, that's all.

—Was it worth it?

She didn't have to think about this, either.

—Yes, it was, she said. Honestly, it was exciting.

—You can go back for more if you want.

—No, she said. It's done. It feels like something I wandered into, something spontaneous. If I went back, it'd be laboured. I'd have to explain why I left. I'd have to tell him I'm Kika's daughter, and if he asked me why I approached him on the train, why I posed for him, why I slept with him, I'd have to admit I really don't know why. Because I really *don't* know. It wasn't anything I planned. And now that it's over, I think it's best to leave it at that.

And for all intents and purposes, that was it, for Kisasi.

Except that it was not. There had been no tidy way to break with Misha. She did not ghost him, as such. She answered the first of his texts and emails by telling him that she had reconsidered the importance of her relationship with Alain, that she adored her partner, and all things considered, he was more important to her—emotionally, spiritually—than Misha and that, although she might wish things were different, there was no reasoning with her psyche. After that, she ignored the (reserved, polite, inquisitive) missives from him, until, some time in the spring, he stopped sending anything at all, bowing to her feelings while wishing that she had treated him a little more "forthrightly."

Years passed. Kisasi moved to Montreal to live with Alain after they were married. She missed Toronto, for a while, and then she didn't, gradually finding it difficult to imagine why she would go back. Her closest friends, though they missed her, were pleased to have somewhere to stay in Montreal.

She thought of Misha van Zandt less and less often until, almost eleven years after the day she'd met him on the train, Alain handed her his laptop, so that she could watch a clip devoted to Misha's life, career, and recent death. By then, Misha had ceased to matter to her, so that his death was a non-event, save that the images of her young mother, as painted by Misha, were shown in the clip she watched and roused her pity for the troubled nineteen-year-old her beautiful mother had been.

The following day, she received an email and then a call from Misha's executor.

—Mrs. Tournier, he said, I'd like to formally invite you to a reading of Misha van Zandt's will, in one week. It will take place in the office of his lawyer. I've sent you an email with the date and time, but I wanted to make sure I spoke to you. I'm not allowed to tell you anything about the will before it's read, but I strongly recommend that you attend. If you're in any kind of financial distress, the estate is authorized to pay your fare to Toronto, from anywhere in the world.

The man's tone of voice, the sombreness of it, captured Kisasi's imagination. It brought a curtain down on Misha's life, more dramatically than the online clip had done. And perhaps because she suddenly felt the loss of a life, she was unexpectedly reminded of a vivid detail: the grey hair on Misha's chest.

—If my husband can come with me, she said, I'll be there.

—I would attend, even if your husband can't make it, said the executor. Misha specifically asked for you to be present, if at all possible.

It was autumn again, but Toronto was now a city from which Kisasi had been estranged. The lawyer's office was on Bay near King, on a top floor from the windows of which you could see the lake stretch out, as if gently reclaiming territory. It was a prospect Kisasi had never seen, and it made the city stranger still, in her mind.

The office was, despite the solemnity of the occasion, despite its oak and cherry wood surfaces, *un*intimidating. And this was because the lawyer himself, John Goldsmith, QC, resembled a mad scientist or absent-minded professor. His hair—grey and white with strata of black running through it—seemed irrepressible. It was like being in the office of an older Sergei Eisenstein, one who'd managed to keep more of his thinning hair. But Mr. Goldsmith's accent was from the country, somewhere among the towns of southern Ontario.

The only people in the office were Misha's executor, whom Kisasi had (she was reminded) first known as Misha's secretary, Mr. Goldsmith, Kisasi, and Alain.

—It's great you could make it, Mr. Goldsmith said. We'd have had to reschedule otherwise. And people are so busy, who knows when we could have done this? I think you showed my secretary the proof that you are who you say you are? So, I'll just get to it. I'll open the envelope, here, so it's official. But the fact is, you're the only beneficiary of Mr. van Zandt's holdings, ownings, goods, and everything. There's nobody else. You get everything, except for the funds Mr. van Zandt left for the official business around this inheritance. I'm getting paid, for instance, and there's a generous amount for Mr. Dubois, here, who's the executor. Not a difficult will to execute, but he gets a million! Kidding, just kidding! All the outlays'll be annotated and the figures sent to you, so you can see everything's above board, okay? But, really, no, that's all there is to it. Congratulations and everything. The rough amount you're inheriting is somewhere between one hundred and fifty and two hundred million, because who knows about property, eh? Final figure could be higher!

It would have been easier to understand Mr. Goldsmith's words if he had spoken more slowly, but it wouldn't have been any easier for Kisasi to take them in.

—There's been a mistake, she said.

—None, answered the lawyer. This will was made years ago, and Mr. van Zandt never changed his mind or the will. If you don't want the money and everything, there's a proviso in the will for that. But he meant it to go to you, and it was our job to make sure you got a chance to keep this inheritance or to turn it down. And now we've done that.

Kisasi looked to Alain.

—We'll take it? Alain said.

—That's not quite how it works, said Mr. Goldsmith. It's Kisasi O'Hara, or by her married name of Kisasi Tournier, who's the one who has to say yes, eh? Mr. van Zandt was quite clear about this.

—But I didn't do anything to deserve this, Kisasi said.

—In my experience . . . can I call you Kisasi? In my experience, Kisasi, other people are not always easy to understand. You may never know what you did for Mr. van Zandt to make you his beneficiary. I certainly don't know, and neither does Mr. Dubois, there. It could be that, at the end, Mr. van Zandt himself might not have remembered his reasons. But he must have had reasons at some point, and this will is like wrestling the consequences of those reasons onto white paper. It's up to you if you want to accept the inheritance or not, but we can both assure you that this will is a codification of Mr. van Zandt's wishes. Everything goes to you, if you want it. Otherwise it goes elsewhere, and you'd have no say in that.

—This is too much to take in all at once, said Kisasi. I'd like some time with my husband to make a decision. It's not just the money; we'd have to take care of his artwork, of the paintings Misha didn't sell . . .

—And deal with houses, taxes, and responsibilities, said Mr. Goldsmith. Mr. Dubois and I will leave the office for a few minutes—say fifteen?—while you think it through a bit. If you need more time, you can have that, but Mr. van Zandt wanted this taken care of sooner rather than later, because he knew people would be anxious to know what would happen to his work.

Now Misha's secretary, Mr. Dubois, spoke for the first time.

—I'd like a minute with Mrs. Tournier, he said. Alone, please, if possible.

And when he and Kisasi were alone, he said

—I think you should accept the inheritance. There's a reason Misha did this and he thought it was a good idea. I'm not allowed to tell you the reason, because he didn't want me to influence your decision. He thought you'd be taking on as much trouble as money, if you agreed. But, still, he didn't forbid me from telling you that there *is* a reason. This is something Misha thought about and wanted.

Kisasi was so shaken that she might have done anything Mr. Dubois suggested, including turning the inheritance down or giving it to him. But hearing that there was reason behind Misha's decision settled her nerves, so that after Dubois had left and she and Alain had shakily talked things over and all had reconvened, Kisasi said

—I'm going to accept the inheritance.

—That's great, said Mr. Goldsmith. Now that you've accepted, we'll get the ball in motion with Mr. Dubois, who'll be dealing with the initial taxes and property taxes. But also, now that you've accepted, I'm authorized to give you this letter from Mr. van Zandt.

He handed Kisasi a clean white letter-sized envelope on which a version of her name was written in Misha's hand: *Kisasi Hedden*.

—

On the train back to Montreal, Kisasi and Alain sat in economy—she by the window, because he'd had the window on the way down. The land was, as it had been eleven years before, a blur of faded colours.

They could, of course, have gone business class or taken a plane or hired a limousine or whatever extravagance they chose. That they chose nothing special was down to Kisasi's suspicion that she had done wrong in accepting the inheritance of an older man with whom she'd slept more than a decade before, but who meant little to her.

Misha's letter, which she hadn't yet read, was in her computer bag, in the pocket she used for her passport. She wasn't afraid to read it, as Alain assumed. There was no reason to be afraid—despite the fact that he had addressed his letter to "Kisasi Hedden" and, in so doing, announced that he'd known Kika was her mother, had known, in other words, that he had slept with his lover's daughter. The emotional weight of the name Hedden was itself enough, Alain said, to keep Kisasi from reading the letter.

But as the train moved away from Kingston station and Alain lay in the seat beside her with his eyes closed, Kisasi felt a sudden annoyance. Since when had she become someone who avoided news, unpleasant or otherwise?

So, she opened, read, and considered Misha's letter.

Dear Kisasi,

When you left me, I was baffled. I never interfere in the lives of people who leave me, but I've never had anyone walk out on me like you did. When you stopped answering my calls and emails, I had no other way to understand you than to look into your background. And just so you know, it would have saved me a lot of pain if you'd told me who you were from the beginning.

Knowing you were Kika's daughter, I had the horrible thought that I was having an affair with my own child. This was unpleasant, and I blame you for it, because after looking into your life, I had to look into Kika's. She'd told me she was going to have an abortion, but I had no way of knowing that she did, until my PI discovered the record of it.

Your mother aborted our son and had you with Francis O'Hara. It is just like Kika to have an abortion and then think better of it and get pregnant again right after. But then, I blame myself that I was never able to convince her that I loved her and wanted our child. I wasn't sure myself, at the time. It's my deepest regret.

As perverse as this will no doubt seem, knowing that you are Kika's daughter has, despite our intimacy, made me think of you as my kin as well. In you, I feel a connection to the one person I truly loved in all my time on Earth . . .

It was, in fact, a long letter. Having established his love for Kika and his belief that Kisasi was something of a daughter to him, Misha went on to detail the trouble she was likely to face dealing with money, houses, artworks, a host of possessions and possibilities. But none of the remaining seven handwritten pages interested Kisasi, because she could not accept that he could think of her as a daughter, given the animal intensity of their couplings. Nothing in how she had used his body said "father," though, to be fair, that word had always been a kind of shallow grave in her psyche, one in which nothing stayed buried.

As if for the first time, a decade late, shame and humiliation struck her. How could she have slept with the man? She was grateful Alain was asleep, that he couldn't see her distress. Nor could she stand the idea of anyone else reading Misha's letter. She was about to destroy it, in fact, when it occurred to her that she was overreacting. Though the shame she felt was sudden and terrible, she reminded herself that she was reading a letter from a man who had recently died, written to tell her about things that had taken place a lifetime ago.

The past preys on the present, but it does no harm, unless you let it. In this instance, she could look on her relationship with Misha van Zandt as a good thing. It had, in a way, precipitated her move to Montreal, being another mark against Toronto, Misha's city. It had also been an invitation to leave her mother's life behind, to do something Kika had not: to marry, without caring how long her marriage would last or what her husband got up to when she was not around.

Rather than destroying the letter, she resolved to let Alain read it as soon as he woke. More: although she had mostly avoided talking about Misha in the decade past, she now looked forward to telling friends about her encounter with the great artist. They would naturally be curious, given her newfound wealth, and she would allow them to read his letter if they wanted. These ideas drove all the shame and humiliation from her mind. And it occurred to her that Kika had told the truth about her name, Kisasi—not so much revenge as defiance.

She felt entirely innocent.

A Misfortune

1.

At the age of six, Amara McNeil shot and killed her father. She had discovered a gun in the bottom drawer of a credenza, its silvery barrel gleaming, attractive because she wasn't sure what it was, though some part of her may have recognized it as belonging to the world of screens and make-believe. And her father had startled her as she held the thing. Spooked, she'd discharged it, the bullet catching him somewhere in the abdomen. There followed: a brief silence, his cries of pain, the wailing of her mother and sisters.

It was a moment Amara had been parsing for forty-one years, and although small details sometimes receded from memory, the vivid ones were inescapable: the handle of the credenza's drawer (ivory), the gun barrel visible though most of the gun was covered by black velvet cloth, the recoil when the gun went off, the sudden quiet that was as bewildering, in retrospect, as the chaos that followed it.

She had adored her father, and forty-one years on, she still dreamed of him—not as he was when she shot him, or not always, but as he had been when tossing her up in the air and then catching her with a loud "whoosh!" before setting her down so one of her sisters could have a turn.

For a long time, Amara believed her father's death was the worst of what the world had to offer. At forty-seven, she knew that there were deprivations and humiliations beyond her imagining. One read about them daily. It wasn't as if she'd built her life around her guilt and sorrow, either. She'd done her best to come to terms with them.

But it did, at times, feel as if guilt and sorrow had covertly steered her circumstances. Was it really a coincidence that two of her closest friends had suffered childhood trauma that afflicted them as Amara's afflicted her? Why was she fascinated by novels and films that depicted the worst in human nature? Whence the need to reread *Dracula* rather than finish *The Wonderful Wizard of Oz*, or to sit through *Funny Games* countless times, before finishing *Annie Hall* or *The Palm Beach Story*?

Her tendency towards darkness, which had grown more pronounced as she approached adolescence, had troubled her family. It had been most troubling to her mother, who walked in on her one day as she was watching raw footage from accident sites—human body parts strewn about a roadway, a digital time code on the bottom right of the screen. It took her mother a moment to realize what Amara was watching, but when she did, she began to cry, which was when Amara, until that moment absorbed in trying to figure out just what body parts she was looking at, first clocked her mother's presence.

Thereafter, and for some years, her mother and sisters treated her with almost excessive compassion, inadvertently rewarding her for the path her psyche had chosen for its recovery. Or, it could be, deliberately encouraging this tendency of hers as something preferable to discussing the death of her father, a subject all of them had tacitly come to accept as *hors-jeu*, too fraught.

In either case, this suited Amara. Curiosity had done her no favours. And for years, playing up her role, Amara wore black clothes and black lipstick. She listened to Throbbing Gristle and Nurse with Wound. She cut herself, her arms and thighs mostly—scars visible when she wished. And her friends were those of her contemporaries who shared not just her tastes but something of her psychic imbalance. A number of them tried to kill themselves; one succeeded.

Time in the city passed in the usual way: innumerable buildings were torn down to make way for newer buildings that would themselves be torn down, the face of the city changing so much that, were it not for Toronto's lake-adjacency, its mutations poised against an expanse of blue, the city might have grown unrecognizable.

That, in any case, is how Amara figured time's passing.

As for its effect on her: the years were kind and unkind in almost equal measure. She fell in love and was loved a number of times. But she fell out of love—or was pushed out—just as often. In her thirties, she took on work as an administrator at York University, but her career stalled, and in her forties, she found herself being nudged aside—gently, for now—by younger peers who, to her embarrassment, she found herself envying. She bought a small house on Cowan Avenue but was forced to be frugal, as she tended to its flaws. Friends and acquaintances began their migrations from friendship, called away from its pleasures by divorces, marriages, children, and aging parents.

Her forties, it seemed, were fated to uncertainty. And to make matters more uncertain still, there was a pandemic, two years into which her mother died after a prolonged illness.

This death was in almost every sense more devastating than her father's had been. For one thing, although Amara was acquainted with the dark shadows and strange light of loss, the pain of her mother's death was more distinct for its slow oncoming. She had grown used to speaking with her mother—once or twice a week—and visited her in Petrolia often. She had come to dread the thought of her mother's death, prefiguring the loss again and again, in a softer but more persistent echo of the aftermath of her father's death.

Then, too, occurring as it did when much of the world was masked and wary, her grief was mixed with a different kind of anxiety. Meetings with her sisters—held to decide what to do about their mother's funeral—took place over video conference, so that their anguish seemed cinematic, as if they were performing for each other. And the funeral itself: the four of them, and very few others, masked in a chapel with a masked prelate, a ritual observed on closed circuit by any who wanted.

Following her mother's cremation and the distribution of the small porcelain vases containing her ashes, there was a reading of her mother's will. She had left property in Sarnia, to be divided equally amongst her daughters. Her personal possessions she left to the discretion of her oldest daughter, Warda. And the modest amount of money she'd saved up was given to her grandchildren. The will was succinct, sad, and clear. And it was very like her mother, one who did not like to leave loose ends.

So, Amara was surprised when, a month after the reading of the will, her eldest sister called her privately to arrange a visit, during which she would give Amara a letter their mother had left for her. More surprising still, Warda said this letter was something the two of them were to keep to themselves.

—Ward, said Amara, you can visit whenever you want. I just finished repainting the spare bedroom. You can break it in. But why so hush-hush?

—No idea, answered Warda. I'll come next Friday.

Which she did, arriving in a cloud of Warda, her tall no-nonsense self bringing childhood with it, bringing back a time when her older sister seemed mythic to Amara. And although, over the years, Amara had fallen out with her two other sisters, she'd never had any disagreements with Warda, preferring to be on her older sister's side.

There was something different about this Warda, though. She seemed hesitant, maybe even troubled. After they'd got current business out of the way—the virus, the dead, and other causes for distress—Warda said

—I'm sorry about the secrecy, Mara, but Mom made me swear to keep this to myself until Dr. Olson died. You remember Dr. Olson? He used to visit us, after father died. His daughter June called me last week. He died around the same time Mom did, about a month ago. Covid, June said. So, here we are.

She handed Amara a sealed envelope.

—This is for you, said Warda.

—You don't know what it's about? asked Amara.

—No, I don't. I've been holding on to that envelope for two years, but I promised not to open it, so I didn't. If you want to tell me what it's about, that's great. But you don't have to. It's between you and Mom, as far as I'm concerned.

—I see, said Amara. Okay, I'll read it later. Come see the guest room. Did I tell you I painted it myself?

2.

Dear Mara,

I don't know where to start. I have wanted to tell you the things I've written here every day since the afternoon your father died. You can't imagine how hard it's been to look on in silence as you suffered, unable to say anything as you lived through the worst that any child could live through.

I want you to know that I've suffered along with you, though I know my suffering was no help to you then and isn't likely to help you now.

First to begin, Mara, you did not kill your father. Your father didn't die from the flesh wound he got from the gunshot. He died because Dr. Olson, our GP in Petrolia, saw to it that he died. I don't know exactly how he did this. He was afraid to tell me, lest I know too much. But Dr. Olson, Brad, did this because we couldn't see any other way to stop your father from hurting us.

You were so young at the time, Mara, I don't know how much you remember about your father. Though he was good to you, he was sometimes very troubled. I imagine Warda remembers more than a few bad moments, but some things must have faded for her, too, except for when we couldn't keep your father's behaviour from other people.

I don't like to speak ill of your father. I never have, because I know Gary had a terrible childhood, worse than any of us. And because he could be so loving and good, as he was with you. Was it wrong to believe that his love for you, Mara, was his real self and that his flaws were something we could all fix together?

I tried my best under difficult circumstances, and when your father died, I was devastated. But I was grateful, too. Grateful to Brad above all. He did what he did because I had asked him for help, and because, over the years, he'd seen what we went through.

It's for his sake that I've kept silent. I swore to keep this tragedy to myself, for Brad's sake. My only regret is that you've had to carry this guilt with you for so long. If I could have done anything, short of breaking my word to Brad, I would have. As it is, Mara, I've told no one any of this. Not even Warda, who is the only one of you girls old enough to really remember the troubles with your father.

I understand if you can't forgive me for my silence. I do wonder if I was right to promise that I'd tell no one. But what I want more than anything else is for you to know you are innocent.

You've done nothing wrong. You never did.

Your loving mother,
Ada

"You were so young," "Brad did this," "Warda remembers": perfectly understandable phrases in any other setting, but not in this one. And the phrases became less clear as she tried to parse them. *What* did Warda remember? Had Dr. Olson murdered her father? If so, why would her mother call him "Brad" and agree to protect him? Was it that Dr. Olson and her mother had been . . .

This last thought was one she could not complete before a wave of shame erased all thinking. It was as if she were trapped in a tawdry and unspeakable drama. It filled her with revulsion to even consider the idea that her mother's lover had murdered her father. There had to be some nobler reason for "Brad," for "Grateful to Brad," for "the troubles with your father," given the mother she knew and loved, given her mother's probity.

Dr. Olson? She could barely remember him: the smell of pipe tobacco, though she never saw him smoke, dark glasses, white shirts, clean shoes, even in winter. There wasn't enough there for her to create a "Brad." Worse: her mother's mentions of "Brad" felt like a betrayal of the long reticence that had been a part of their relationship, part of the intimacy they'd had as mother and daughter.

She had assumed that her mother's unwillingness to talk about the whole "misfortune" had been meant to shield her daughter, to protect her from "the worst any child could live through." What was she to make of that silence now?

The letter said both too little and too much. Amara forced herself to read the words and phrases over and over, though the shame and revulsion grew with each reading. The letter was a venomous spider. And it was impossible to dissociate its venom from the memory of her mother who, through some terrible miscalculation, had managed neither to assuage her daughter's guilt nor bring her peace of mind.

If anything, for some time after putting the letter aside, Amara relived the misery of her father's death—all the little details—but with a depth of humiliation that had not previously been part of her memory. The guilt she'd felt before reading her mother's letter now seemed purer, almost virtuous.

3.

Warda was not intrusive. It wasn't in her nature. When Amara came downstairs after reading their mother's letter and pleaded a headache and sudden exhaustion, Warda expressed concern but showed no curiosity.

Nor, the following morning, did she seem interested in the letter she'd been safekeeping. Warda, soul of discretion, a living echo of their mother, down to her very features and generous body, seemed more interested in Parkdale, a neighbourhood she'd always liked for its "unpretentious" feel.

As they walked along King Street heading to Liberty Village, she complained about the Longo's and PetSmart and Winners . . . so many new franchises in glossy buildings. It was only as they sat in a coffee shop—which, though new, met her approval—that Warda said

—Have you read Mom's letter?

The question came without emphasis, as if the letter were just another subject between them, no more urgent than houses, children, or health. But it felt, to Amara, as if Warda knew something. And so, to test her, Amara said

—Yes. She wanted me to know that she forgave me for shooting Dad.

—Oh! said Warda. Is that it? I wonder why she wanted to wait till Dr. Olson died, then? I thought maybe she was protecting him.

—Protect him why? asked Amara.

—Well, I don't know. Why else wait for him to die, though? She was staring at Amara, an eyebrow slightly raised.

—I have no idea, said Amara. There's nothing in the letter that mentions him. I think she blamed herself for what happened, and she just wanted to apologize.

—She definitely blamed herself. I mean, it's not like she could have stopped a six-year-old from being curious. And what was the point of keeping so many guns around the house, anyway? Honestly, Dad was obsessed. After I had Michael and Edwige, I really wondered how anyone could leave a loaded gun where kids could get to it. I suppose it was a different time. When men were men and women were nervous is how Doug says it. Mom carried this guilt with her all these years. But it was obviously an accident. You don't blame yourself anymore, do you?

—No, no, said Amara. Not anymore. A long time ago, maybe.

—That's what I thought, said Warda. So, the Dr. Olson thing is just a mystery?

Amara drank her coffee, nodding her head in agreement.

—It was hard for Mom, said Warda, living in Petrolia. She used to complain that everybody knew her business or wanted to. She felt like we were in a fishbowl. Which is why we left, I guess.

—What was Dad like? asked Amara.

Warda looked at her directly—interested, all at once.

—I don't think you've ever asked me that, she said. Just as well, because the thought of him is pretty painful. He wasn't a good person, Mara. Mom wouldn't let us say anything bad about him, but I wasn't sad when he died. None of us was, except you and Mom.

Out of nowhere, Amara recalled the smell of their father's aftershave, and the way he would put shaving cream on his face and pretend he was rabid, growling like a dog. It was a good memory, leading as it did back to a time she'd always imagined as idyllic. The memory—the feel of it—in no way corresponded to what Warda had just said. Nor did Warda's words correspond to what Amara remembered of the grief that followed his death.

—I know I was only six, she said pointedly, but I remember Dad's funeral. I remember *everyone* crying.

—There's no point arguing about things that happened forty years ago, answered Warda, but I think Fern and Ruth will agree with me. I'm not saying we didn't love Dad. It's just that it was different for us. He wasn't the Dad you had. With us, he could be a little . . . *impetuous*. And that's all I'll say about it.

If you want to hear more, ask Fern, though I imagine she's buried as much as she can.

Something in Amara was deeply aggrieved by these words. Despite her usual deference to Warda, she was almost desperate to protect her father, a desperation made more painful by the fact that there seemed no one else to defend him. How bitter it was that the one who longed to speak on his behalf was the one who'd shot him!

She kept this desperation to herself. She drank from her coffee and bit the almond croissant she and Warda were sharing: powdered sugar, almond paste, a brittle shedding of flakes. The reason for her hiding her emotions: she was wedded to the clarity that accompanied the idea—the fact—that she had killed her father, even more so, having heard her sister's efforts to tear the man down, having endured the tawdriness of her mother's letter.

It seemed to Amara, as she bit into the croissant, that her mother and sister were both trying to make things better for her, trying to lessen her guilt. Perhaps they still remembered her as she had been at fourteen, susceptible to darkness. And they were frightened for her.

But they had failed to convince her that she was innocent, that her father had been a troubled man, that she had not killed him. And she was buoyed by the relief that accompanied their failure.

4.

For the rest of Warda's visit, Amara tried to avoid the subject of their mother and father, but it was not easy. For one thing, she felt compelled to ask Warda if their father had done anything "unforgivable."

—It depends what you mean by unforgivable, Warda answered. He never molested us, if that's what you mean. Did he touch you?

—No, said Amara at once.

And again the image of her father's "rabid" face came to her, along with the sound of his voice calling their mother's name.

Ada! Where's my coffee?

Ada! Where did you put my lunch?

Ada! What are you doing?

Always the same asking or beseeching, on the edge of anger.

—No, she repeated, he never touched me. Why would you ask that?

—You're the one who brought it up, said Warda.

But she then waved a hand, dismissing the subject.

—Let's go out somewhere for supper, she said. My treat.

And that was that.

That was more or less that, in fact, for the remainder of their time together. Neither sister alluded directly to their childhood during the last two days of Warda's visit. They spoke, instead, of Ruth and Fern, of Warda's children, of Toronto, of Toronto Island, of the state of democracy, et cetera. And when it came time for Warda to leave, Amara took the afternoon off, accompanying her sister to Union Station, waiting with her until her boarding call—Train 60, Track 17, east towards Ottawa, where her son lived.

Their parting was as poignant as it usually was. Amara's love for her sister was not the least changed by what had passed between them—their mother's letter, the discussion about their father's personality. If anything, the fact that they had *not* talked about these things for two days was restorative—restorative of the silence her mother and sisters had always maintained around family matters. A careful silence, as it now seemed.

Amara felt relief as she walked out of the train station and decided, because the day was warm and the sky was blue, to walk home along the lakeshore, hurrying through the mingle of exhaust and stale air, shadows and noise, jackhammers and music that afflict pedestrians as they walk south on Bay Street down to the relative quiet by the water.

After that, what else could it be but pleasure to see the lake, to feel it?

And as she walked along the shore, she looked out at the water, which was not blue at all—as it invariably was in her imagination—but various and changing so that, in places, it was as gunmetal or grey as a cloudy sky before rain. Here and there it was blue or blueish, while, in the distance, touched by some errant light, it was bright green. And it occurred to her that, contrary to her assumptions about the city's changes, the lake was more various and changeable than Toronto was. She had always thought of the city as "ever-changing," but, obviously, it changed physically much less often than the lake beside it. More than that, when she thought of the city's inhabitants, it occurred to her that, from a certain angle, they were always the same: their faces different but their stories limited and drab.

Even her misfortune, when you considered it coldly, was more of the same human sadness. How many children had accidentally—or purposely, for that matter—shot a parent? Too many to count, no doubt. She herself had long given up on googling "child shoots parent." And although her story was vivid to her, wasn't it, in the end, more of the human noise that drifted across the water, dissipating long before it reached the middle of the lake?

At Spadina and Queen's Quay, she wondered how far the sound of a city actually travels over water. And turning to look at the lake, she thought of her father, poor man, his story as tawdry as hers, the ways in which humans betrayed each other more limited and certainly more predictable than the evolutions of cloud cover and water colour beside her. This thought was as comforting as the discretion that had reasserted itself between her and her sister.

5.

That evening, Amara stayed in and ordered momos from Little Tibet. But otherwise, she returned to the life she had made for herself. She deliberately returned. She did not think about her sisters, did not think about her father, and tried not to think about her mother.

She failed to avoid thinking about her mother, however, because as she turned on her computer to stream an episode of something vacuous, she happened to push aside the envelope containing her mother's letter. And how odd that a white envelope (on which her mother had written her name) could cause such distress.

What was she supposed to do, now, about the envelope and its letter? She could not leave it on her desk. She did not want to think about it every time she sat down. Nor did she want to put it somewhere "safe," somewhere someone else—one of her sisters, say, on a visit—might find it and read her mother's words.

For any number of reasons, she did not want to destroy her mother's letter, either. It was, for one thing, the only letter her mother had ever written to her, and there was something moving and intimate about this. It was, besides, two pages of her mother's handwriting, and as such, it held something of her mother's essence. It felt as if burning the letter would be a burning of her mother, a being she had, of course, adored.

And yet, burn the letter is what she did.

Taking it from its envelope and reading it again, it occurred to Amara at last that the letter was not true. The letter was a touching effort by her mother to free her from guilt, touching and, for all that, slightly desperate. Because of course she *had* shot and killed her father. It was inconceivable that Dr. Olson—of whom she had a sudden and vivid memory: the man tossing her up in the air, as her father had done—it was inconceivable that such a kind man had, what?, murdered her father and allowed her to take the blame?

Her mother had clearly had kindness in mind, not truth. Moreover, the kindness had been meant for her alone. Why else write the letter and then leave it with Warda—Warda, who would have died rather than break the promise to keep it to herself? No, there was no doubt that this kindness had been meant only for Amara.

It was in this spirit, imagining she was keeping a private mitzvah private, that she burned her mother's letter: setting fire to the envelope and letter by the flame of her gas stove, leaving the pages to burn in the nicked and yellowed porcelain of her kitchen sink.

6.

In the weeks that followed, any number of variations of her situation occurred to Amara, most of them bringing their share of humiliation: that her mother had written the truth, that her mother and Dr. Olson had been lovers and they had done her poor father in, that her father had been a violent man and Dr. Olson's intervention had saved them from his abuse.

Along with these scenarios, there came an unwanted solidity to her memories of Dr. Olson: the smell of him around the house after her father's death, the tone of his voice—troubling to her, now—as he spoke her mother's name: Aydie, not Ada.

She put these versions resolutely aside. She held on to her own guilt as if it were a thing that shielded her from further humiliation; as if it were both essential, an irreducible portion of her—who was she without it?—and yet in need of protection.

This guilt was part of a peculiar mechanism, since guilt was only real when it caused her pain, and it caused her pain only when she imagined her father as she had known him: kind, funny, loving. The pain she felt brought this good father with it and allowed her a grief that was also essential to her. Amara, of course, did not see her guilt this way, but she felt it: the paradox, her distress bringing her comfort, her pain protecting her from whatever lay just beneath her mother's words.

In this way, Amara clung to her guilt until, after a few months, the whole episode—letter, humiliation, distress, refusal—began to fade, becoming a dimmer memory, a forgetting, even, so that, six months later, she could once again begin her own story, when telling it to herself, as she always had before, and with almost as much confidence: at the age of six, Amara McNeil shot and killed her father.

The Bridle Path

After Witold Gombrowicz

I'm more or less indifferent to money—the fact of it, I mean. My father tried to pass on his conviction that money is important. But he was a poor Trinidadian immigrant who'd worked himself up to the rank of manager at a clothing shop in Yorkville. He had grown up penniless, while I had never known poverty. So, it wasn't possible for me to understand his attitude to money.

The thing my father *did* pass on was his fascination with the wealthy. He did this inadvertently, I think. When trying to teach me about the world, he made sure to mention that all men are created equal, that a poor man was not *morally* inferior to one with money. But in his unguarded moments, when he was trying to convey harsh truths, he would allow that poverty might be a sign of ignorance or laziness. If I hoped to get ahead in life, it would be better for me if I had a few dollars in my pocket.

But there was another side to him. I remember being at his shop as he was helping an obviously wealthy gentleman try on a bespoke suit. It was the first time I had seen my father so servile. You couldn't have said that he was fawning. There was still a dignity to him. But it was a servile dignity, a willingness to disappear, if asked.

Meanwhile, the gentleman was unshowy, nothing like the cliché of the wealthy man. If my father was dignified in servility, the gentleman—a visiting European noble, as it turned out—was dignified in power. His influence was not on display, but it wasn't hidden, either. And this balance was the source of a charm that stayed with me. Before this encounter, I'd had a vague idea of what status meant. Afterwards, I had a model for it.

This was also the moment when my ideas about nobility evolved. I couldn't help wondering if the European gentleman was, in fact, morally superior by virtue of wealth and status. Did *noblesse* actually *oblige*, or was the obligation voluntary? The question was impossible to answer without direct experience. And my prospects of gaining experience were limited. I was not, after all, high-born. So, I was not often in the company of those I wanted to observe.

My desire to be around the wealthy is the main reason I became a lawyer. I elected to specialize in tax law, because I assumed my clients would be those with wealth or those with access to it. And my assumptions were right. I did—and do—spend time among the wealthy. That said, until a lawyer achieves a certain standing, none of the clients are enthusiastic about speaking to him, and it wasn't until I was made a partner at Morris, Miner, and Jewel that I began to fraternize—if you can call it that—with some of our wealthier clients.

My father was pleased I became a lawyer. He assumed I would make much money, and he believed that familiarity with the "higher-ups" would cure me of the desire to be around them. But I was surprised by his hypocrisy. He himself had praised the wealthy, shown deference to them, advised me to make as much money as I could and hang around those who had it. But in his heart, he must have felt either scorn for them, or jealousy, or resentment.

Not that such feelings are wrong per se. I have seen wealthy men and women behaving badly. Not just criminally, but with disregard for basic decency. One sees this in all classes of people, however. In a crisis, people behave badly—*un point c'est tout*. There are few among us who face distress with equanimity.

All of this was on my mind when I met Edward Bryson.

I met Edward by chance. His wife, Miranda, had decided that she wanted a divorce. This was something she had decided any number of times before. And each time she had, her lawyers would warn us that they'd need a full accounting of Edward's wealth and holdings.

No one believed she would divorce her husband, not even her own lawyers. She had cried wolf so often that her lawyers' request was treated as pro forma, something done to make Miranda feel better. As Edward's lawyers, we would draft a letter of response, officially stating our willingness to accept any court-ordered demand for information. And as a number of my peers had already dealt with Miranda and her lawyers, it was up to me to draft the letter, file it, and attend to the silence that was almost certain to follow.

This time, however, silence did not follow. Miranda, it seemed, was serious. She had, in the words of her lawyer, caught Edward "in flagrante delicto with a young person." For this reason, she was determined to punish her husband.

Miranda was immensely rich, richer than Edward. Any money she might get from a divorce was "a drop in the bucket." What she was really after—what she wanted—was to have him suffer a bit.

When we spoke, her lawyer said to me

—You know, Gordon, off the record: Miranda was traumatized by this whole affair. She wants Edward to admit how little money he has compared to her. That's her idea of punishment.

I took this for banter. I would not—*could* not—change Edward's tax records, the number of his assets, one way or the other. And Miranda's lawyer knew this. Also, to be honest, I did not believe that a man worth hundreds of millions could be punished by being forced to own up to it. So, I thanked him for his words and put them out of mind.

I was curious, though, about the kind of man Edward Bryson might be. Or, at any rate, curious about the man described by Miranda's lawyer. So, although there was no reason to contact him, I called Edward, the pretext being an exchange about Miranda's lawyer.

I don't know what I expected. I didn't think he'd ask to see me in person. But that is what happened. His secretary invited me to his home on the Bridle Path, a pleasant surprise, as I've always loved walking from Sunnybrook Park up to the Botanical Garden and then, among the mansions, to Windfields Park.

I was among the mansions when it struck me that, despite my many wanderings in the Bridle Path, I had never actually entered any of the homes or even stepped onto their grounds. So I was intimidated as I approached the Brysons' property, as I buzzed at the front gates, as I was answered by a woman with an unplaceable accent, as the grilled gates slid open to allow me in. I was ill at ease and distracted.

I don't know what impression I made on Edward. I remember most of my impressions, though. The woman who answered when I rang at the gate—her accent, as it turned out, Moldovan—met me at the front door and led me to a lounge: light wood wainscotting, lightly varnished wooden floor. On the floor there was a blue carpet, on which Arabic script was interwoven in red. The windows looked out onto the gravel driveway and a bordered green hillock. On the opposite side of the room from the windows, there was a large fireplace, before which there was an elaborately fashioned metal screen, in which you could make out the words "Life Is Freedom, Freedom Is Leisure." Near the fireplace, there was a blue Diane sofa, a coffee table on which there were old copies of *Nomenus Quarterly*, a dark armchair and, near it, a side table with a modest-looking lamp.

My overall impression was of a tastefulness just on the right side of showy.

I was sitting on the sofa when Edward came in.

—I'm sorry to keep you waiting, Gordon, he said. I've just had a call from Miranda's lawyer, and it looks like Miranda doesn't want to divorce me after all. I'm sorry you had to see us like this, at our worst. But that's what marriage is about, sometimes, isn't it? Are you married?

I stood up to shake his hand.

—No, I answered, no, I'm not.

—So much the better, he said. At least *you* don't have a wife accusing you of sleeping with her boyfriend.

I suddenly felt uncomfortable. Edward had not released my hand and he was looking at me, not unkindly but in a way that suggested an expectation of some sort. I tried to reassure him. I said

—I didn't believe all that, anyway.

It seemed my words offended him.

He dropped my hand and said

—I see.

The feeling of having given offence was almost immediately swept aside.

—How wonderful to meet a tax lawyer who believes in me! But you came all the way out here for nothing. So, why don't we celebrate our meeting, at least? My dealer just brought me a very old Benromach. Let's have a taste, together.

And this we did, Edward sitting in the armchair while I sat on the sofa.

It was in these moments, as he asked me about myself, my life, and my aspirations, that I took in his appearance: handsome to the point of being almost womanly, about six feet tall, slightly taller than me, with blond hair, dark eyebrows, a strong jaw, brown eyes, broad shoulders, and long-fingered hands. Two fingers of his left hand were oddly angled and looked as if they'd been broken, while his ears were almost flush to his skull. He moved economically, with no unnecessary shifts of position. But this near-stillness was broken by one of the things that characterized him: his right eyelid "stuttered." That is, it half opened or half closed sporadically. I assumed there was something in his eye, but after a while it was clear the movement was a tic. Assuming that he was sensitive about it, I tried not to stare at the right side of his face.

You'd have thought, my being the son of a clothier, that I'd remember what Edward was wearing when we first met. I assume it was something simple but finely made, almost certainly bespoke and English. But then, as my father liked to say, the point of clothes, for those with taste, is not to show off. The point is to leave an impression of good taste. And this Edward's clothes did, though I recall only flashes of white and grey.

When we'd finished our Scotch and said goodbye, I was left feeling that the two of us might have been, under other circumstances, friends. This, though Edward had not said a single memorable thing about himself and I could not tell what he thought of me.

Months passed and I was at an office party. It was New Year's, and I had drunk too much prosecco. Also, I had recounted my visit to the Brysons' and gone on about Edward's generosity. Bob Morris—son of Richard Morris, the Morris of Morris, Miner, and Jewel—finally spoke up.

—You don't know Edward Bryson, he said. He's not generous.

I again related my meeting with Edward, but "Little Dick," as Bob is known behind his back, was dismissive. I mentioned the fifty-year-old Benromach Edward had offered me and suggested that Bob could not appreciate generosity, because Bob was not a wealthy man.

—Listen, Bob said, Ed Bryson uses fifty-year-old Scotch in his barbecue sauce. You're not special. But since you like him so much, I'll see that you get a proper invite to his place. I'm sure you'll enjoy yourself.

Even tipsy, I could hear the scorn in Little Dick's voice. But I felt a great joy at being threatened with the very thing I wanted.

—Yes, I answered, please.

I didn't expect Bob Morris to do what he claimed he could. He'd been as drunk as I was. I assumed he'd been letting off steam by puffing himself up, pretending that he knew the Brysons well enough to get me an invitation to their home. The next time I saw him at the office, I was conciliatory. I was sorry to have pushed him to make such a promise.

He, on the other hand, treated me as he always did—with indifference, as if nothing had changed between us, as if he felt no obligations. We spoke about changes in federal tax policy and the fate of certain loopholes.

But then in early March, I got an email from Edward Bryson. Its subject read: *Equinox.* And after the "Dear Gordon," Edward thanked me for "defending his honour" and invited me to celebrate the spring equinox with him and his wife, Miranda de Kerouaille, Marchioness of Portsmouth. The equinox being only two weeks away, he hoped I'd be free and asked me to RSVP.

That Edward mentioned my "defence of his honour" was proof that Bob Morris had spoken to him about me and had, true to his word, landed me this invitation. I thanked him for it, too, admitting that I hadn't expected him to follow through on his New Year's promise.

—You can thank me afterwards, he answered.

It was seven o'clock and dark when I arrived at the Brysons'. The house was alive, the way many-windowed houses are at night when all the lights are on. I was met at the door by a young boy dressed up in butler's livery.

—Good evening, sir, he said. May we take your coat?

The boy, who looked to be around eleven, was angelic: blue eyes, long lashes, and tousled hair. His expression was one of concentration. His tongue stuck out slightly, like a cat startled while drinking milk. He looked as if he were lost in his role.

He didn't take my coat far. He handed it to an older child who waited for it at the entrance to the room where Edward and I had shared a drink. This boy was also dressed up in livery, but he was plump, dark-haired, and, by the looks of it, bored and unhappy.

—Thank you, the older boy said.

He retreated into the room without looking at me.

The Brysons' home—their property—was grander than I could have told from my initial experience of it. For one thing, it was a compound. Its two main buildings were joined by a short arcade: clear glass, through which you could look up at the sky or onto two outbuildings, which were themselves like cottages and which, this evening, were lit up.

I followed the boy through to the second house. It was like following a fawn, a being unselfconsciously self-conscious, as he led the way to a high-ceilinged room around which a number of couples stood together.

There was no one I knew. The Brysons were not there, nor could I tell what kind of people I was with. Everyone was decently dressed. But, here and there, the place smelled of talcum powder or sweat or the kind of perfume I associate with my grandmother. There was something common—that unkind word—to the gathering.

Not that this put me off. Not at all. To me, the talcum powder and body odour offered unexpected proof of the Brysons' generosity and largesse, their disregard for social standing, their broad-mindedness. It was a credit to them that they entertained those who were manifestly outside of their social realm.

As my young guide had abandoned me to the room, leaving after an awkward bow, I walked around, not too concerned with catching anyone's eye. There was a bar at one end of the room. Behind it were shelves of alcohol, whiskies mostly. The man tending bar was tall, pale-skinned, and dark-haired, a mèche hanging onto his brow as if painted there. He was dressed in the same livery as the boys had worn, as if the theme of the evening were something old-fashioned, like "Butlers," rather than "Equinox."

Having secured a drink, I waited with everyone else for the Brysons who, to all appearances, had forgotten their own gathering. They were so late that, after an hour, I began to wonder if we had all come on the wrong day. They did arrive, though, and their entrance was surprisingly low-key. I was speaking to an accountant and his partner, a computer programmer—both of them punishingly dull—when, as I turned away, there Edward and Miranda were, casually speaking with a group of people.

I couldn't help feeling admiration for them, their presence being like the coming of a noble idea, a feeling clearly shared by others in the room, whose pleasure at meeting the couple was almost palpable.

This was the first time I saw Miranda Bryson in person. I'd seen photos of her, of course. For years, she and Edward had been regular attendees at film festivals and award ceremonies. There were countless images of Miranda around. She was tall and compelling. I knew she was in her fifties, but I could not have guessed her age otherwise. Her brown hair was up in a curly bun, its loose locks framing her face. Her eyebrows were dark, but her eyes were a dark blue, made bluer set against her bright-red lipstick. Though she was dressed in a white shirt with a black half-jacket and black pants, her beauty was such that butler's livery could not demean it.

I waited at the edge of the group greeting the Brysons. Beside Miranda—and, here, I wondered if I should call her Miranda, Mrs. Bryson, or Marchioness—was the young boy who had met me at the door. She seemed delighted by him but in a distracted way. She ruffled his hair and, from time to time, rubbed his cheek.

At some point, she must have noticed me watching her. She squeezed the child's cheek, and though we had not officially been introduced, she smiled at me and said

—His flesh is so soft, I can't help wondering how it would taste.

Hearing this, Edward said with mock-solemnity

—Miranda, do stop playing with your food.

Those nearby laughed. Miranda looked at the child and said

—But Bruce doesn't mind. Do you, Bruce?

The boy blushed.

—No, he said.

There was, once again, laughter, but I couldn't see the point of it. Bruce's affection for Miranda was touching, I suppose, but the crowd's amusement confirmed my impression that the room was filled with mediocrities, all of them there thanks to the Brysons' pity.

Catching sight of me, Edward approached with his hand held out.

—Gordon, my knight in shining armour! How are you? It's nice you could make it. Are you having a good time?

—Yes, I am, I answered. Your home is terrific.

—I know, he said. Miranda has her dark side, but she knows how to arrange a room. She's a *marchioness*, after all. She'd be the first to tell you about her exquisite taste. Have you tried the bar? There are all sorts of expensive whiskies, I hear.

—You haven't seen the bar? I asked.

—No, he answered. I don't drink often. And even then, only with people I like.

He winked at me and smiled.

I don't mind admitting I was charmed. It was pleasant to hear that, as far as Edward was concerned, I was an exception, a person he liked. It was this pleasure that drove me to tell him how much I admired what he and his wife were doing this evening.

—What do you mean? he asked.

—I mean, I said, your kindness in inviting people into your home who are so obviously beneath you. It's really generous.

Edward looked at me, then, as if he were having trouble taking my words in. But he brightened up, almost immediately.

—Do you think so? he asked. I mean, we have these gatherings every year for tradespeople who've helped us out. I hope we don't come across as superior.

—No, no, I said, not at all. It's more that I admire how you are with common people.

Edward laughed.

—We're not royalty, he said, and we're not nobles, even if Miranda likes to pretend we are. But it's nice of you to play along. I knew you were special the moment we met. Let me introduce you to Miranda.

He put a hand on my shoulder and guided me towards his wife. Before he introduced us, though, he spoke into her ear while looking in my direction. Miranda smiled as she put out her hand.

—Miranda Bryson, she said.

—Gordon Millbank, I answered. It's a pleasure to meet you.

—Ed told me how highly you think of us, she said. I'd say *you're* the generous one. We're having a small gathering next week, for a happy few. Why don't you and your partner come to dinner with us? We'll have a chance to talk without all these . . . *tradespeople* around.

—I'd be honoured, I answered.

Miranda pursed her lips, the small o they formed unplaceable among smile, pout, and kiss. Then she turned away, and again, I was charmed. And this charm went some way towards making the rest of the evening bearable. Once the other guests saw that Miranda and I had interacted, I could feel them warm to me. The couple whose company I'd endured approached.

—I didn't know you were friends with Miranda, said the accountant.

—No, no, I answered. We just met. She was being kind.

They smiled as if we were getting along, but I excused myself and escaped to the bar where I drank a whisky that the barman recommended, something old and amber that tasted of iodine, the sea, and caramel.

I don't know what Bob Morris expected when he recommended me to Edward Bryson. I think he meant to teach me a lesson or two. The usual, no doubt: the wealthy are not like "us," you are not like them, there are more things in Heaven and Earth than are dreamt of in your philosophy, and so on.

But when I mentioned that Miranda had invited me to dinner, he said

—I thought she'd find you entertaining.

He said this without conviction and his face was impassive. I couldn't read him at all. Still, I was pleased at the thought that Miranda and I were sympatico, that it had been clear to Bob that she would like me. And I carried this sense of connection with me when I visited the Brysons for dinner.

The evening began well. It was a cloudless late afternoon, and warm. I walked part of the way to the house on Bridle Path, taking in the nicely kept surroundings, the smell of the trees and grounds and, unexpectedly, grilled meats—mansions and barbecue being unrelated, in my imagination.

The gate was opened by Edward himself. He walked from the house to greet me, shaking my hand once the gate had slid away between us.

—Would you like to see the property? he asked. I'll be your tour guide.

—I'd be honoured, I said.

I followed Edward around the Brysons' compound, becoming acquainted at last with the expanse of their home.

I felt like I was finally getting to know the Brysons, as I got to know their property. I'd begun with the room where Edward and I shared a drink, had then experienced the place at night, and now enjoyed this tour of the grounds: five buildings around a cobblestone courtyard—two multi-storey houses, a rustic cottage, a garage, and a building that had served as servants' quarters "back in the day." Beyond the buildings, there was a wide grassy expanse: a field for horses, whose barn was acres away.

—The horses are Miranda's idea, said Edward. It's her latest hobby.

—What was her hobby before? I asked.

—Llamas, I think. I really can't keep up with her. I'm just glad the nudism's over.

He smiled wistfully, or ruefully, I wasn't sure which, and maybe because he saw I was bewildered, he answered a question I hadn't asked.

—No, he said. Not just Miranda. For a few months, last year, *all* the homeowners on the Bridle Path went around naked. It was oppressively fleshy.

Here, for the first time, I doubted Edward's words.

—Well, I said, I guess all things come to an end.

—That's true, said Edward. And nicely biblical! Let me show you the storehouse.

The "storehouse" was in the basement of the cottage. In fact, the cottage was a façade of sorts. Its upper floor was exactly as you'd expect from a rustic home, and it was used as a guest house. The basement, though, was marvellous and intimidating. I followed Edward down some stairs, expecting to find a dirt floor, a furnace, water heaters, et cetera. Instead, there was a platinum room with a single door that led to further steps down. These steps led to a suite of different-sized rooms. In the first, there were shelves of supplies, tins and tins of food, jars of preserves. Then came a large kitchen, bedrooms, living rooms, a walk-in freezer, and even a mini-slaughterhouse, with butcher's blocks and an array of knives.

—These knives are *my* fad, said Edward. I've had most of them made for me personally, in Japan. Aren't they beautiful? Here, hold this one.

As I held the knife, I was filled with admiration, not just for the object—a mizunara-handled kiritsuke—but for the impressively organized bunker. Here was proof of what I took to be Edward's forethought, his refined sensibility at work.

—This is my happy place, he said, smiling. I feel like I come back to myself when I'm down here.

After a quiet moment, he said

—Let's go back up. The others will be waiting for us.

The "others" in question were three couples and a dining companion for me, as I had come on my own. There was Miranda's brother Maurice and his wife, visiting from their home in Poitiers. There were the Hallers and the Smythes. And, finally, there was my companion, a tall blond woman who smiled faintly when we were introduced.

—This is Huguette, said Edward. She's your "and one" for the evening. Don't you think she's beautiful? You two were made for each other!

He was teasing her and she answered as if peeved.

—Eddy, she said, will you stop!

Though it seemed to me that Huguette was annoyed, all of those present laughed. All except me, of course, because I didn't know her well enough to gauge whether I should laugh or not. I smiled, instead, as if in on the joke.

Despite my confusion, this part of the evening went well, too. All of them were rich, of course, but they all struck me as wealthy, too. I mean, they all had a great deal of money, but they possessed charm, culture, and, Huguette included, a certain grace. They were relaxed in each other's company, and after a few minutes, I relaxed as well. I found myself talking about tax law with the Hallers—who, to be fair, were being polite—and about Scotch with the Smythes, both of whom knew a great deal about it, having often visited Scotland and toured distilleries from the Highlands to the Lowlands.

—Ardbeg! said Mr. Haller. My first taste of Uigeadail!

I assumed that Huguette was not much of a talker, so I spoke mostly to the others. But I had the feeling that this was annoying to her, that she had expectations of me. So, I asked how she knew the Brysons.

—Can't you think of a more banal question? she said.

—Yes, I answered, I could ask you about the weather.

She looked, then, as if she were suddenly curious about me.

—Touché, she said.

And went on to tell me that she had once worked for the Brysons, that she'd been a realtor before she married her late husband.

As Huguette spoke, Miranda approached.

—You weren't just any old realtor, said Miranda. You had your own agency! Gordon, don't let her fool you. Hughie's a rider, not a horse!

She took my hand and put it in Huguette's.

Huguette's hand was warm and dry, though I couldn't help feeling its warmth was due to Miranda's presence, not mine. Still, the fact that she held my hand, loosely, seemed significant.

—That's enough business, said Miranda. Dinner's coming.

(Huguette let my hand fall, as we approached the table.)

Various young people, in white shirts and black pants, were shepherding the first course our way: cups of morel mushroom tea, plates of endive and pear salad.

—Sit! said Miranda to her guests. Chef has made something special.

I took great pleasure in all of this. The servers were discreet, the first courses were delicious, the company was entertaining. It felt as if I'd arrived somewhere I belonged. So, it caught me off guard when, with the main course, the atmosphere changed.

Miranda said

—Oh! It's the Bruce Bourguignon!

At least, that's what I heard, and trying to be witty, I smilingly corrected her.

—Do you mean *Boeuf* Bourguignon? I asked.

She stopped, then, and stared at me. I had made a mistake.

—What would be the point of *Boeuf* Bourguignon? she answered. Anyone can make that. This is *Bruce* Bourguignon! You remember that lovely boy you met at our evening for people who work for us? Well, this is him.

Miranda's expression was unreadable, as if she were wearing a mask of her own face. It was a strange joke, this "Bruce Bourguignon," and I must have shown my dismay. Edward, looking at me, raised an eyebrow and said

—Now Miranda, you don't want Gordon to get funny ideas, do you? God knows what he'll end up thinking about people like us.

Addressing Edward, Miranda's brother said

—Wait. Does this nause really think we're cannibals?

Edward laughed.

—You shouldn't call our guest a nause. He's a very, very good accountant! Anyway, Gordon, you do know that eating children's part of our culture, don't you? There's a wonderful family portrait by Goya of Saturn eating his kids, and when you think about it, Swift's "Modest Proposal" is practically a cookbook!

At this, everyone laughed, myself included. I had been chastised—what with being called an "accountant" and all—but I accepted it. Still, it was too late. I'd offended Miranda, and from then on, her words had an edge to them.

—Do tell me if you find a finger, she said. They're too bony to eat, but the marrow is delicious.

Nor was there any way for me to escape her bitterness. If I apologized, I'd have to say what I was apologizing for. I'd have to admit either that I'd found her comments tasteless or that I really believed we were about to eat the child whose cheeks she'd caressed a few months before.

To make matters worse, my regret—my disappointment in my own temerity—likely read as a kind of seriousness. And this, no doubt, encouraged Miranda and her brother to tease me, mercilessly.

—You should have been here last week, her brother said. The Carl-paccio was delicious!

As if my embarrassment weren't obvious enough, the suggestion that we were eating *Bruce* Bourguignon ruined my appetite. When I took up a fatty piece of meat from my plate, I couldn't help wondering what it might be like to eat human flesh, a thought that brought me cruelly back to the knives Edward had shown me before dinner. It was a miracle that I managed to keep my food down. Of course, to have stopped eating would have brought on more scorn, more derision.

By the time the third course came, they had moved on. Miranda and her brother now poked fun at Edward, at one point going so far as to commiserate with *me* that I had Edward for an acquaintance. To my relief, I was being led back into the fold.

The rest of the evening was uncomfortable. I was self-conscious. I resigned myself to the consequences of my faux pas, while resolving not to be so ridiculous in future and making the most of my conversations with the others.

After dessert and wine, Huguette—who was leaving early—asked if she could drive me home. Feeling that I did not want to overstay my welcome, I left with her, though I turned down the drive home, walking instead along the dark sidewalk-less streets in the Bridle Path, all the way to Yonge and Lawrence, from where I took a taxi home.

Before we parted, Huguette smiled and said

—It was nice meeting you. I hope we see each other again.

Which struck me as pure and unadulterated pity.

I was disappointed in myself, but I took some comfort from the fact that, after all, this had been my first real encounter with the kind of people I had admired from afar. It was natural that I should miss certain signs and indications, that I should be ignorant of the rules that governed the small world made by the Brysons and their friends.

The awkwardness of my dinner with the Brysons had been, to some extent, inevitable. In fact, it was a relief to see the evening as a test of my *savoir faire*, my ability to learn the rules. I hoped there would be other occasions to prove myself.

On the Monday after my dinner with the Brysons, Bob Morris came into my office. The pretext was that he needed someone higher up—me, perhaps?—to verify the work done by one of our younger colleagues. I waved him away, passing the responsibility on to someone else, as he must have known I would. But before he left my office, he asked if I was still enchanted by Edward.

—Yes, I said. I had a wonderful time. I'm still enchanted.

—Oh, he said. I heard you had problems with the main course.

—No, I said. I didn't.

—You're a better man than me, then, he said. I'd have trouble eating kids.

I did not give him the satisfaction of seeing my face. I ignored him and went on peering at an irrelevant article on New Keynesians until he left. He was smirking, I imagine. I could hear the amusement in his voice. He must have thought that he'd achieved what he wanted: a chastening for me. In his mind, I suppose, I'd been put in my place.

But although I *had* been shown my place, I no longer felt chastened. *Au contraire*, I had the feeling that I would see the Brysons again, and I was looking forward to it. Whatever the case, none of this was any of Bob Morris's business.

As if to reward my optimism, a week later, I got a text from Huguette, asking if I'd like to meet for dinner. And when I met her at Scaramouche, she rose from her chair and embraced me as if we were friends.

—It's nice to see you, she said.

—Likewise, I answered.

I ordered the scallops with spiced cauliflower and ate as Huguette spoke about trivial things: the buffoonery of our late mayor, the recent changes in weather, the difficulty in maintaining a home in Forest Hill. She spoke so freely, I began to wonder if I'd somehow forgotten that we were intimates.

I could sense something hidden, however, something waiting, as though I were being judged. But it wasn't until dessert that she finally asked me about myself.

—What do you want out of life? she said.

A question that took me by surprise. The kind of question I hate, leading as it inevitably does to clichés. I want to do what I like. I want to enjoy enjoyable things. I don't want to end up like my father. Honestly, my aspirations are the least interesting part of me.

—Why do you want to know? I asked.

—No reason really, she said. I'm just curious. Miranda invited me to a dinner party next week, and Ed suggested I should bring you.

—He did? Why?

Huguette laughed.

—I'll be honest, I said. I thought I'd made a bad impression.

Huguette looked out the windows of Scaramouche: the city skyline, sunlight fading.

—It wasn't a bad impression, she said. Miranda doesn't *dislike* you, but Ed's the one who wants you to be there. He thinks you'd be a faithful companion.

—But what about you? I asked. Do you want me with you?

I meant only to ask, Was there anyone she'd have preferred accompany her? But Huguette looked at me, surprised, before she answered, as if with regret

—Don't take this personally, but I prefer women.

I went home that night feeling grateful for Edward's kindness, grateful that he and Miranda were giving me a chance to correct the impression of haplessness I'd given them, of gaucherie. It was a relief, as well, to know that I could feel at ease with Huguette. Knowing that she "preferred women"—whatever that meant exactly, as she hadn't specified whether her preference was social or sexual—I relaxed in her company, and when the evening was over and she had, at her own insistence, paid for everything, I accepted her ride home and asked her in for coffee.

She turned me down, kindly, and added

—Maybe some other time.

In asking what I wanted from life, Huguette was looking out for her friends—as well, it turned out, as herself—probing my fitness to be among them. That the two of us would become intimates was the last thing on my mind, the last thing I'd have predicted. I, myself, prefer the company of men—socially, I mean. But her question stayed with me, because it called to mind a memory I'd been avoiding: my father as he helped a gentleman put on his jacket.

The details of that moment—which I described at the beginning of this account—returned to me with clarity: my father's face, his discretion, the way he held the man's coat up for him to try on and, then, the way he smoothed the ripples on the jacket's shoulders. Beyond that, the look on my father's face as he examined the suit: eyes wide open, mouth pursed, and a smile that could express whatever the onlooker wished—fondness, concern, pleasure, disappointment, approval.

In my father's demeanour, there was distance. He did not look the man in the face, that went without saying. My father was open to interpretation. And this openness was what he would have called his duty. Of the two men in that moment—one dignified in servility, the other dignified in power—I naturally chose the one I assumed was masterful—the wealthy one—because I could not see that both were masterful, that tact met tact. They both kept a respectful distance—though only one of them could have breached the conventions without consequence.

That moment was the beginning of my fascination with the wealthy—as opposed to the rich. And it was the beginning of a turning away from my father, a rejection of his servility, the moment that made my relationship to Huguette and my friendship with the Brysons possible, likely even.

I don't regret any of this. Most sons turn away from their fathers, if they don't turn towards them. But in considering Huguette's question about my aspirations, it occurred to me that, in a sense, I had unwittingly ended up on my father's side.

In that moment, as he held the coat up for the European gentleman, my father would have been noting and interpreting and reacting to every sign or signal the man put out: a tilt of the head, a smile, a shrug of the shoulders, a look in the mirror, a hand pushed out from the sleeve and then retracted. My father was constantly deciphering, reading, unravelling, and surmising. And so it is for me, with the Brysons.

As disconcerting as it is to realize that I have become my father, it's comforting as well. I understand how much I underestimated him, for one thing. And for another, I see how all the contradictions I held against him were the result of a very difficult and constant task—translation from one station to the next. It would have been more unusual if he had been *consistent* in his attitude towards wealthy clients.

I take comfort as well in the mistakes I've made in my reading of Miranda and Edward. These mistakes have been an avenue to our friendship, because I have learned from them. Take, for instance, the moment when I stupidly corrected Miranda's pronunciation of "Boeuf." Though she teased me for an hour afterwards, she appreciated—so Huguette has since told me—the way I accepted my rebuke. It was also in that moment, as he saw Miranda teasing me, that Edward took my side. In a word, the ways I have been wrong have brought me closer to the Brysons and, of course, to Huguette. Although, of course, I remain on a kind of knife's edge.

These days, no dinner party goes by without one of us suggesting that the food we're eating has something to do with human flesh. It is funny and private, and I've even had the pleasure of seeing other guests confused by our "cannibalism"—though, of course, none of us has ever eaten a child.

Pu Songling: An Appreciation

To do good without intending it merits no reward,
though it is still good. To do evil without intending it
merits no punishment, though it is still evil.
Pu Songling, *Tales from a Chinese Studio*

1. An Apprentice

Having been a much-honoured lecturer at the University of Toronto, Médard Albouy retired at the age of seventy in order to find an apprentice to whom he could pass on all of the learning—of medicine both light and dark—that he'd accumulated in a lifetime of study.

This search of his was unexpectedly arduous. For one thing, Professor Albouy, no longer affiliated with the university, found it difficult to attract suitable candidates. Those he approached—including some of his own best students—turned him down when they learned he would be teaching "superstition" and, just as disobliging to them, that they'd receive no university credits for listening to him.

Tired of looking for a candidate among the university's students, Professor Albouy let it be known that he would teach *any*one—educated or not—who showed the will and aptitude to learn. Word of this got out, but although he interviewed a number of candidates, none was suitable, most having in mind that they would learn to punish their enemies with voodoo or obeah and then quit. Among these candidates, there was a subset who wished to simply pay him to punish their enemies.

So, after a year of looking, Médard—now simply *Mr.* Albouy—gave up his quest for an apprentice, feeling (with some bitterness) that he would sooner cut off a finger than share any of the precious things he'd carefully culled from a life's work. Perversely, it was when he abandoned his search that the city seemed to realize what it had missed. Candidates—serious candidates, some of whom he might have accepted just weeks before—petitioned him during the day, asking to be considered for apprenticeship.

But having decided *against* taking on an apprentice, Médard set an impossible requirement for anyone wishing to learn from him: they were to bring something dead back to life in front of him. He would, he said, gladly mentor anyone who could do this. There being none who could reanimate the dead, the number of candidates fell to zero. All the hopeful gave up, and Mr. Albouy was free to study, write, gather medicines, and practice the medical arts as he wished, in peace.

One evening, as he was writing down the medicinal effects of willow sap, ground cumin, and warfarin, he heard a faint tapping, as if the windblown branch of a tree were rhythmically ticking on his door, then stopping, then ticking again. As he lived on the eighth floor of an apartment building, the tree branch was unlikely. On opening his door, he was faced with a tall woman—five foot eleven—who was dressed in a grey two-piece suit, white shirt, and black Blundstones. She was light-skinned and slim, her white hair (a modest pompadour) lay on top of her head like a kind of wing, while the sides and back were buzzcut.

Her outfit was distracting, but something about her spirit put him at ease. She looked at him for a moment, before respectfully offering him a white plate on which a mushroom omelette lay.

—This is for you, Mr. Albouy, she said.

And when he'd taken the plate, she stepped back.

—What do you want me to do with this? he asked.

The plate was warm and the omelette smelled good, but he was not hungry.

—The mushrooms were dead, but the omelette is alive, she answered. I'm thinking of becoming your apprentice.

He wasn't sure it was prudent to look at her directly, there being a chance that she was mentally unstable. He wondered if she was pulling his leg. He looked around, to see if they were being filmed, and seeing no one else, he said

—I won't eat this, because I'm not hungry. But I disagree about the omelette being alive.

The young woman, for her part, seemed to have no difficulty looking at him directly. She held his gaze until he began to feel awkward.

—People always talk about mushrooms bringing dishes to life, she said. But you weren't being metaphorical?

—I'm not a poet, Médard said. If you'd like to be my apprentice, you'll have to bring something actually dead back to actual life. And I'd prefer you do this during the day.

—I understand, she answered. My name is Lucinda Hsu. I work during the day. Would you mind if I returned in three days, at the same time?

—It's seven in the evening, said Médard. It's a little late. But if you're going to bring something back to life in three days, at seven o'clock, I'll be happy to see it.

Before he could say anything else, Lucinda had taken the omelette from him and made her way down the stairs.

Three days passed, and at seven o'clock in the evening, there was the same gentle knocking at his door. Even though he was expecting it, the knock seemed to him so delicate that he could not associate it with the woman he'd met. Lucinda had not been wraithlike or retiring.

It was her, however, dressed much as she had been: suit and Blundstones, but with a blue shirt this time. Beneath one arm she was holding a shoebox, the top of which had been crudely punctured five or six times.

After greeting him and entering his apartment, she said

—I've brought you a dead rat.

—Bring it into my office, he answered.

And led her into a large square room—no doubt once used as a bedroom—in the centre of which there was a solid wooden desk and, more remarkably, floor-to-ceiling shelves against three of the room's walls. On the shelves, bottles and boxes, phials, containers, and plants. Lucinda paused on entering, taking a moment to look around before nodding. A lock of white hair fell across her face, which prompted Médard's surmise that it was unusual to see a young woman of colour with white hair.

—Do you mind? Lucinda asked.

But she did not wait for an answer, instead placing the box on his desk, lifting its cover and withdrawing a large immobile rat from within it. She then passed the rat to Médard who, at a loss for what to do, put his palms together so that the rat lay unmoving on them.

—Let's agree that the rat is dead, said Lucinda.

And it did appear that the rat, its white fur groomed as if for a court appearance, was not alive.

—All right, said Médard, let's say the rat is dead.

At these words, Lucinda spoke in a language that sounded like French and patted the rat on the side of the head as if waking a friend; to no one's surprise, a frisson shook the creature and it came to life, sitting up in Médard's palms, sniffing its way, as rats will, and agilely jumping to Lucinda's palm before climbing up her arm to perch on her shoulder.

—Is this what you had in mind? Lucinda asked.

The truth was that Médard Albouy had nothing in particular in mind. He hadn't imagined that anyone would try to convince him they could raise the dead. So, he had not tried to imagine what bringing a rat—or any creature—back to life would look like. He had a strong suspicion, however, that the rat had not been dead. If it had, would there have been any need for perforations in the shoebox? On the other hand, he did not want to call the young woman a liar. Something about her interested him. If the rat hadn't been dead, it had been impeccably trained and that in itself was remarkable.

—I'm not saying I don't believe you, he said, but I'm not convinced your rat was positively dead.

Both the rat—who was now on Lucinda's shoulder—and the young woman looked at him fixedly. It was as if each had one eyebrow arched, though, of course, the rat did not have eyebrows as such.

—Well, said Lucinda, I guess we're at an impasse. What do you suggest?

Why, Médard wondered, should he be the one to break the impasse?

—If you'll come back in two days, he answered, I'll provide the dead animal. If you can revive it, I'll take you as my apprentice.

Lucinda and the rat on her shoulder both seemed to regard this as reasonable.

—Then I'll see you in two days, Lucinda said.

She then raised a hand in farewell and saw herself and her companion out.

Two days later, she returned.

Médard was uncomfortably aware of how absurd it had been to demand that his apprentice bring the dead to life. It had been peevish and small of him. He wasn't certain that Lucinda was an appropriate candidate, but asking her to do the impossible was counterproductive. She would fail, because the task *was* impossible, and he would never know if she would or would not have made a good apprentice. Still, he had set the condition himself and had turned down worthy candidates because of it. There was nothing to do now but go through with the test.

That said, he cheated.

On the desk in Médard's office, there was a full-sized African grey parrot (*Psittacus erithacus*—thirteen inches from crown to tail) laid out on a blue cloth, unmoving, its tail feathers a flash of red beneath its dark-grey wings, against its light-grey thorax. Its eyes were closed; it looked like a sleeping infant.

Lucinda's demeanour on seeing the parrot was interesting. She ignored Médard. She approached the bird and put her face close to its head. Then she circled the desk, examining the parrot from every angle. When after a silent quarter hour, she spoke, it was to scold Mr. Albouy—gently, but without hiding her disappointment.

—What you did is dangerous, she said.

—How can it be dangerous if the bird is dead? he asked.

Rather than answer, Lucinda began to explore his office, slowly going from shelf to shelf, wall to wall until she found all the dried plants she had, evidently, been searching for. She held them in the palm of one hand and breathed in their scent.

It occurred to Médard that, to play his part correctly, he should have asked her what she was doing. But he knew from the plants she'd chosen exactly what she was up to.

Using a copper mortar and pestle she took from a shelf, Lucinda ground the plants to dust. Then placing two pinches of this dust on her palm, she approached the African grey, leaned forward, and blew the dust in the parrot's face.

The parrot stirred, groaned as if waking from sleep, and said

—Ahhh . . . fuck me backwards . . .

—I apologize, said Médard quickly, my cleaning lady's son thought it was funny to teach Edna this, years ago. I never know when she's going to come out with it.

—That's not the problem, Lucinda said. I was worried she was really dead. This isn't something you do all the time, is it?

The young woman was as talented as he was, perhaps more. She had, by observation, understood the drug that he'd used to put Edna in a zombie state and had, with great elegance, devised an antidote that was more efficient than his. Edna, now fully awake, settled on a perch near the door and, rather than cursing, imitated the sound of a train passing in the distance—its lonely whistle—with impressive fidelity.

Feeling that the young woman was owed an apology, Médard recounted how he had sought an apprentice, how he had been discouraged, how his discouragement had led to the absurd situation they had just lived through. And, no, he had never before put Edna in a trance. He had done this to give Lucinda a way to fulfil his condition without really fulfilling it.

He then asked if Lucinda would consider allowing him to be her mentor. The word "apprentice" now seemed out of place and petty. Rather than him teaching her, handing down his experience as if he were some sort of demiurge, he wished to be a caretaker of her immense talent. The feeling was much closer to humility than any he had anticipated when he first imagined taking an apprentice.

Years later, on his deathbed, Médard remembered with pleasure how he had almost dismissed Lucinda Hsu. The pleasure came from both the love he bore a woman he thought of as a daughter and from the agreeable realization that in asking to be his apprentice, she had been testing him, not the other way around.

2. Lunar Caustic

Médard Albouy did not dislike people. He had studied medicine and magic out of respect for those who stood to benefit most from his work: people. But he was one of those who love the idea of humanity while mistrusting specific instances of it.

His passion was for the science of helping, the particularities of helping, the panoplies and instruments of help. As veterinary science did not appeal to him, humans were his focus, though he liked to keep his distance from the majority of them.

Lucinda Hsu, his apprentice, was his opposite, where people and medicine were concerned. What interested Lucinda was the human: stories, emotions, gripes, joys, superstitions, and prayers. For her, magic (a manifestation of longing) and medicine (a formal magic) were interesting because they led to the human, because they allowed the human to persist. The science of medicine was worthy of pursuit, insofar as it was like a hand cupped to protect a faltering flame.

These differing attitudes were complementary. In fact, it would have been difficult to find a more suited mentor and apprentice. On the other hand, their experiences of the world were so different that it led Médard in particular to wonder if he or Lucinda had taken a wrong turn somewhere. He did not want the life of "entanglements" that Lucinda lived.

Lucinda's life was indeed filled with entanglements, but she would have called them encounters. These were caused, in part, by her personality: open, kind, obviously clever, an expert and sympathetic listener. There were none she would ignore, if they were sincere. Her encounters were occasioned by her learning, as well. She had taken a degree in medicine at McMaster and then travelled for five years with Doctors Without Borders, exhausting an inheritance she had received from a grandfather who, though he'd hoped for a grandson, accepted that a granddaughter who practiced medicine was not entirely worthless.

Having practiced urgent and heartbreaking medicine in extreme situations, Lucinda returned to Canada where, shell-shocked and exhausted, she worked as a simple clerk for the Shoppers Drug Mart in a modest neighbourhood, Parkdale. A peaceful job, you'd have thought, but her innate sympathy for others meant that, once people discovered she was a licensed MD, Lucinda was constantly asked for advice about small things (cold sores, cankers) and medium things (infections, fevers) and major complaints of all sorts, from IBS to cancers.

Lucinda had other qualities that made encounters almost unavoidable. She was a tall light-skinned Black woman with prematurely white hair who usually wore two-piece suits. Her height, race, and white hair were not a source of concern or self-consciousness. She did not think about them, unless asked to. Her style of dress, however, had begun as a way of mocking the grandfather who'd so desperately wanted a grandson. After his death, she had accepted his legacy but, to her family's dismay, she resolved to keep wearing suits until the inheritance ran out. But by the time her grandfather's funds had been spent, she found that she enjoyed wearing suits. For one thing, her suits intimidated the people she wanted to intimidate: those who judged her for her appearance. For another, her way of dressing attracted the kind of men and women she found attractive, those whose curiosity about her sometimes led to very pleasant interludes.

People in the neighbourhood talked about her. They told stories about her kindness and her great knowledge. So, when someone in Parkdale could not get a doctor through official means—because they had no health card, no legal right to be in the country, no funds, and so on—they would seek Lucinda out and she would help if she could.

A case in point . . . one Sunday in spring of 2021, as Lucinda was walking home from Liberty Village, she became aware that she was being followed. It was not difficult to notice this, because her pursuer was not subtle. The woman—older, Black, short and stocky—had been trying to keep up with her. Whenever Lucinda slowed down, however, the woman slowed down, too. The rigamarole seemed so ludicrous that Lucinda finally turned to confront the woman.

—Do you want to tell me something? she asked.

—Madame le médecin, said the woman, vous parlez français?

The woman spoke very little English, but she had been told about Lucinda, and although she was hesitant to talk about her problem, she believed she was in need of a doctor.

—Pas médecin quelconque! she added.

"Not just any doctor"? Lucinda was puzzled—not by the idea that the woman needed a special sort of doctor, but by the question of whom the woman imagined her to be. She apologized and told the woman that she *might* be able to help her find the right doctor, but more than that she likely could not do, as she was no sort of specialist.

Having confronted her, Lucinda understood why the woman had only half-heartedly trailed her. It seemed she did not know what she wanted, could not decide what to ask or how to ask it. But then, as if gathering her courage or, at least, resigned to her humiliation, the woman said

—S'il vous plaît, Madame le médecin, venez avec moi. Il faut que vous veniez.

—Où ça? asked Lucinda. Chez vous?

Yes, the woman—Miriam Hoarau, a stranger—wanted Lucinda to come with her to a house which was somewhere behind them, off Springhurst. Most would have been wary, but Lucinda was moved by the woman's distress. So, she put aside her doubts about following an unknown person to an unknown house.

As they stepped from the first-floor landing into Miriam's apartment, Lucinda felt a sudden disquiet. The two were alone and she anticipated a request to examine some private part—a breast with a hard cancerous growth, for instance. But after hesitating, Miriam instead opened the door to a small bedroom, which was largely taken up by a double bed. On the bed, there was an older woman who, to Lucinda, appeared to be barely alive beneath the greying sheets. Disconcerting as the body in the bed was, however, it was not the most alarming thing about the room, because on the bed with Madame Hoarau, Miriam's mother, were five ravens: three to one side of her body, two to the other.

The ravens were fully grown, each about thirteen or fourteen inches tall. They were like quiet observers and relatively still, though they seemed wary when the bedroom door was opened. They shifted place, one of them hopping over Madame Hoarau's body, so that there were now four to one side of her.

It was alarming to see the birds—like five small ruffians—on the bed. But Miriam was something more than alarmed. Rather than enter the bedroom, she stood by the door, clearly frightened. It was uncanny to be plunged into such a scene, but Lucinda was more puzzled than anything else.

—Mais qu'est-ce qui se passe avec ces corbeaux? she asked.

Miriam coaxed her from the room before answering. It had been a month since her mother had fallen ill, and at first, they thought she had a cold—nothing that strong rum, lemon juice, and salt couldn't take care of. Two days into her sickness, however, the first of the "mauvais esprits" came: a single raven entered the bedroom through the window.

They assumed the bird had entered by chance, and Miriam had tried to lead it out, luring it towards the window with a piece of bread. The raven, however, was not interested in bread. So, having done what they could without resorting to violence, they called the humane society which, eventually, sent a man with a net who trapped the bird and, as if annoyed at them, advised them to keep their windows closed. Which they did, not wishing to trouble the authorities any more than they had.

But closing the window made things worse. Mother and daughter, who shared the bed, were awoken one night by loud and repeated tapping against the bedroom window. Opening the curtain, Miriam could see nothing but the streetlight on Springhurst, and night itself beyond the streetlight's halo. The tapping began again, but on drawing the curtain this time, Miriam was frightened by a raven flying towards her and flinging a stone against the windowpane. And these attacks on the pane went on until the window cracked.

Now, of course, they were terrified. Added to the feeling of being objects of an incomprehensible mind was the banal reality that they could not afford to have the window broken. Miriam, who worked cleaning houses, barely made enough to replace it. Besides which, she did not want anyone to know her mother was living with her. She had signed a lease asserting that she was the only tenant. She could not risk losing this place, which she could only just afford.

Terrified or not, they were forced to open the window and let the raven in.

But the raven—*ravens*—would not be so easily accommodated. The women moved out of the bedroom, Madame Hoarau sleeping on the narrow sofa, her daughter on the floor beside her. They soon found, however, that the ravens were not interested in the bedroom. They clawed at the bedroom door, cawing loudly day and night, until the landlord himself asked if Miriam was keeping birds and reminded her that no pets were allowed.

What were they to do? They could not give up the apartment, with Madame Hoarau still sick and the cost of moving prohibitive. But it was unthinkable that they share their space with what were, to Miriam, malevolent creatures. As it was, the ravens shat all over the bedroom and the smell of them was increasingly strong, despite the closed door and open bedroom window.

It looked as if they would have no choice but to leave or to throw themselves at the feet of the landlord, in the hope that his humanity—his concern for those whose needs were obvious—would protect them. But then Madame Hoarau decided to "accept her fate," convinced that the mauvais esprits were after her alone—convinced because, having lived longer than her daughter, it seemed reasonable to assume she was the greater sinner. One afternoon, when Miriam was out cleaning, Madame Hoarau struggled up from the sofa and entered the bedroom, prepared to give up her life for her daughter's sake.

—Ça fait deux jours, Madame le médecin! Et maman n'a pas mangé.

Her mother had been lying in the bed for two days, growing weaker, not eating. Though she was afraid of the ravens, Miriam ventured into the room to bring her food and water; this, despite the harassment of the ravens who seemed inclined, at times, to let her approach and uninclined at others, so that Miriam did not know how the birds would treat her—that is, whether they would flap around in a fury or passively allow her to approach.

The only good thing, if you could call it that, about her mother's decision to enter the bedroom was that it became clear Madame Hoarau was indeed the one the ravens wanted. With her in the bed, the birds were relatively peaceful, standing guard over her body, climbing in and out the half-closed window when they wanted. Of course, now Miriam worried that someone would notice the ravens' comings and goings, that she and her mother would again attract the landlord's attention.

In recounting all of this to Médard, Lucinda described the distress of the Hoaraus in great detail. It was their pitiful situation that led her to promise she would do whatever she could for them. That said, she had no idea how to deal with the ravens, no great knowledge of bird habits.

—Did you notice anything unusual about the ravens? Médard asked.

—Not about how they looked, Lucinda answered. There were five of them when I first went into the bedroom, and then a few more came and the ones who were already there made room for them.

—Did they peck at the woman, Médard asked, or attack her in any way?

—They didn't attack, Lucinda answered. They were aggressive but *not* aggressive at the same time. If the whole thing hadn't been so scary, you'd have said the ravens were at church: one or two of them would go to Madame Hoarau's head, and the rest would make room for them and move down to her feet. And then they'd change places again, like they all wanted to look at her.

—A ritual, Médard said. That's interesting. Look and see if I have some lunar caustic on the second shelf there.

The request was so unexpected that Lucinda tilted her head to look at him. Seeing this, Médard laughed.

—Yes, yes, he said, silver nitrate, lunar caustic. I know that sounds random, but what you just described is like something I saw in England, years ago, when I was younger. It was rooks we were dealing with in Aldeburgh, and they were very noisy.

—You're going to give silver nitrate to the ravens? asked Lucinda.

He smiled at her, getting up from his desk with some difficulty, before rooting among the bottles on a shelf behind him.

—Where you're wrong, he said, is that you think the problem's with the ravens.

He took down a dark container of silver nitrate.

—I want you to give a small amount of this to your Madame Hoarau, he said. A small amount! Ten micrograms in a cup of water. Once a day for three days. Let's see what happens.

The dose was not dangerous, but the thought of using silver nitrate—not on the birds but on Madame Hoarau—was incomprehensible to Lucinda. What possible benefit could there be to it, especially in such small amounts?

Médard grimaced as he sat back in his chair.

—When I was in Aldeburgh as a young man, he said, there was a famous Spanish soprano called "La Cuerva Encantadora" who'd come to sing at the Aldeburgh festival. At the time, I thought they called her "the enchanting raven" because she had long black hair, but it turned out she was La Cuerva Encantadora because she attracted crows and ravens wherever she went. Which is why she never toured outside of Patagonia, New Zealand, and parts of the Caribbean, where there aren't any corvids. She only agreed to sing at Aldeburgh because Robert Brook, who was *the* expert on corvids, happened to live in Snape Maltings, where La Cuerva was going to sing. Professor Brook was my friend's father, and he was the one who gave lunar caustic to La Cuerva, to help her with her condition. I don't know if your Madame Hoarau has the same condition as La Cuerva, but the silver nitrate's worth a try.

—

When they talked about the case five days later—that is, when the ravens had gone and Madame Hoarau was quietly recovering—the whole business still seemed baffling to Lucinda. Médard, who was not an expert on corvids, was also unsure of how the dose of silver nitrate worked, but he remembered Professor Brook's explanation . . .

Through no fault of her own, the smell of La Cuerva had been like a drug to the ravens—like an aphrodisiac, say, or something trance-inducing. Worse than that, the ravens had become addicted to the woman, literally addicted: reluctant to leave her side, breathing in her exhalations while forsaking their lives and nests. In administering a touch of silver nitrate, they had lightly changed her chemistry, so that, in effect, her smell became unpleasant to the ravens, maybe even sick-making.

—Why silver nitrate of all things? Lucinda asked.

—I don't know, Médard answered. That case with La Cuerva happened when I was in my twenties. It's a miracle it stuck with me. Well, not a miracle, but the thing I find fascinating is how a person's body can produce something to intoxicate certain birds. And then how the slightest change—a little bit of lunar caustic—can produce the opposite. Corvids loathe even a hint of silver nitrate.

—That is fascinating, Lucinda said, but were there any side effects?

—It's funny you should ask, Médard answered. I hadn't kept up with the La Cuerva. But I looked her up online, while we were waiting to see what would happen with Madame Hoarau. And it turns out there was a side effect. La Cuerva was sometimes attacked by crows for the rest of her life. They turned on her. Not enough to discourage her from touring, but still: there you are.

—Ahh, Lucinda said.

3. Uncertain Ground

Lucinda Hsu sought out Médard Albouy because he was one of the few scholars she'd heard of who treated black magic as a worthy part of medicine. She had attended a number of his lectures and seen for herself the kind of man he was: cantankerous, droll, and provocative but always serious about medicine and the possibility of magic.

She did not ask to be considered when Professor Albouy began his search for an apprentice because, at the time, she was burned out, so exhausted that she abandoned medicine. She chose, rather, to work at a pharmacy—a Shoppers Drug Mart that belonged to a friend—where she was wildly overqualified. So, for a time, she was a clerk, learning the whereabouts of stationery, mouthwash, "fresh food," and over-the-counter pills of various sorts.

The work, not entirely mindless but simple and uncomplicated, demanded only patience, memory, and a sympathy for others which was, in any case, almost instinctive to her. The work met her needs so well that it was a year before she began to think of a return to medicine. It wasn't that she missed the work or her fellow doctors or even the wonderful smell of hospitals, a industrial fragrance she associated with adventure. Rather, she had been lying in bed with her closest friend, Liz, gossiping.

It was sometime in early evening, and they had been talking about their childhoods—the differences in their popularity: Liz with many friends, Lucinda with few. It was late summer. A butterscotch light came through the bedroom window, and as Liz turned to answer her phone, Lucinda saw that on her friend's left shoulder blade there was the tattoo of a tree frog. The tattoo was colourful, the eyes of the frog orange-red circles with a tiny black lens in each; its skin lime green with indigo markings on its legs. She wondered why her friend had chosen to live with the tree frog and then she thought about blood, benzalkonium wipes, and allergies to Dettol.

Just so, a flood of memories came to her, including a moment from a lecture by Professor Albouy about poisons and their usefulness. In a sense, Médard Albouy was like a signpost in the distance, pointing to a place she suddenly wanted to revisit.

One Friday afternoon in 2022, three years after she had first visited Professor Albouy and sometime after they had dropped the pretense of an apprenticeship, Lucinda and Médard sat together in his office, sipping the Calvados that she had bought for him at a shop in Paris, where Lucinda had spent the spring.

Knowing that Calvados was his only indulgence—a memory of his first trip to France as a young man—and that Médard never drank unless she drank with him, Lucinda had poured two drams, one in each of the narrow-rimmed snifters he kept for the purpose. Because she herself almost never drank, hated both the taste and the effect of alcohol, the Calvados was more of a fragrance than a drink, a hint of apples that had accompanied a handful of their conversations. And in fact, they had finished a thoughtful consideration of conjuration, spellcasting, and Nietzsche when Médard said

—If I were a god, I'd be moved by all those rhythmic appeals.

—Would you? asked Lucinda. I sometimes wonder what people pray for most. Money, I think, and the death of others. Some of these spells seem like such beautiful ways to ask for death.

—That's true, said Médard. I tend to forget about the malevolence behind the rhythm. As I've gotten older, I tend to see things in a better light than they deserve.

—It's because you're good-natured, Lucinda said.

—Maybe, said Médard. Or maybe it's because I don't deal with people as often as you do. And the word "malevolent" makes me think of church. And I'm not a fan of churches.

—Churches? Lucinda said. They have their terrain, don't you think?

—Terrain? Médard answered. That's an interesting word. Do you mean good and evil and sin and grace? I suppose you could call those terrains. But they're slippery ground for an atheist. I can deal with the notion of good, because people have been going on about it since Plato and Aristotle. But I'm allergic to the idea of evil. It always strikes me as grandiose. It's easier to think about narcissism and spitefulness. But, you know, Lu, I accept that there are things I might never understand. I'm not even sure that understanding is such a great goal. It's more about having a healthy balance between knowledge and ignorance.

Lucinda smiled.

—Do you mean fifty-fifty? she asked.

—No, no, Médard answered. I'd rather have more ignorance than knowledge.

It suddenly seemed remarkable to Lucinda that Médard could meticulously consider and catalogue spells and conjurations from around the world while being noncommittal about things at the heart of magic: good, evil, gods and demons. It was the main difference between them, she thought, because she certainly believed in good and evil, sin and redemption.

On the other hand, she, too, was happy to live with a healthy quotient of unknowing. There were things on the border of darkness and light about which she was almost grateful to be ignorant.

—I was in Kingston, she said, at the Hôtel Dieu. A few years ago.

Lucinda was in Kingston for a refresher course on post-mortem detection of poisons at the Hôtel Dieu Hospital—the Dieu, for short. She was not a pathologist, but she had been invited by a friend, Mare Crawford, an administrator at the Dieu who knew of her fascination with toxicology.

The three days of lectures and camaraderie—pathologists being the most entertaining of all specialists—had been so enjoyable that Lucinda, feeling herself beholden and wishing to repay Mare's kindness, stayed in Kingston for a few days, volunteering for night duty at the Dieu's Urgent Care Centre.

As it happened, her first night—a Friday—was as frantic as a makeshift medic's unit in wartime. There had been two bus accidents. The bodies of the dead, dying, and injured could barely be accommodated by the emergency wards in town, and the shortage of doctors was alarming. What had begun as an act of thanks became a hair-raising twenty hours of emergency diagnosis, consultation, life-saving surgery, and defeat. Nor were all the victims from the bus accidents. It was a weekend, so there were the usual stabbings, gunshot wounds, assaults, and sexual mishaps; the full complement of tragic turns, slight wounds, deaths, and recoveries.

One case, though, from near the end of Lucinda's shift, when night had fallen again, was unusual. A double homicide or murder-suicide—a young woman, an older man. Husband and wife. For lack of space, their bodies had been sent to the old morgue in the Dieu's basement, though that part of the hospital was no longer officially in use.

Lucinda herself had seen the couple, had checked for vital signs, had confirmed their deaths from gunshot wounds: she to the chest, he to the neck. So, she was surprised when an intern, flustered, came up from the morgue to tell her that the gentleman was still alive.

—What do you mean alive? she asked.

She had seen all manner of corpse movements in her time, from those that had sat up to those whose hands had raised as if they were asking a question, from the farting and tumescent dead to a corpse that had somehow tipped itself from its stretcher.

—He's breathing, said the intern. It's spooky.

Nor was this unheard of. She had once seen a man begin to breathe again a half an hour after he'd stopped.

—Let's see, she said.

And smiled to let the intern know that everything was fine.

Lucinda was not intimidated by death. Moreover, she was relieved to visit the old morgue, to get away from the Urgent Care Centre, to examine a part of the Dieu built in the 1840s.

Insofar as she had anticipated the charm of a historic room, Lucinda was disappointed. The old morgue, badly lit, dusty despite the hasty cleaning it had received, was drab, windowless, cold, and smaller than she'd imagined it would be. It was, she thought, like a garage for the dead, only slightly eerie for being ancient. In the room, there were three corpses neatly parked against a far wall, and two, side by side, against the wall to the right of the entrance. The two nearest were the bodies of the young woman and her husband. And, as the intern had said, the body of the husband was drawing breath, erratically.

All thoughts of atmosphere and history evaporated. Lucinda felt for the man's pulse and found one. She listened for a heartbeat and heard one. He had bled onto the cold platinum-coloured trolley on which he'd been put, naked but for his socks, though he was covered by a white sheet. For whatever reason, she had, earlier, mistaken him for dead. This fact both annoyed and astonished her, and she called up for assistance from the intern.

It was, no doubt, because of her astonishment that Lucinda was not as surprised as she might have been when the body of the man's wife rose up to sitting position, displacing the sheet covering her, looking straight ahead before speaking.

—Don't let him . . . , it said.

Here, Médard interrupted Lucinda's account to tease her.

—You misdiagnosed two deaths? I'm having a hard time believing this, Lu.

—I know, Lucinda answered. I'd been going for twenty hours straight. So, I wasn't at my best. But I'd say, on the whole, I might have been wrong about the husband, but I'm not sure I was wrong about the wife. She was dead, by almost any definition you choose.

—So, a dead woman spoke to you?

—I thought so, at the time. I'm not sure, now.

Lucinda's attention was divided. It was important to tend to the husband at once, to get him to an operating room where he could receive blood and further attention to his injury: a rough gaping wound where part of his neck had been.

But seeing as the woman, too, was alive, or seemed to be, she went quickly to the other side of the rectangle made by the two trolleys. She held the woman's wrist to feel for a pulse. There was no pulse. She shone a light into the corpse's eye nearest her, checking for any reaction. The eye did not move, nor did the pupil contract. Though it was gruesome to do so—because a bullet had entered through the woman's left breast and destroyed her heart—she listened, ear against the woman's cold chest, for a heartbeat, for the drawing of breath. There was no heartbeat, and there was no breathing.

By all that we know about bodies and the science of bodies, it was not possible for the woman to have spoken, and even less possible for the woman to speak again, as she did while Lucinda's ear was against her breast.

—Let him die, the corpse said.

Lucinda drew back and, in that moment, became entirely Hippocratic. Every other aspect of her personality fled to a distant corner of her psyche.

—I'm a doctor, she said. It's my duty to save him.

—Then I've failed, said the corpse. Help me lie down.

Lucinda did as she was asked, pushing against the woman's breast while holding her thigh down. It was this moment the nurse saw as he entered the morgue.

—Can I help you, Doctor?

—Take that one to an operating room, Lucinda answered. He's still alive. He'll need blood immediately. I'll take care of this one.

Lucinda did not realize she'd been traumatized until days later when, home again, she was still troubled by what she'd gone through. Mistaking a man for dead was one thing. But her doubts about the woman's state were even more serious, creating as they did a conflict between her learning (the woman was dead, scholastically speaking) and her intuition (the woman, in speaking, was surely alive).

Even more unsettling was the sensation that she had done something wrong, that it had been wrong to save the man whose neck was torn. She had followed protocol. She had handled the situation properly, and yet it felt as if she had not.

—Did you ever keep track of him? Médard asked.

On top of everything else she liked about him, Médard was an intense listener. She looked at his face: rugged, a pleasant triangle made more triangular by his haircut—grey hair sticking up, unruly on the top, though neatly combed on the sides—his light brown eyes beneath his dark eyebrows. She had not known him long enough to be certain of it, but she was confident that Médard was a good man. He had been a good teacher.

—I did keep track of him, she answered. For about a year.

—Was he a bad man?

—Yes, I think he was.

To begin with, she was not the kind to mistrust her instincts. Beyond the fact of a corpse having spoken—and it had been humiliating to wheel a body in rigor mortis into an operating room to check for vital signs—there was the request made by the corpse. To have spoken those final words—"Do not let him live"—meant either that the woman had been unhealthily obsessed with her husband or that the man merited the obsession.

This uncertainty troubled Lucinda for months, bringing into question her decision to save the corpse's husband. Of course, the theoretically correct answer was within her as well: *one is not meant to care for the good and allow the bad to die.*

No sane person would choose the responsibility of sorting the good from the bad on the operating table. Both the good and the bad suffered, and suffering was the issue. But this idea brought her less comfort than it should, because if suffering was the issue, what was she to make of the possibility that

Mr. Gleeson's wife—the dead woman—wanted him dead precisely because he caused suffering—and who knew what kind of suffering that might be?

A year after the incident at the Dieu, wanting some idea of the man's personality, Lucinda decided to visit Mr. Gleeson at his home in Kingston. Not wanting to intrude, to keep things as professional as possible, she called him first, explaining who she was and enquiring into his well-being.

—How lucky am I, he said, that a doctor's interested in me? Why don't you come and see for yourself. My neck's better, but I have other problems.

Gleeson's home was in Reddendale, a neighbourhood so blandly Canadian that she might have been anywhere in the country. The house itself was just as unplaceable: beige bricks, yellow aluminum siding on the addition atop the garage, no large windows, a tall pine tree in the front yard obscuring part of the house from the street.

—How nice of you to come, he said, how nice.

Lucinda's first thought, as the storm door closed behind her, was that she could almost certainly take him, if she had to. It was an unusual thought for her. Mr. Gleeson was short, stocky, and had wispy mutton chop sideburns, but his words were all politeness, unambiguously welcoming. He was not aggressive, but the inside of his house was almost pointedly bland: it was as nondescript as the neighbourhood, so that she felt nowhere in acres of nowhere.

—What did you want to know? he asked.

—I don't know if they told you at the hospital, she said, but the first time I saw you, I took your vital signs and I marked you down as dead. It's a little embarrassing.

—Don't worry about that, he said. Anyone can make a mistake.

—If you don't mind my asking, Lucinda said, what happened to you? Were you and your wife attacked?

—I don't like talking about it, he said, but if you have to know, my wife tried to kill me.

—Oh, I'm sorry I brought it up. It must be a painful subject.

Without looking at her, looking down rather at the coffee table between them, he said

—It's nice of you to take an interest in me. Why don't I make us some tea? I'll tell you about my poor Melanie. She lost her mind, you know.

—If it's not too much trouble, I'd love some tea, Lucinda answered.

—No trouble at all! said Mr. Gleeson. I was just boiling some water before you came.

She had a mind to leave right then. She couldn't have said what was wrong, but something was. As he went to the kitchen, she stood up and walked about the living room, with its gas fireplace and its exercise bike facing a large television. On the fireplace mantle, there was a framed picture of Mr. Gleeson and his wife at Disney World, wearing Mickey Mouse ears.

Mr. Gleeson returned with a wooden tray on which there were: two cups (on one of which there was a Union Jack; on the other, an Italian tricolour), a silver spoon, and a sugar bowl, on which there was a flag of India. After setting the tray on the coffee table, he put the tricolour before her and kept the Union Jack for himself.

—Here you are, he said.

And she was suddenly—fortuitously—reminded of a game she used to play with her sisters: sugar and salt. Two cups of tea: one with sugar in it, the other salt. The object was to get the person facing you to drink the tea with salt. The one who drank first, and would thus know if her cup was salted or not, was observed by the other who then had a choice to stick with their cup or trade for her sister's cup. The winner was the one who avoided the salted tea by getting the other one to drink it. And the best way to do that was to convince your sister that *you* had the cup with sugar in it, if you were the taster.

It was an unexpected, joyful memory. Lucinda smiled, remembering her sisters drinking from the "poisoned cups." Of course, her older sister, Ruth, was the champion among the four of them, because she loved the taste of tea and salt and showed genuine displeasure if she drank from the tea with sugar and well-feigned displeasure when she got the one with salt.

Smiling at Mr. Gleeson, Lucinda said

—Thank you.

And was about to drink from the tea when she twigged to two things: the smell of the tea was musky, just a little, but enough to put her in mind of tomato leaves, and Mr. Gleeson was looking at her carefully, smiling in his turn.

So, Lucinda did what she had done as a child when playing salt and sugar: she brought the cup to her lips, imitated the sound of sipping, and gave a slight sigh of happiness, lightly smacking her lips before putting the cup down on the coffee table. Mr. Gleeson took a drink from his cup and put his down on the table as well.

—So, said Lucinda, let me take a look at your neck.

—You sound like a vampire, Mr. Gleeson said, giggling. I hope you don't bite.

As she examined his scar—the darkened skin in an elongated ellipse around the discoloured area where the flesh had been torn away—she wondered if there *was* something in her tea and, beyond that, why he would poison her at all. At the thought, she was almost overcome by the feeling of irreality, by the imperceptible passage from a familiar world to another that only looked like it.

—It's cleaned up nicely, she said.

And on heading back to the couch where she was sitting, with her body between Mr. Gleeson and the table, she switched cups, taking the one with the Union Jack and, as before, pretending to sip the tea.

—You were going to tell me about your wife, she said.

—Oh yes! said Mr. Gleeson. So I was!

He was one of those men who will be victims or nothing at all. He was absorbed by the story of his wife's deceit, by his terrible luck in choosing a young woman who pretended to love him, who betrayed him. He was so absorbed in the telling that he took up the cup before him and drank the tea as if he were thirsty, finishing it.

Now, of course, she was committed to staying with Mr. Gleeson, observing him until she was sure he had *not* been poisoned. Whatever world this was, it was not one in which she could blithely cause the death of another. If he had been poisoned, and if the dose was strong, he might show signs of it in as little as fifteen or twenty minutes. If not, she would leave in half an hour.

That said, having looked at his neck and listened to him talk about his wife, what further reason could there be for her to stay? There was no subject that needed airing with him, unless it was to ask him if the tea he'd drunk was poisoned.

Mr. Gleeson, however, came to her assistance. He was, he said, glad to have a doctor in his company and wondered if she'd mind talking about herself.

—What's it like, he asked, to have life and death in your hands?

—I don't think about it that way, Lucinda answered. Surgery would be too intimidating, if you did.

—I don't agree, he answered. You must know you have this power. Maybe you don't think about it consciously, but you must know you have it. If I had it, I'd accept it.

—I'm sure you're right, she said.

—No, no, no, he said. Don't be condescending. I'd like to know what you think.

—What I think, she said, is that there are things that help you focus and things that don't. Thinking about my so-called power wouldn't help me; so, I don't. But what work do you do?

He was the owner of a handful of Tim Hortons around southern Ontario. He didn't mind telling her about that at all: the ins and outs of the business, the way to run a franchise, and, yes, the power he had as an owner. He was sure that this, in the end, was what had turned his wife against him. She couldn't stand to see him prosper.

A half an hour passed—not quickly—and Lucinda was convinced that she'd been overcautious, that Mr. Gleeson was an odd duck but not more than that. He was so obsessed with his own life that it was difficult to imagine him plotting the deaths of others. In the end, she thought, his wife had had her own reasons to want him dead. Whatever they might have been, they were none of her business.

When he came to a break in his descriptions of management, Lucinda stood up, looked at her phone, and said

—Mr. Gleeson, I've got to make a call.

But Mr. Gleeson no longer seemed to notice her at all. He continued speaking, but his words now seemed directed at someone beyond her. And as Lucinda looked towards the television, the exercise bike turned itself on and its pedals began to move up and down as if someone were using it. The sight was comical. It was unnerving as well—the hair on the back of her neck stood up—but her first thought was that, whatever was happening, it was too early in the afternoon on a sunny day for anything truly supernatural.

While she was trying to figure out why he had programmed the bike to start on its own, Mr. Gleeson began a conversation—both sides of a conversation. He would say a few words in his own voice, then answer himself in a woman's voice, which she recognized as that of the corpse at the Dieu.

Lucinda was fascinated more than she was frightened. For one thing, Gleeson's conversation was as crushingly banal as his monologue on management had been. He and his wife seemed to be planning a trip to Florida, and he was asking what he was meant to pack and was she sure that they should drive along the coast, since they did that every year. Meanwhile, his wife answered that she wasn't interested in the coast, that she'd seen enough of the I-95, that she wanted to visit Atlanta, that they could stop in Cincinnati.

After a few minutes of this bickering, Mr. Gleeson turned towards her and, in his wife's voice, said

—What are you waiting for? You can go.

And Lucinda—now properly unnerved—went.

Lucinda brought the Calvados towards her, could smell it as it approached: cooked apples and alcohol. No wonder, she thought, that the French expression for losing consciousness was "tomber dans les pommes"—falling into apples. It seemed so French to equate a loss of the senses with an assault by one of them.

—I'd have left sooner, said Médard.

—I left, Lucinda said, but I called an ambulance as soon as I got out of there.

—You thought it was belladonna?

—Yes, Lucinda said, and I was right. The tea was poisoned, and the dose must have been massive. By the time they found him, he was pretty much done for. There wasn't enough pilocarpine in the world to save him. My fingerprints were all over the teacups, and I was the one who called the ambulance. So, I was a person of interest in the investigation, *the* person of interest before they found that one of the rooms in the house was like a nursery for poisons. And then, too, there were human remains in his basement freezer.

They sat quietly together, as Médard took her story in.

—So, he said, Gleeson was the one speaking in his wife's voice at the Dieu?

—Yes, said Lucinda, that's what I think, too. It makes sense about the talking corpse. But that's not the thing that stays with me. The thing that bothers me, when I think about it, is that I can't say for sure *who* poisoned Mr. Gleeson. You could say he poisoned himself, because I had no idea what was in the tea. Or you could say that if I thought the tea was poisoned, I should have thrown it away, not let him drink it. So, I poisoned him. Which is what one of the detectives said.

—The man wasn't innocent, Médard answered.

—I'm not saying he was innocent, but, you know, Professor, I'm not on this Earth to kill anyone, and I don't like the feeling that I did kill him, that I'm responsible.

—Is this what you had in mind when we were talking about knowledge and ignorance?

—Yes, Lucinda answered. What you said made me think about what percentage I'd want of knowledge to ignorance. I'd want to know more than not know, because I don't deal with doubt all that well.

—Now, said Médard, I see what you meant by churches having their own terrain. They're about dealing in doubt, aren't they?

—I think so, said Lucinda. Doubt and mystery. Whether you believe in God or not, church is a good place to think those things.

Médard considered her words before gently answering.

—It's one of the many places, he said, where you can think about those things—an operating theatre, a movie theatre, anywhere people congregate there's going to be doubt and mystery.

Lucinda smiled at his tone and, with a feeling of sympathy for the older man before her, took a small mouthful of Calvados.

—Do you go to church, Lu? Médard asked.

—Never, Lucinda answered.

By which she meant that she rarely went, except for funerals, to see off the ones she loved, and weddings, to see them hopeful. She did not rule churchgoing out completely, however, because she believed that a time for mystery was coming, would come for all, and this interested her a great deal.

4. A Ghost Story

In the last years of his life, Médard did not see Lucinda as frequently as he would have liked. This was in part because he was often ill and not fit for company. The arthritis that had afflicted both of his parents had come for him, as if angrily returning for something it forgot. Added to that were the usual complaints—a susceptibility to flus and viruses, an irritation with the new city, a tiredness that makes it difficult to accomplish two objectives in the same day—groceries and banking, for instance.

What's more, Lucinda, having found an even deeper love for medicine, rediscovered a longing to help those in faraway places. So, she was away, in places Médard would not have visited even if he could.

Her sojourns abroad disturbed him as much as her absence. He was worried for her, though he knew it was useless to worry. How surprising to discover these paternal feelings so late in life! But there you are: some versions of love make their way to you at least as surely as arthritis.

Lucinda, who was as fond of Médard as he was of her, knew that he missed her. He never failed to tell her so. She worried about him as much as he worried about her. He had few friends or even acquaintances whose company he could abide for long. All his life he had, by his own admission, put his work before friendship, and now that he was in his eighties, he was paying for his preference. It made her wonder why he had accepted her, but also why she was amused by his flaws—his cynicism and grouchiness, his coldness towards others. Could it be that she alone understood his flaws as the signs of a shyness he struggled to overcome? Maybe, but these were questions she did not dwell on. Whenever she was home—that is, in Toronto—she visited Médard after seeing her own parents first.

Some months before Médard's death, Lucinda returned home from Kenya by way of Montmartre where, of course, she had bought a Calvados from the Repaire de Bacchus at the top of Rue Lepic. This was now a signal place and part of her ritual of homecoming, though she did not drink Calvados and there were fifteen bottles of the spirit in a cupboard beside Médard's sink, only one of which had been opened—and not much taken from it, either.

(By the time Lucinda died, there would be fifty-five bottles of Calvados in her bedroom closet—the fifteen she had inherited from Médard, twenty-nine she'd bought on her way home from France, and the eleven she was given by her friends who, knowing her ritual, had taken to buying Calvados for her.)

Lucinda had gone to Kenya after a hair-raising time in Côte d'Ivoire where she had felt constantly in danger. The exhilaration of having escaped with her life was such that she allowed herself a sojourn at Hemingways Watamu, a resort steps away from the Indian Ocean.

—It's one of my favourite places, she said. Very peaceful. There's nothing to do but look at the ocean and go to sleep early. The perfect place after Côte d'Ivoire. But . . . you remember what happened in Kingston a few years ago?

—The talking corpse? Médard asked. You mean there was another one?

—Not exactly, Lucinda answered, but there was a corpse.

She had driven from Mombasa, early in the morning, in light rain that had stopped somewhere around Mtwapa. From there, the hours to Watamu had gone by as if in a brief dream—blue sky, warm morning, the smell of damp sand and verdure.

Perhaps—given how tired she was, how jetlagged—she might have spent a few days in Mombasa, recovering. But she had turned away from the city as soon as she could, chasing the quiet of Watamu, as if silence were sunlight. And she arrived around eight in the morning, going out for a walk after letting the resort know she was there.

It was then, in morning quiet, walking down to the ocean with the sound of the ocean itself an ocean, that she felt how tired she was, how lightly connected to reality. This feeling was intensified, first, by the sight of men in white linen raking the seaweed back into the ocean to keep the sand clean. And then, further along, by a number of people standing beside a palm tree that leaned—at about 60 degrees—towards the water.

—Where are the police? a woman asked.

—He told you, a man answered. The station doesn't open till eight.

It was on hearing these words that Lucinda noticed that someone in a dress—a woman, it turned out—had climbed halfway up the tree and, it seemed, refused to come down. A young man beneath the tree, in obvious distress, called out from time to time.

—Mum! Come down! You have to come down!

As she reached the spectator nearest to her, a man in plaid swim trunks, Lucinda asked

—What's going on?

—I don't know, he answered. Looks like that fellow's mother doesn't want to come down from the tree. She's frightened is what I'm thinking.

Wanting only peace, Lucinda thought of walking on. But her curiosity, though dulled by fatigue, got the better of her.

It was not usual, after all, to see a woman who looked to be in her fifties or sixties (long white hair streaked with strands of black) stuck in a tree like an unfortunate moggie.

As she approached, Lucinda saw that the woman was quite still, hugging the tree for dear life, you'd have said. The wind moved what moved around her: her hair, her dress, the leaves of the palm tree above and beyond her.

—Has anyone tried to help her down? she asked.

Her question was met by a curious embarrassment. The spectators, her son included, were clearly waiting for the woman to come down on her own. Lucinda might have tried to climb the tree herself, but she was tired and not certain that she wouldn't fall if she did. So, the question she'd asked was her only contribution to the . . .

Here, Médard, who seemed dismayed, interrupted Lucinda's story.

—The woman in the tree was dead? he asked.

—Yes, Lucinda answered, she was.

—Did you get a chance to examine the body?

—No, Lucinda said, I didn't. I assumed she'd come down eventually. So, there wasn't any reason for me to stick around. I only found out that she died in the tree when I was leaving Watamu. I was at the front desk waiting to check out, and someone who'd been at the tree when I was started talking to me about it. Out of the blue. He was still shaken up. He said, "Isn't it strange the way life is? I never would have guessed that poor woman was dead." She hadn't been hanging on to the tree at all. She'd been in rigor. I asked why she'd climbed the tree in the first place. And the answer to that was that no one knew. Not even her son, who was devastated, as you can imagine.

I couldn't help wondering if they had to break her arms and legs to get her down, and naturally, I thought about the corpse at the Dieu. But how did you guess she was dead?

Médard, who had poured himself a thimble's worth of Calvados and held onto his glass while Lucinda told her story, put the drink down cautiously, as if he might miss the desk.

—I didn't guess so much, he said. I remembered something I'd been meaning to tell you for some time. About bodies in rigor. It's quite a coincidence, but I once dealt with a corpse in a tree, too. It wasn't in Africa, though. It was in Hornepayne, where I'd gone when I came back from England. I was in my twenties, and I was like you, back then. I was idealistic. I wanted to do medicine in a small town. Or so I thought.

In those days, Hornepayne was little more than an unexpected train stop in northern Ontario—a formerly grand but then-dilapidated station with a few streets and small houses nearby. A population of less than a thousand. A random outpost—amidst the rock, trees, and small lakes—that owed its existence to the Canadian National Railroad.

No doctor could have made a living in Hornepayne alone. Which did not deter Médard when his hair was dark and he could, for the sake of his ideals, abide the company of others. He had inherited his father's '65 Volkswagen Type 3. This was how he made his way to more remote communities, having established himself in Hornepayne—that is, having rented a room in a house two streets from the train station.

He was there for six months, which was longer than Dr. Kurtesz—whose office Médard shared—thought he would last. Hornepayne taught Médard that he was better suited for medicine without patients, in part because in the face of want, poverty, and great need, he could not stand the fact of his own inadequacy. He was both too much, in that his presence raised the hopes of those in smaller towns who needed medical attention, and not enough, in that he could do little more than hand out Band-Aids and give children shots for measles.

This wasn't strictly speaking true, or at least it wasn't the whole story. Médard was kind and attentive, and people were grateful for Band-Aids and inoculations, for the ear of someone who could help, for the respect he showed them. Their regard for him was a great part of his service. The problem was with his despair at not being able to do more.

Then, too, there was the effect on him of the land itself—the solitude of roads that were not quite roads, the indifference of the crags and stony cliffs, and a presence that was almost strong enough to be called a voice: the forest. These things worked on him, but not in the way his despair did. The land pricked his sense of mystery. And this was even before the incident in Owl's Beak, just north of Hornepayne, where he had gone on a Sunday morning in September, called there by a woman whose sister-in-law's corpse had climbed a tree.

Her sister-in-law's corpse had climbed a tree. Said that way, the incident sounds macabre, but not nearly as macabre as the story behind it.

Médard arrived in Owl's Beak, a settlement of some fifty people, around eight in the morning and, as Lucinda had in Watamu, saw a group of people staring up at a maple, to the trunk of which a woman seemed to be clinging. About six feet further up, a young man in socks and underwear lay as if caught in a crux where several branches forked.

A woman tugged at Médard's elbow.

—Dr. Albouy, she said, that's my sister-in-law. It's my sister-in-law's body, but she's not supposed to be up there.

Her voice sounded more puzzled than anything else.

—You must be Mrs. Barker? Médard said. Was your sister-in-law unwell?

—Unwell? said the woman. No, she wasn't unwell. She died two days ago.

And so, belatedly, Médard noticed that Mrs. Barker's sister-in-law, Helen, dressed in a plain black dress that fell just below her knees, was rigid, clearly in rigor. Her skin was ashen, save for her legs, where the blood had drained and the skin was a shade of purple.

—Who's the man up the tree? Médard asked. Does he have anything to do with this?

It was some trick, if he had, Médard thought. For one thing, the woman's fingers—of both hands—were plunged into the tree trunk, as if it were made of bread dough.

Here, Lucinda interrupted him.

—That's very disturbing, she said.

—It was, Médard answered. I felt like I was dreaming. A very lucid dream. I can remember the details to this day: the black dress, the discolouration of her legs, the trouble it took to get the body down from the tree, the face of the young man who turned out to be one of three men who'd come from . . .

—Ah, Lucinda said, so he was involved. Was it part of a ritual or something?

—No, no, Médard answered. Nothing that straightforward. After they pulled Helen Barker from the tree, the man above her came to, like he'd been sleeping. And to be honest, that was more alarming than the corpse, because I'd assumed he was dead, too.

—I'm confused, Lucinda said. Did he confess to putting the corpse in the tree?

—In a way, Médard answered, but not the way you're thinking.

Helen Barker had died of natural causes, it seemed, while visiting her brother in Owl's Beak. And having no appropriate conveyance, her family had to wait a few days for a hearse to come from Kapuskasing, where Helen lived and where the Barkers had a family plot.

Her brother and his wife were by no means wealthy. They ran a bed and breakfast in town, the only place that received visitors. The B & B was rarely busy, rarely full. But as it happened, Helen died on a Friday when all of the rooms (four of them, on the second floor) had been rented. So, her body was laid out on a small cot in the heated coach house behind the house, a sheet covering her corpse, a white screen giving it privacy—in a manner of speaking.

An inconvenience because the next day, three young men, who were lumberjacking in a camp some five kilometres out of Owl's Beak, had come into town with friends and stayed up drinking till eleven o'clock. Too unsteady to walk home, they needed somewhere to sleep. And the coach house would have been suitable, the Barkers said, were it not for Helen's body.

But the young men were persistent, happy to pay three times the cost of the room, and undaunted by the thought of sleeping with a corpse. There was, to the Barkers' minds, no answer to this. In particular, Helen's sister-in-law encouraged her husband to accept the proposition, on the grounds that Helen herself would have approved.

So, three more cots were set up in the coach house, a modest distance from the screen, and the men fell asleep almost at once, moonlight illuminating the single spacious room through two windows that faced west.

This was a particularly important point for the young man recounting what had happened: moonlight, as illuminating as only the moon can be when there are no clouds, no streetlamps, no lights from cars and trucks. In other words, he could clearly see when he woke up—light sleeper that he was—the corpse push back the screen and walk to the cot nearest her where she stopped, leaned over the body of his sleeping friend as if to kiss him, and drew in his spirit, as if she were drawing the flame off a candle.

You can imagine the effect this had on the young man. Whether what he'd seen was real or imagined, he was terrified, not knowing whether to stay quiet or run. In the end, unsure that his legs would carry him, he stayed as still as he could, helped by the fact that the woman retired noiselessly behind the screen.

He had no idea how long this state of fright held him, but just as he'd found the will to wake his remaining friend and sneak out of the coach house, the corpse again came from behind the screen and went to the bed that held the second man. For the same purpose, it seemed. It bent over the sleeping man and drew the life out of him, so that now the only living presence in the place was his own.

Perhaps he snorted. Maybe he gasped. For whatever reason, the corpse did not retire behind its screen. Instead it approached his cot—its greyish skin platinum by moonlight, its dress like a hovering shadow. The man leapt from his cot and ran from the coach house, pursued by the corpse itself.

—

Médard was not smiling, exactly. His expression was unreadable.

—Are you making this up? Lucinda asked.

—No, Lu, he answered. I'm just remembering how absurd it was to hear all this. What are you meant to say when someone tells you a corpse chased him up a tree?

—Do you think he believed what he was saying? Lucinda asked.

—He did, Médard answered. And I examined the bodies of his friends. They were dead. Of heart attacks, we found out later. He nearly died from fright himself. I'm not saying I believed the story, exactly, but you've got to admit it was a weird one to make up. Not to mention the corpse being halfway up the tree.

—Why did the corpse stop climbing? Lucinda asked.

—Dawn, apparently, Médard answered. I mean, the real answer is "I don't know," but according to the young man the corpse stopped climbing right around where dawn light hit the tree.

As if in relief at telling her this thing he'd long been meaning to tell her, Médard carefully picked up his glass of Calvados and drank some.

—I was young when that happened, he said. It left an impression. I'd say it was responsible for me turning from practicing to research. To the kind of research I've done all my life. I suppose you could say my door was opened to certain things. I have no idea how that corpse and that man got up that maple tree. But there you are. I've been wondering about it for sixty years.

5. A Late Dream

One night just after his eighty-first birthday, Médard Albouy dreamed that he was sitting at a desk in an impossibly large and high-ceilinged lecture hall, one so grand that he could not see the front of it from where he sat, nor yet the back of it, either.

The place was not unpleasant. There were floor-to-ceiling windows along one of its walls. And although he was too far from the windows to get a good view of the outside world, he could see an unbroken sky across which a single cardinal flew, like a red needle stitching an unwound bolt of blue.

He was taking an exam, it seemed, but he felt untroubled, because he was confident he knew the answers to all the questions, though the exam was several hundred pages thick, and whenever he looked at the questions, they seemed unrelated to anything he'd studied:

11. What is a rabbit when tied to a sofa?
155. If three numbers, then list the cities.
3116. When is a lake most likely to yield?
When an ocean?

And so it was: although Médard had no idea what the exam was about, he *did* know the answers:

11. Western
155. Panaji, Goodnight, Gone
3116. Midnight. Never.

Added to the pleasure of knowing the answers—a pleasure he'd often experienced when taking exams, because he was meticulous in his preparations—was the presence of his friends from university, many of whom he had not seen for years. The joy of being with his classmates was so intense that it was a moment before he realized that all those in the desks nearest him had been dead for years. Some had died decades earlier, like Jock Harvey who, soon after matriculation, had been struck by a motorcycle in Rome, where he'd gone to celebrate.

(Jock was in the desk beside Médard's: still young, intently staring at a page of the exam, the only trace of his accident being a patch of dried blood, a reddish clot between his precisely rounded hairline and the top of his back. How little death had changed him!)

The realization that, among the students around him, he was the only one still alive altered Médard's mood. It seemed to him, as he was writing on a theme—"The medulla oblongata as first principle and last cause"—that the line between life and death was trivial. He was curious about being on one side of the line while those around him were on the other.

He was about to tap the shoulder of the man in front of him—Fred Rasmussen, as it happened, dead of cancer at fifty-three—when he was stopped by a preceptor.

—You can't speak to anyone until you finish the exam, the man said. But if you'd like to finish sooner, you can skip to the final essay. If your answer is good, you're free to speak to whomever you like.

It was a reasonable offer, and Médard was pleased. The subject of the final essay was barely legible. There were missing words, words too faint to read, and (perhaps) a melange of languages:

Hypno . . . thé . . . : con . . . justif . . . - 1055 - 2009

But as with the questions on the first pages of the exam, Médard was confident that he understood perfectly. In an hour that passed like seconds, he wrote a lucid and beautiful essay on therapeutic hypnosis, beginning with the earliest instance of hypnotism in Europe (a woman in eleventh-century Lyon hypnotized at the threshold of her home by a rhythmically swaying wind chime to its modern use by cattlemen who, to make animal flesh more tender, hypnotize cows before killing them).

The preceptor, moved by Médard's essay, congratulated him on passing the exam *summa cum laude Dei* and welcomed him to the city where he would be working as a physician.

—What city? asked Médard.

Without answering, the preceptor pointed towards the window from which there could be seen a magnificent city, a Paris of the mind, a city one forever approaches without reaching, a kind of urban horizon. It was, Médard immediately realized, *his* city, one he could no more refuse than he could refuse his own soul.

And yet he was reluctant, feeling that he still had duties and responsibilities.

—I'm honoured, he said, to be given this opportunity, but I would like time to take care of matters at home.

—It would be a shame, said the preceptor, to let you go for even a minute, when you're capable of the kind of insight you've shown in this essay. What sort of matters do you need to take care of?

—I have an apprentice, Médard answered. I have things I'd like to share with her.

—Ah, said the preceptor, you mean . . .

(Here the man took a yellow Moleskine notebook from his pocket and turned to its final page.)

—Lucinda Hsu? She is a wonderful doctor! You've been a fine mentor to her, but do you think she'd be better if she were more like you?

—That's not what I meant, said Médard. I meant that there are things I know that would be of help to her.

—That's an honourable sentiment, said the preceptor, and as we all admire Dr. Hsu, I hesitate to stop you. But I wonder if there is anything you know that Dr. Hsu would not discover on her own if she needed. Isn't it also true, Médard, that . . .

(Here the preceptor consulted the yellow notebook.)

— . . . what we don't know is as important as what we do? You used to start your lectures by saying ignorance is our greatest resource, didn't you? I'll tell you what: if you can name one thing that Dr. Hsu needs from you, any lack that makes her less able than you, I'll give you time to pass it on. After that, there are so many here who would enjoy your insight.

This, too, sounded reasonable, and at the outset, Médard was certain he could think of a dozen things that would be crucial to Lucinda. But as they occurred to him and as he spoke them, their importance waned.

—She doesn't know, he said, that the green June beetle when ground with sundried Scotch bonnets makes a paste that removes warts.

—That's true, said the preceptor, but what *you* don't know is that brown June beetles are better for warts, and less tricky to use. Dr. Hsu knows this already.

—Does she? Médard asked. But does she know that spiderwebs contain vitamin K and are a gentler anticoagulant than the . . .

The preceptor interrupted him, gently.

—Médard, please. Everybody knows this. And Dr. Hsu herself has used spiderweb in field hospitals that would terrify you.

And so it went for a dozen "important things" Lucinda needed to know. After each of Médard's examples, the preceptor would point out that Médard's own ignorance was perhaps as deep as Lucinda's, and yet: he had been a good doctor, a beloved lecturer, a respected researcher. His ignorance had not kept him from his accomplishments, far from it.

Médard, at last, saw the obvious. He might be useful to Lucinda, but he was by no means essential. And if he had accomplished anything where his apprentice was concerned, it was in imparting the love and fascination he had for a discipline to which they had both devoted their lives.

There could be nothing deeper than this, Médard accepted, nothing greater for him to pass on. There remained only the small details which, as the preceptor had pointed out, would come to Lucinda if she needed them.

With this thought, Médard's connection to his home wavered; his connection to his city was altered—as was his connection to the sky and to the placid blue-green lake: Lake Ontario, which, in this, his final dream, seemed to stretch on eternally so that, standing as he suddenly was at the foot of Jameson staring out at the water, he could see on the lake's far shore a version of Toronto, his beloved city, looking serenely back on itself.

Consolation

Five years before my mother died, we had a violent argument—a thing that had never happened before. She was in her early eighties and still driving, and because I am an inveterate back-seat driver, on one of our outings I suggested she take a road she did not want to take. She resented it and I could feel her anger growing.

Once we got home, she came at me, all 110 pounds of her flailing, screaming, and cursing. It was like being assaulted by a very short scarecrow. I shouted back at her and pushed her to the ground without meaning to and left her house, resolved never to speak to her again.

I did not speak to her for almost two years. A mistake, because in the time it took for me to overcome my hurt feelings, dementia gradually took hold of her, so that the woman I made up with was no longer the one I had angered. The argument between us had been, as I now think, a signal moment in her decline, the beginnings of an irrationality, an anger, and a confusion: all characteristic of the vascular dementia that erased her before she died.

At her funeral, several years after we'd made up and not long after she'd forgotten my name, I was overcome by emotion. Not the emotion I expected, however. As her coffin rested on its bier in the aisle between two banks of pews and as my older sister spoke of how much we had loved her, most of my thoughts were of my father, her ex-husband, who had died ten years before her.

This was as disheartening as it was emotionally tangled. I missed my father, of course, but I felt the injustice of his presence, as if even here, at my mother's funeral, his memory was as vivid as hers, his absence almost as striking.

My father is often in my thoughts, but here his memory—the many fragments of him I harbour—was an intrusion.

The last time I saw my father, we spoke about love. I had helped him to make a difficult decision about a medical intervention that, given his weakened state, might or might not kill him outright. He saw that I was troubled and tried to reassure me.

—Any decision that's made with love can't be wrong, he said, whatever the outcome.

I was moved by this, so I assented. I did not—and do not—believe that decisions made with love can't be wrong. In fact, I wonder if they are not more often wrong than right. What moved me was his conviction, his belief that love is a guiding light. So, when I agreed with him—as opposed to arguing with him, as I normally would—it was to allow him whatever consolation his belief in love allowed.

He lay back on the bed, tired. His face was gaunt, and he was now thinner than he had been since his boyhood, but he was still handsome, his hair a statesmanlike white.

We were in a private room at the Riverside hospital. It was spring. The tree outside his window was newly minted green, and somewhere among its leaves there were birds, mostly out of sight, whose presences I could sometimes catch, in glimpses of black, red, and white, or divine from the sudden, slight shaking of a branch.

My father had been a fairly loving parent to me and my three sisters. It is no surprise that two of them became doctors—a fact that filled him with relief as much as pride. I can, with equal justice, say that I became a lawyer due to his influence. About this, his feelings were mixed. By the time I passed my bar exam, he had spent more time with lawyers than he wanted, having been through three divorces. Still, he accepted that the profession was "venerable," that it would make me money, and in any case, he was proud of me.

All of that said, he had been a terrible husband to our mother: unfaithful, untruthful, unkind. And when he died, a month after I saw him for the last time, none of us was surprised that she refused to attend his funeral. It was grace enough that she called each of us to say

—I'm sorry you lost your father. I hope you can understand why I won't be going to his funeral.

It was hard not to wonder how she'd take the news of my father's deathbed faith in love. I imagined she'd shut her eyes and frown. But thinking back on all this, I'm not so sure. She had, over the years, insisted on her indifference to him and his fate. Perhaps she'd have politely acknowledged his spiritual growth and left it at that. In any case, at the time, I was too upset by my father's death to talk about it with anyone who did not love him.

I've always felt a kind of perversity in my relationships to my mother and father. It's as if I got to know them in reverse. As an infant, whose instinct it was to observe and manipulate them, I knew them instinctively: knew when to smile for them, knew when to make the noises that made them happy, knew how to annoy them into giving me food and water.

Whether I actually knew them or not, they were not problematic until, when I was three, I was separated from them for a year while I lived with my grandmother in Trinidad. On meeting my parents again, I found them strange. We had somehow passed from closeness to wariness. And this fog of mistrust lasted till I was myself a parent; after which, they began to evolve in my mind—as they are evolving still, even after their deaths.

My father, Kenneth Robertson, was born in Belmont, Trinidad, in 1931, at a time when Belmont was poor and unaccommodating. He was, for the rest of his life, ashamed of his origins, embarrassed by all of it: by Belmont itself and by Bedford Lane, the narrow street on which he and his four brothers lived, so close to the houses across from them that they could, on Fridays and Saturdays, hear their neighbour beating his wife, her cries, the whining of their children, and the barking of a pothound they'd fed once and which would not go away.

The five boys slept in a small bedroom, three on one bed (one up, one down, one up) and two on another. They were so used to the bedbugs that afflicted them that when my father's eldest brother decided to sun out their mattresses—thus killing the bedbugs—none of them could sleep, so uncomfortable were they on un-infested bedding.

You'd have thought, given my father's loathing for Belmont, that the place was a vacuum from which no light could escape. But this was far from the case. I don't know if humiliation drove the other boys as viciously as it drove my father, but on a street where there were only a handful of houses, seven boys—including my father and his brother Prentice—went on to become doctors. This fact, which my father sometimes alluded to, was the one good thing about Bedford Lane that he would allow. Everything else was excrement or ashes, rats or pothounds.

The fact that Bedford Lane had created so many doctors did not surprise me, largely because I had no idea until I visited Trinidad in my teens just how difficult it must have been for boys born without money to make it to medical school on the back of sheer diligence, a diligence rewarded by a government that, after all, needed doctors.

For girls without money, it was, at the time, impossible.

And this is where my mother, Helen Joseph, comes in. Her family was not as poor as my father's. My grandfather worked for the *Trinidad Guardian* until, older, he bought a sweet shop in San Juan with his savings. Not that a sweet shop in San Juan could, in the fifties, lead to a life of luxury, but it kept them from hunger and, I believe, gave my mother a sense that life was open. She was not humiliated by her origins. It was my father who did the humiliating.

That he could humiliate her was due in part to the fact that they had known each other since their earliest childhood, that he was her first love. I don't know that she was the first girl he slept with, but she was, perhaps, the first one who stayed seduced after he seduced her. He had promised (she said) to love her until they were both in their nineties and fit only for lying in each other's arms, staring happily at the moon and listening to the kiskadees.

Was she moved by this cliché, or was it simply the beauty of him—a young light-skinned Black man, just over six feet tall, broad-shouldered, with long eyelashes and oval eyes—his sense of humour, his ambition to better himself? These were all qualities that any number of women found difficult to ignore.

As my mother tells it, he began sleeping with other women as soon as he got into medical school, and kept at it obsessively while they were married. But in the early days of their marriage, he was faithful. She was the one he loved, and she was the one guiding him. Which is just as well, as she was the one who believed in their future, in the possibilities that lay before them, despite their births on a small island, miles and nautical miles away from the worlds they heard about on BBC Radio's foreign service.

The reason they chose Canada—as opposed to, say, any of a hundred places with older, more interesting cultures—is banal. At my mother's instigation, my father applied to medical schools in Canada and the United States. He was accepted in a number of places, but they knew someone who knew someone who lived in Ottawa. So, Ottawa—with its medical school—is where they moved.

Canada turned out to be a good place for my father, a larger pond in which to swim. It took longer for the rightness of her decision to become clear to my mother. She had always intended to return to Trinidad and missed it terribly. But as the years passed and Trinidad sank into a violent lawlessness that made it gradually unrecognizable, my mother accepted that she had left at the right time and that, in choosing Canada, she had chanced upon a stable world that suited her, despite the heartbreak and humiliation she had to bear in the name of marriage.

Decades after their divorce, I asked her

—Why didn't you leave Dad sooner?

—I almost did, she answered, except for that idiot John Waller.

Bellefeuille, when we moved there in 1967, was a small town with a thousand inhabitants. It had once been somewhere important, one of a handful of places in Ontario where crude oil was discovered. It had, at one end of it, a mansion built by someone in the 1800s, a place that had been abandoned and then kept up and then abandoned again. At the other end of town, two miles away, the main street turned suddenly from asphalt to gravel road, as if Bellefeuille, having lost its mind, wandered off into farmlands and farm fields where the byways lost their names and took on numbers (10th Line, 8th Line, RR 7, County Road 5) or remained nameless.

The town was a hiccup of modest buildings and mediocre streets in the face of fields, creeks, trees, and ponds. It was a good place to grow up. There was always somewhere wooded nearby where you could escape from adults. Plus, there was room between houses, huge backyards and interesting fauna—skunks, mice, moles, beavers, groundhogs, toads, tree frogs, snakes, carp, leeches, and noisy birds.

(If I had been born in Canada, there is a chance I'd have been happy there.)

We had been living in Bellefeuille for a few years, following my father's graduation from the University of Ottawa and his internship at Toronto General. He'd been recruited by Dr. Eli Behar, a Jewish man whose new medical centre was in need of doctors.

Dr. Behar's Jewishness was significant, in that he was already regarded with suspicion by those in town who were either openly or discreetly antisemitic. He was tolerated, by those who tolerated him, as the son of Menachem Behar, who had been the town's tailor for fifty years. But his inviting a Black doctor to Bellefeuille tested everyone's patience. What next? A Negro priest? Negro judges? Black Mounties?

Despite this, my father, who got along well with women and men, took no more than six or seven months to establish himself as a "good doctor." He was funny, likeable, and irreproachably professional, where medicine was concerned. Moreover, these were the days of house calls, which he made without complaint, and he had a good bedside manner. Going into his patients' homes led to an intimacy which encouraged trust which led to word about the Black doctor being a good guy which led to the stunning surmise that while other Black people might be problematic this one wasn't. So when, two years after coming to Bellefeuille, my father tired of working for Dr. Behar and struck out on his own, he took most of his patients with him and he found more than enough work to support his family.

I imagine my father felt gratified by his accomplishment. And if so, it must have spurred his conviction that sleeping with his patients was acceptable; his due, even. He had dragged himself out of the pit that was Bedford Lane and arrived at this outpost of civilization where he could do useful things for people—examine their bodies for flaws, deliver babies, prescribe medication, recommend specialists in Sarnia. His reward for escaping from Belmont was the authority that being a doctor conferred, an authority that brought power, an aphrodisiac that must have been as arousing for the women he slept with as it was for him.

This, in any case, is my understanding. I assume that class, race, and revenge are what drove him to sleep with his patients, though sleeping with his patients could—and should—have cost him his profession. At the same time, I wonder what he was looking for in the small-town women who came to see him.

I wonder about those women as often as I do about my father. What were they thinking when they looked at Dr. Robertson? We were the only Black people in town, the only ones within a ten-mile radius or so. The ideas they had about Black men would have come mostly from television, I imagine. My father used to complain that his patients would regularly tell him how much he looked like Malcolm X, how much like Martin Luther King, like Redd Foxx, like Flip Wilson, like Richard Pryor, though none of those men looked alike and none looked like my father. He was a kind of bellwether, a reminder (to men and women in Bellefeuille) of which Black man was then prominent in American culture.

This was around the time of the race riots in Detroit, whose tellings and retellings were like campfire horror stories for white people. So, it seems unlikely that the women he slept with, though they knew him physically, actually slept with Ken Robertson, the man himself. Yet, here, too, I find myself at a kind of border. My father was handsome, personable, and, according to my mother, very good in bed. It's quite possible that for most of the women he slept with, he was less a Black man than simply a man who, as one might expect of a doctor, knew his way around a woman's body. In which case, race may not have had anything to do with it at all, where sex was involved.

During one of the most unnecessary conversations I've ever had with my mother, she told me more than I wanted to know about fucking my father. To her mind, "good in bed" was principally a matter of experience. As my father had slept with a good number of women, he knew how to please her. It was not, as far as she was concerned, a matter of seduction and chocolates. It was mechanics, mixed, of course, with affection.

In any event, the Wallers entered our lives, shortly after my father set up his own office on Eureka Street. They entered our home like bringers of good tiding. For one thing, they were the first white people, aside from the Behars, whom I remember my parents entertaining. It was the whole business, too: the house clean, my mother in makeup, my father wearing a jacket and smelling of aftershave. Then the hors d'oeuvres—shrimp cocktail, baby fingers arranged around a red sauce that smelled of horseradish; smoked oysters, glistening tabs neatly arranged on a plate beside white crackers; pearl onions and olives in their own bowls; and cheese on a wooden board. It was all the things that made my toes curl, when I was eleven, and which, on top of that, meant that adults were congregating and that I was to be seen, not heard.

I remember a handful of sharp details about Mrs. Waller. She was, I think, in a white dress with red criss-crossing lines on it, and she was what was called "busty" in those days, a word I associated with pigeons. Her hair was blond, and it hung down to the middle of her back, unfussed with. She had a necklace with a pendant of some sort, and her eyeshadow was blueish, as was the style then, though I'd never seen it in Bellefeuille.

It was her husband who left the deeper impression that evening. He was a tall dark-haired man, physically imposing and wide. About his clothes, I remember that his jacket was brown corduroy and slightly too small for him. He wore it over a white shirt and blue jeans. And, to me, the jeans were impressive. They weren't the kind of thing one wore on evenings out, even I knew that. But he was the kind of man who was proud of being a car salesman in Sarnia, the kind who would not—or, maybe, could not—put on airs.

When, out of politeness, I said, as I was instructed to say

—Good evening, Mr. Waller.

He laughed out loud, a false laugh, and answered

—To hell with that shit! My name's John. My father was Mr. Waller.

I liked him immediately. He was exactly the kind of adult to thrill an eleven-year-old, a plain-speaking menefreghista who wore the clothes I would have chosen, had I been an adult. What my mother and father thought of him would have been much more complicated. To begin with, he was at their house wearing casual clothes and using the language of the street. It was one thing to refuse to stand on ceremony when you were at home. It was something else to sneer at the courtesy my parents' generosity should have elicited. Was he simply ignorant and graceless? Or was he, rather, spitting in the soup of the Black people who'd invited him to dinner?

Adding to the complexities of the question—and to the resentment that having to ask it would have occasioned—was the fact that John would have provoked them. The man must have reminded my father of the Belmont from which he'd escaped—a place where ceremony of any sort would have been regarded as pretentious. To my father, John Waller's behaviour must have stunk of mildew and kerosene.

It would not have helped that John allowed himself—to my delight—to turn down the shrimp cocktail and French cheese. Nor would it have helped that he barely touched the stewed chicken, callaloo, and fried plantains that my parents served. Even his wife chided him for this, assuring him that the food was wonderful while thanking my parents for their graciousness.

—I can't help it, he answered. I'm used to Canadian food. Anything spicy keeps me up at night farting like a pug.

His face was red, suggesting embarrassment, but his tone was defiant. No doubt, his wife had forced him to come to this evening and who knows but that this was his way of getting back at her. And, again, my eleven-year-old self was in John's corner. I disagreed about the stewed chicken—my favourite food—but his discomfort was a mirror of my own, and besides, I found the idea that he farted like a small dog endlessly funny.

Nowadays, being twice the age of all the adults at that soiree and knowing its aftermath, I'm sympathetic to Mr. Waller for other reasons. Given that John and my parents had nothing in common, whose idea had it been to bring them together? It is clear that neither my mother—who dryly offered to make John a grilled cheese sandwich—nor John himself would have conceived of such a thing. It would have to have been Mrs. Waller or my father. In which case, it is likely that they were already sleeping together and that this evening was some sort of false flag, a way to throw their respective spouses off track by bringing friendship into the equation, the idea being that friends do not betray friends, nor fuck them, either.

I'm almost certain that my parents never went for dinner at the Wallers', and I don't know if my mother ever saw Sarah Waller again. I did, though, on two occasions when my father took me with him to the Wallers' home just out of town, off the 10th Line.

(It was my father's not-so-secret wish that I take up medicine. He would have been grateful to have his son become a doctor, relieved that I would not suffer the poverty that he had, that I would be self-sufficient. The house calls I made with him—maybe a dozen, in total—were meant to pique my interest in medicine. But they did the opposite. I found it oppressive entering what I mostly remember as darkened homes and being told to wait while my father saw to the ailing, while someone from the household—husband, wife, whoever—tried to keep me company, though their minds were elsewhere and their distress was, at times, raw. I found these visits more and more embarrassing until, after a time, I refused to go with him—a step away from medicine, unwittingly provoked by my father himself.)

The first house call at the Wallers' was, perhaps, just that—a doctor's visit, simply. The front door was answered by the Wallers' eldest daughter, Madeleine, my age, who let us in and followed my father to the bedroom where Mrs. Waller was lying in bed. My father, who had come to give Mrs. Waller a needle, closed the door to the room. Madeleine and I could hear moaning and coughing, and then Mrs. Waller let out a wail.

When I later asked my father why Mrs. Waller had cried out, he answered that the needle had hurt her. And I accepted this because there was no false emphasis in his delivery, nothing in his tone to suggest a lie or an incomplete truth. His answer was all so matter-of-fact that I didn't bother to ask what the needle was for, nor did I wonder why a grown woman should cry out at receiving one.

The second house call at the Wallers' was different, in fact and in my memory. For one thing, my father insisted that I *and* my sister Hecate come with him. I can't say for sure, but it seems likely that we were meant to keep the Wallers' daughters—Madeleine and Cynthia—busy, it being summer and school being out.

When we rang at the door, Mrs. Waller herself answered. She did not look ill, and the house smelled of the apple crumble she had, she said, just made, and would we children like a piece? There was nothing gloomy about the home. All the curtains were open, so that my first impressions were of bright sun and the taste of apples and brown sugar.

Mrs. Waller was in a light and floral dress that stopped just above her knees and through which the sun passed, allowing a view of her body that was occluded when she was not in the light. I was confused by these glimpses of her body and then embarrassed for her. She asked my father if he wanted a glass of dandelion wine. And to my surprise, he said yes. He had, of course, brought his black leather bag with him, and picking it up, he said to me

—Sam, I want you to stay and mind the girls while Mrs. Waller and I go to her room. I'm going to give her a shot of B12 to help her get over her anemia.

I was at the beginning of that time in life when anything that hints at the sexual is fascinating but beyond articulation. It did not occur to me, for instance, that Mrs. Waller had worn that dress with nothing underneath it in order to please my father. I assumed, rather, that I was the only one who could see through it, that it was an accident, that she had dressed in a hurry. And yet, at the same time, I did know, and I was suddenly interested in what my father and Mrs. Waller were going to do in the room. So while during other house calls, I quietly endured the waiting, this time I left Madeleine, Cynthia, and Hecate playing with their dolls in the yard, and went inside on the pretext that I wanted a glass of water.

The kitchen was at the other end of the house from the Wallers' bedroom, and I remember feeling I would certainly get punished if I were caught, though no one had forbidden me from going to the room. I went as quietly as I could along the hall that led to the bedroom, tiptoeing as one does at that age, using one's whole body for silence—shoulders raised, hands forward like cat's paws, feet lifted higher than needed at each step. And as a result, I could hear, well before I got to the door, the sound of Mrs. Waller—wordless, but as if quietly and arrhythmically complaining in a high, childish voice—the more subdued and deeper sound of my father's breathing, and the sound of something dully, rhythmically knocking against a wall.

—What are you doing?

At Cynthia's loudly chirped question, all sound ceased from the bedroom, until Mrs. Waller called out

—Cynthia! Go play in the yard!

I put my finger to my lips and shepherded Cynthia back to the yard. I knew that I knew something I wasn't supposed to know, though I didn't know what it was.

Reflecting on that moment now, fifty years and a bit later, it seems more complicated, not less. Beyond the penis-and-vagina tumult, there must have been worlds of fantasy. I mean, what did my father and Mrs. Waller think they were doing that was worth risking discovery by their children or crushing their respective spouses or setting fire to the lives they were leading? Or did they think at all, as opposed to surrendering to the joy of wanting and being wanted, though their surrender would have an unpredictable effect on those around them?

One of those effects is that the word "anemia" is erotic to me.

Another word: "passion"—from the Latin *pati*, to suffer—an idea that's like a chasm, going as it does from Christ being crucified to a man quietly touching the inner thigh of his friend's wife beneath a dinner table. So, my father and Mrs. Waller were passionate, and that passion left its mark.

(I think of this moment as the first one in my professional life, if for no other reason than that I've spent decades litigating it. At times, I wonder if I heard what I thought I heard. At times I wonder how I would prove it. If counsel proposed that what I heard were two people building a bird feeder—one crying out from splinters, one exhausted after trying to hold the feeder up—what could I answer? Over the years, I've come up with countless proposals of that sort, each as absurd as the last, all impossible to refute. But what was—what remains—influential about the moment is not what I believed was happening between my father and Mrs. Waller. It wasn't the moral turpitude that interested me. It is the questioning of the moment's significance that sent me on my way.)

My father's affair with Mrs. Waller went on for quite a while, it seems, though my mother did not find out about it until a year after the Wallers had come to our house for dinner.

It wasn't that she didn't know my father was screwing other women. She had, for instance, found a used condom in the garbage pail of his office one day while, to help save money, she was cleaning the place herself. When confronted, he denied that the condom was his—which left open the possibility that someone had broken into the office, had sex while there, and disposed of the condom in the pail. My mother knew that this was unlikely, but then . . . people had already broken into his office looking for drugs. It was not impossible that hooligans should have had sex there as well.

Also, as unlikely as this horny break-in was, she wanted it to be true. My mother wanted all the signs to mean what she wanted them to mean or else be meaningless. The woman who'd stared at her defiantly at a town meeting was not one of my father's lovers. The lace panties she found in our basement had nothing to do with my father. The perfume that clung to him for weeks before dissipating belonged to "a patient who had lost her sense of smell"—my father's explanation. The working late on weekends, the being too tired to have sex with her for months on end, and so on and on. My mother admitted, when we spoke about her life in Bellefeuille, that these details were obviously significant, but at the time she treated them ruthlessly.

It was hard work for my mother to deny, to forget, to forgive, to banish. So, it's not surprising that the news of my father's affair with Mrs. Waller had to come by extraordinary means, in order to overcome her barriers to knowing. And the means, in this case, were out of the ordinary. One day, John called my mother and asked to meet her. Though she could hear that he was distraught, she wanted nothing to do with him.

—What is it you want, Mr. Waller?

—I'm going to kill your husband, he said, if he doesn't stop harassing my wife! I'll kill him!

—What are you telling me for? my mother asked. If you're going to kill him, you're going to kill him. Why do you need to see me?

He hadn't expected this response, it seemed. In fact, it must have shaken him deeply so that, upset and angry as he was, he began to cry, a thing that annoyed my mother even more. Mr. Waller loved his wife. He was crushed. He was going to lose his daughters, everything he had because "your husband can't keep his pecker in his pants."

If my mother was annoyed at the beginning of the conversation, she was enraged by this point.

—If your idiot of a wife would stop taking it out of his pants, we wouldn't be here, would we?

In the past, when my father's infidelities came to light, my mother had not had to deal with husbands or boyfriends. She knew the usual triangles his infidelity generated. She knew what it was to have his women inform her that they loved her husband or let her know that she wasn't the only one who'd slept with him or tearfully confess their regret at having slept with her husband. These were humiliating encounters, but my mother believed she understood the language of women, even white women. She knew the tone and words that distinguished genuine regret from the heartfelt confessions that, like something poisoned, were meant to hurt her and to destroy her family.

Dealing with Mr. Waller was different. My mother did not believe that he would kill her husband, but Mr. Waller's self-pity, his "blubbering" as she called it, his pathetic incapacity to murder my father were more humiliating, because she was not used to dealing with husbands and because being asked to sympathize with Mr. Waller, to acknowledge his pain as if he were the victim and her humiliation counted for nothing, was a further degradation.

This all being the case, you'd have thought that Mr. Waller's call would be a final provocation, a humiliation that would drive her to end her marriage and leave my father. It almost was. But according to my mother, it was the absurdity of Mr. Waller's call that convinced her to stay with my father. The idea that there were men in the world as immature as John Waller—that "damned Baby Huey"—put my father in a much better light, one that was sufficient to hold her interest.

In telling me all this, she added

—Anyway, it's better the devil you know.

But hearing my mother say this was like hearing someone say they'd prefer to live with Beelzebub for fear of finding Satan. It was odd. And, of course, her decision—hanging up on Mr. Waller, remaining faithful to my father—was one she would regret when my father finally left her for another woman; left her, that is, even after she got down on her knees and pleaded with him to stay for his family's sake, if not for hers.

Stranger still, she held her decision to stay with my father—and all the humiliation that followed it—against John Waller, so that when she told me about his call, she was once again furious, not at my father for sleeping with John's wife but at the man himself who, in the end, got what he wanted. My father stopped sleeping with Sarah Waller.

Why he stopped sleeping with her has puzzled me. It had to be love, no? For my mother, I mean. Or was he worried that Mr. Waller would shoot him? Or was it pride in his reputation that drove him to abandon Mrs. Waller? Not being ruled by my sexual desires—being, in fact, wary of them, being my father's opposite—I could not believe he would endanger his family and reputation for the sake of a little interchooksy—to use his word.

Pride is the answer I find most convincing. I believe he wanted to be a pillar of the community, a man so admired—despite his origins, despite his colour—that the people of Bellefeuille would invite him and his family to wave at them from a special float in the Santa Claus parade. And this they did, one cold December day that I do not remember fondly.

For all that, he went on sleeping with his patients, constantly risking his reputation.

Nor do I believe my mother's "better the devil you know." Her fear of the unknown is unconvincing as the reason she stayed with my father after his affair with Mrs. Waller. She was herself a complicated person, fiercely independent but in thrall to my father or fascinated by him or, maybe, in love with her own creation, which, having coaxed him from Trinidad and supported him through medical school, is what he was. Whatever he did, however he hurt her, my mother could still look at him and think "I made you! You owe me." Something of that emotion almost certainly influenced her decision to stay. It is easy to imagine Galatea leaving Pygmalion, but much harder for me to imagine the reverse.

Or perhaps she loved him: simply, truly, from the depths of herself, while believing that he loved her, too, that he must, after all they had shared, that for the sake of his family he would remain with her.

It may be that my father's behaviour was influential on my decision to study law. But I'm certain he was at the root of my inclination to family law, my field. I have never looked on the unhappiness of families without wishing to help. And although I am not particularly sentimental—perhaps, at times, not sentimental enough—it is difficult not to see myself in the children of bad marriages.

But years of considering these fraught unions has led me to the small miracle of unhappiness. I don't mean, of course, that unhappiness is desirable. I mean that it sometimes comes at you from so very far back. For instance, I often felt the impact of Bedford Lane on my father's behaviour—his need for valorization, his struggle for a sense of self-worth, his shame at his origin. What surprises me is that the lane—houses close to each other, the sound of a man beating his wife because he has spent the little money he has on drink, the dogs that rush at strangers—has had its influence on me as well, through my father.

I understand his difficulties with self-worth, his feeling unworthy of love. And although I did not live on Bedford Lane, I feel touched by the squalor it represented to him. As such, it's difficult not to wonder how far the misery goes back—like wondering about light from a distant star and marvelling at its persistence—and how far forward. Do my own daughters feel the presence of Bedford Lane in me?

Sometime after my father's funeral, my eldest, Dora, surprised me by asking

—Dad, did you love your father?

—Of course, I answered. Why are you asking me that?

I was upset that what I thought of as the truth of my feelings, the strength of my affection, was not obvious.

—You never talked about him, she answered. I always thought you didn't like him.

And though I was upset, it was with Dora's question that I really began to piece together what I knew and felt about Kenneth Robertson—his origins, the things that had formed him, our moments together, his fear that I might fall back to the pit he'd climbed from: Bedford Lane, Belmont, Trinidad and Tobago, the West Indies.

In a word, it was after his death that I became more inclined to love my father for who he was. And it is perhaps not too surprising that thoughts of him intruded on my mother's funeral, because my mother's death was a moment in my relationship with my father.

When I visited my father on his deathbed and he spoke about love's guidance leading to the right decisions, I wondered if he knew how devastating his behaviour had sometimes been.

—Did you love my mother? I asked.

—Yes, he answered, of course. But we were so young . . .

—What about that woman you had the affair with in Bellefeuille? Sarah Waller.

—Sarah Waller? I don't know Sarah Waller.

—Mom said her husband threatened to kill you. She must have told you about it.

He laughed, as far as his pain would allow.

—I think I'd remember that, don't you?

His pain overcame him, then, and I went to find a nurse in the ward. By the time the nurse had come and the morphine had kicked in, the subject had changed. But given how he'd answered my questions, I'm convinced he didn't want to talk about the past. He had clearly lied to me. I could see the recognition on his face when he heard Sarah's name. That said, I wasn't sure what he was hiding—shame, love, longing, nostalgia, humiliation? Or nothing so dramatic. He may have simply wanted peace, to lie in his hospital bed, with a notion of love to lessen his apprehension. Because, as a doctor, he must have known that his death was likely and soon to come.

At his death, my mother showed little emotion, aside from the concern she felt for our grief. I don't believe her indifference was convincing, though. I can't say that she still loved my father, but I could always sense . . . something, an occasional struggle for equanimity when he was mentioned. How could it be otherwise, when he was the man whom she'd begged to stay with her, pleading for her family's sake? And he'd said no, because he had moved on.

It occurs to me, as I imagine my mother pleading for her family's sake, how much more present she has been in my life. My father's presence was, relatively, fleeting. There were always reasons and he was usually gone, in my childhood. And yet the distress I feel when I think about my parents, when I feel distress at all, is to do with him. He has the larger profile in my psyche, while occupying a much narrower place in my memories.

I'm almost certain that I share this sense of paradox with my mother and sisters.

Years after my father's death, my mother had a series of small strokes that left her with vascular dementia, a dementia that was as surprising for what it left as what it took away. It took away most of her recent memories and then, gradually, most of her distant ones as well. What remained were some two dozen memories that she returned to again and again, as if her self were a receding tide that gradually exposed these hard, bright moments: her father crying when she left Trinidad, a friend who fell down stairs to his death, a letter given to her by an unsuspected admirer, a woman who said something unpleasant to her at a funeral.

Among these irreducible memories was the moment my father assured her that he would love her until they were both in their nineties: moongazing, listening to the kiskadees. This promise of his—made when they were in their teens—would come up, sometimes as often as ten or twenty times in half an hour: returning, returning, returning.

—Do you know what your father said to me?

At first, she spoke of my father's promise with anger. She was still Helen enough to be bitter. But as time passed, she would mention it as if it were an unusual fact, one she could not place, one she found confusing, though she was certain it had significance. By the end of her life, it was clear that my father's avowal of love was more or less meaningless to her, so that I wasn't sure what to feel when, months before she died, my father's words and all the memories that had hitherto remained passed into silence, as she stopped speaking altogether.

She was thin, then, her white hair slick, as if pasted to her skull, combed to keep it neat. Her skin was still brown but slightly dull, her wrists delicate-looking. I have no idea, of course, which shard of memory stayed with her longest, if any one of them did. Knowing that my father's promise to love her had been an unpleasant memory, it seems odd to hope it stayed till the end, but I do, while hoping that she knew his vision of moons and birdsong was not durable.

My father's belief in love's guidance was, at least to a certain extent, an overcoming of the shame within him, an overcoming of the doubt and uncertainty, a way forward. Which is why I felt he was welcome to whatever consolation it offered.

But for my mother, because her death was such a long going-away, I like to think of her as she had been before dementia took her: strong-willed, wary, scornful of my father's words. Not bitter, but not fooled, either. Imagining her like that, it's possible for me to hope that some part of the love my young father felt for her still touched her, before vanishing along with everything else.

An Elegy

In Memoriam Harry Mathews, 1930–2017

My earliest experience of language came when I was two or three years old. I was in Trinidad, at the home of my grandparents and in the company of my grandmother Hilda and her mother, Ada. I had not realized I was speaking a language until Hilda and Ada began to speak to each other in a different one, patois.

In those days, the older generation spoke patois when they didn't want children to know what they were talking about. So, what I most vividly remember is my confusion. I was old enough to realize that the sounds of "patois"—a name I didn't learn till much later—were not English. But I understood *something* of what Gramma Hilda was saying to Gramma Ada. My confusion came from hovering on the verge of understanding without passing through.

My parents had left me and my sister, Thecla, in Trinidad when they'd left for Canada, where my father was to study medicine. They had left us in the care of their families: my uncle Kenneth, my grandparents Hilda and Rudolph, and my great-grandmother Ada. But it was only with my great-grandmother that I ever felt loved.

I was her first great-grandchild and the love I felt for and from Ada Homer is one that still resonates, sixty years after her death. So, the shock of being suddenly unable to understand her—like finding the door to your own room locked—was sharp enough to make me wonder about the sounds I was hearing. Why couldn't I understand them? How could there be a barrier between myself and Gramma Ada? This sense of barrier brought with it a feeling of shame, as if I were at fault for not understanding. It is a shame at the heart of my relationship to language.

Three or four years after this moment in Trinidad, I had my first experience of French. This moment was less personal, but it was just as indelible and humiliating.

Having brought us to Canada, my parents decided to send me and my sister to a French grade school. My father (still studying medicine) and my mother (a legal secretary) believed it would be best if their children were bilingual, like Ottawa itself. An interesting decision, a good one, I think. But 1963 was before the vogue for "French immersion" in English schools. So, we were sent to a French school—École Garneau—not far from where we lived, a French school where I, at the age of six, was expected to learn the language and get along with it.

And I did, eventually, get along with it. I learned French quickly because I had to, because I felt oppressively self-conscious in class, whenever I was asked a question. But the strangeness of my first day at Garneau has stayed with me as vividly as the moment I heard Ada and Hilda speaking in patois.

—Comment t'appelles-tu?

The teacher, a young woman, asked me this a number of times before I realized she was asking my name. I remember she said the words more and more slowly, until someone said, in English, "Your name!" She immediately corrected them.

—En français! she said.

I became, at that exact moment, an English speaker. That is, I understood that *I* was an English speaker. I also understood, in that moment, that although English is my mother tongue, it might not have been.

The political fact of English, the reasons I spoke it, did not come to me until much later. English was not some random inheritance but the by-product of one world power (the English) taking over the island of Trinidad from another (the Spanish). And patois, incomprehensible to both, would have been a way for the indigenous bystanders to keep certain things to themselves.

I was born in Trinidad to a family with Carib, Chinese, French, and African roots. I still think it unfortunate that I never learned patois or, for that matter, the Garifuna of my great-grandfather.

While we were at École Garneau, my sister and I, I began to have a recurring nightmare that stayed with me until my teens. In this dream, I am in what I take to be Ottawa and I'm happily getting along with the people around me. The dream always starts happily, which is why my dream-self never suspects what's coming. But then someone begins to talk to me, and to my shame, I realize I don't understand what they are saying. For whatever reason, the person believes I am pretending not to understand, and my pretense offends them. They become angry, as do all the people around us. It's usually at this moment that I realize I'm not in Ottawa. The crowd becomes aggressive—shouting at me in a language I don't know—until I back away and begin running, pursued by murderous strangers.

Why they are murderous, I don't know. It seems almost random that my psyche should imagine itself in such operatic danger for want of a language. But it did.

—

Given the disjunctions of my early life—the loss of home and certainty, the estrangement from language—it would not have been unusual for me to spend some of my life in search of home and certainty. In fact, that's what I thought I was doing. I imagined my work—my writing—as a psychic equivalent of the search for home.

(As a young reader, I preferred the *Odyssey* over the *Iliad*. No question.)

(As an older reader, I find Cavafy's "Ithaca" moving, however often I read it.)

But the paradox of any quest for home is that it is, at the same time, a rejection of home. How could it be otherwise, since home is internal and non-home is infinite? The surprise, here, is that it took me so long to understand the extent to which I refused to accept home while searching for it and that I had, without realizing it, become obsessed with the unhomely, with the strange.

(An aside about the word "unhomely." "Unhomely" doesn't quite work, here. According to *Merriam-Webster*, it means uninviting. Worse, given how we normally use "homely," it could be taken to mean something that is un-ugly. But it is so close to the right word: *unheimlich*, a German word that is literally "un-home-like" and means "scary," "sinister," "weird." But how interesting that for English the word "homely" should mean unattractive. In psychosexual terms, this is probably for the best. In any case, I'm drawn to the idea of the "unhomelike" as sinister or weird, despite the fact that, for all intents and purposes, this negatively describes most of the known universe.)

It's not as if the signs of my refusal of home weren't there . . .

When my family moved from Ottawa to Petrolia, a small town in southern Ontario, I told everyone that my name was Paul. So, for a year or so, I was Paul Alexis. I was Paul until my parents had enough and insisted that my friends, teachers, et cetera call me André, a name I resent to this day.

When "Paul" was taken from me, I embraced my nickname: Axle, from axle grease: i.e., black. Despite the racist overtones, it was a nickname I myself suggested to my new classmates when I was sent to school in London, Ontario. And so there are, to this day, people who know me as Axle, first, and André second—not many, though, a quickly diminishing number.

When I was a teenager, home itself—the place where my parents lived—was so unbearable to me that I lived, for six months or so, not in my bedroom but in the basement, on a mattress beside the furnace, as far away as I could get from home while being, technically, at home. In fact, something about the smell of an oil furnace still calms me, though I didn't choose the close for its smell. It was a place where I could fit a mattress, where there was a plug for a little lamp, where I could hear nothing but the heartbeat of the furnace as it worked.

When writing my first novel, in my thirties, I left my daughter with her mother and, abandoning my apartment, wrote in an off-season resort, alone by a small lake—White Lake, near Sharbot Lake—north of Kingston, Ontario: two kilometres from the nearest human, hundreds away from anyone I knew.

It is difficult to find home when neither you nor those around you are certain who you are and when no physical place corresponds to it. If I have a home, it is in Trinidad, circa 1957. But that place ceased to be, decades ago. My Trinidad is now only a handful of impressions: a bird flying towards me while I am held in someone's arms, the taste of a "congaree" (a millipede) that I dug out of the ground and bit, the sugary smell of my grandfather's store, the feeling of wearing a mustard poultice beneath my clothes in very hot weather, the taste of castor oil, the smell of the Caribbean Sea, the fear of rainfall.

—

Leaving is creative, as are isolation and uncertainty. This is a cliché that stretches from Virginia Woolf's plea for a room of her own and Kafka's complaint that there is never enough silence when one is writing all the way to the accepted wisdom that the feeling of not knowing what one is doing is important to any truly creative endeavour.

But there is something more to leaving for me, and perhaps for others who emigrated when very young. Yes, I do write better when I am alone and isolated, but I suspect this is because the separation and isolation bring back my early childhood: a time when my parents left me, when I was taken from Trinidad, when I finally understood that I was trapped in Canada. I suspect this primal feeling triggers the urge to turn inward and that turn is crucial for the writer that I am.

All of which is to say that leaving Toronto (my home, almost) to write—these minor emigrations—have kept me in touch with my immigrant self—the self that is *déboussolé*—and this immigrant self is my most creative. It is the self for whom an understanding of symbols, sounds, and language are linked to survival. Of course, this reliance on the immigrant within me has had consequences—predictable and unpredictable—for how I write and how I think about literature.

(An aside about compasses: the English word "disoriented" is lovely, suggesting as it does that knowing the direction of the Orient/the east is crucial for knowing where one is. But I prefer the French word "déboussolé," deriving as it does from the French word for compass—*boussole*—and suggesting the state of being without a compass, unable to tell north from south, east from west. It puts the emphasis on the instrument—the compass—and its loss, the lostness not only of direction but of the means for telling direction. This feels closer to the confusion I felt as a boy adrift in Canada: home lost, along with the means to find it.)

Predictably, much of my work is a re-creation of the bewilderment that was a dominant emotion of my childhood self—bewilderment and resentment. Rather than directly expressing this bewilderment, however, I have tried to create worlds in which a sympathetic reader will feel a familiarity while struggling to interpret the appearance of certain things, certain signs, certain utterances.

The easiest way to accomplish this is, of course, with genres.

In the same way as ancient Greek tragedians relied on their audiences' knowledge of shared stories and myths, one can use the conventions of, say, detective fiction to bring a reader to a familiar situation: here is the crime and—after a bit of rummaging—here is the culprit.

Moving, in work to work, from one genre to the next is almost as important to me as genre itself: from detective fiction to romance, from romance to pastoral, from pastoral to apologue, and so on. I'm careful to observe the conventions of a genre. It would be a fatuous game otherwise. But the pleasure of moving from genre to genre is intense and twofold: first, the reader's expectations can be subverted or met, and second, when I begin writing in an unfamiliar genre, there is the fear that I don't know what I'm doing, that I'm poaching on foreign ground. This fear—the sense that there are conventions and rules that you haven't mastered, that you might not master—is an almost perfect corollary (intellectually, emotionally) to my first emotions on coming to Canada. Fear is a means of opening my mind to new avenues, while forcing me to use my own resources, though these come from another place—literary fiction, mostly.

I have always felt that the question "How is one meant to

fit in, in Canada?" has something in common with the question "How does one create a plot for a detective story?," not only because they make me similarly anxious but because they suggest terrains—geographic and literary—and exploration of terrain.

Genres allow me a kind of emigration. But just as important to me are my wanderings through the novels and stories of writers whose work—whose *worlds*—I admire. And I mean "wandering" as a reader and as a writer.

As a reader, I'm anarchic in my travels. I've loved books of all genres and subjects: ancient and modern. As a writer, I feel encompassed and enchanted in worlds created by a limited set of authors, mostly writers of fiction: Tolstoy, Joyce, Proust, Beckett, Bulgakov, Austen, Kawabata, Queneau, Harry Mathews, Italo Calvino, Henry James, Tommaso Landolfi, Michael Ondaatje, Margaret Laurence, Witold Gombrowicz; a few handfuls more.

These are the writers who have, to varying degrees, influenced my work, either by suggesting avenues and approaches to fiction—Jane Austen's look at the pitfalls of romantic alliances, Queneau's play with structure, Kawabata's use of images—or by calling to mind a question that can best be written as "What would that be like?" To take James Joyce, for example: "What would it be like to write about a single day in the life of my city?" Or "What would it be like to write a novel using a previously existing structure, as *Ulysses* uses the *Odyssey*?" Or "What would it be like to write a long interior monologue?"

Whether or not I actually answer—for myself, that is—the questions suggested by another writer's work, the questions themselves are influential in changing how I think about writing or fiction. More, they have led me to my own approach. But having arrived at my own set of concerns, I think about the work of others less, as I write, and about my own obsessions more: nature, home, death, elegy, rebirth. And from time to time I regret—resent even—the collection of mannerisms and awkwardness that, according to Hemingway, is what critics will call a writer's style.

(It's not just in my way of writing, either. I remember having an argument with my father about the nature of love and responsibility. I made a cutting remark that felt nicely weighted and poised. My father looked at me with what was, at first, approval and then with derision.

—That's just the kind of thing people write, isn't it? he said.

He could not help admiring the sentence, but he wasn't convinced by it.)

(An aside about the Closerie des Lilas: this essay was written at the bar of the Closerie in Paris. I had gone there to see what Ernest Hemingway's favourite café looked like. And without choosing a particular spot, I sat at the bar where, after a moment, I noticed a brass plaque before me: *Hemingway*, it said. I asked the bartender, a young man, if this was where Hemingway used to write. He had no idea, but one of the older servers assured me that if that particular place wasn't the only spot Hemingway chose at the bar, it was certainly one of the places where he wrote. Amused, I ordered a beer and, after the beer, decided to write at the bar, standing up—which was surprisingly comfortable. I was interrupted, first, by a group of young people from Michigan who politely asked me to move, so they could take a picture of the plaque. And about fifteen minutes later, an eastern European couple—in their sixties, by the look of them—were shown the plaque and, seeing me writing, asked "How do you dare?" Meaning that it took nerve to write where a man they worshipped had written things that meant so much to them. They consoled themselves by adding "Well, he probably didn't write at the bar." I politely agreed, but I knew that Hemingway liked to write standing up. In all likelihood, he *had* written at the bar. In any case, I came to the Closerie des Lilas every day for two weeks. I'm sure I meant something symbolic by the act, but no one noticed after that first day, and anyway, the bar at the Closerie isn't a particularly inspiring altar.)

It is axiomatic that a writer is meant to find their own voice. But my own wish—a fantasy—is that I might write like, say, Tommaso Landolfi or Jane Austen, while nourishing my own obsessions and exploring the ground I know. That's not how Art works, though, and what I resent about my style, about the way I write, is its inevitability. Given my estrangements from language, my search for fluency, my sense of guilt if I write other than—by my own definition—"well," these words, here, were probably unavoidable.

I have found a home in my own language, and to some extent, I dislike it.

Garifuna, a language native to parts of South America and the Caribbean, was the language of my great-grandfather, John Modest. The language, also known as Black Carib or Kalipuna, has fewer than 20,000 speakers world-wide and is endangered. To my knowledge, this is its first appearance in literary fiction, though the Garifuna transcribed in this book is the evocation of an echo of a tongue spoken in Trinidad, a hundred years ago.

—André Alexis